I0691431

# SMILE FOR ME

## BOOKS BY JAN THOMPSON

**Protector Sweethearts** (6 Books)
JanThompson.com/protector

**Defender Sweethearts** (6 Books)
JanThompson.com/defender

**Binary Hackers** (4 Books)
JanThompson.com/binary

**Seaside Chapel** (6 Books)
JanThompson.com/seaside

**Savannah Sweethearts** (11 Books)
JanThompson.com/savannah

**Vacation Sweethearts** (8 Books)
JanThompson.com/vacation

Keep up with Jan Thompson's book news:
JanThompson.com/newsletter

# SMILE FOR ME

## VACATION SWEETHEARTS BOOK 1

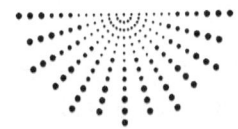

JAN THOMPSON

GEORGIA
PRESS

# SMILE FOR ME (VACATION SWEETHEARTS BOOK 1)

Copyright © 2016 by Jan Edttii Lim Thompson

Author Website: JanThompson.com
Book News: JanThompson.com/newsletter
Published by Georgia Press LLC

All rights reserved. No part of this publication may be reproduced, distributed, or transmitted in any form or by any means, including photocopying, recording, or other electronic or mechanical methods, without the prior written permission of the publisher.

This book is a work of fiction. All characters, persons, places, events, and things either are the product of the author's active imagination or are used fictitiously.

Scripture quotations are from the New King James Version®. Copyright © 1982 by Thomas Nelson. Used by permission. All rights reserved.

The lyrics for the "I Surrender All" hymn penned by Judson W. Van DeVenter in the 19th century are in the public domain.

Cover Design: Deranged Doctor Design

First eBook Edition: June 2016
ISBN: 978-1-944188-12-2

First Paperback Edition: December 2016
Paperback ISBN 978-1-9441-8820-7

*To my Lord and Savior, Jesus Christ, who died on the cross to save me from my sins and rose again from the grave to give me eternal life in heaven.*

*For God so loved the world that He gave His only begotten Son, that whoever believes in Him should not perish but have everlasting life.*
*—John 3:16*

# READ THE VACATION SWEETHEARTS PREQUEL FOR FREE

When art gallery archivist Sheryl Breckenridge tries to get world-famous sculptor Winton Pace to display his artwork at Simon's Gallery, she doesn't expect him to fall in love with her. Will she reciprocate in this friends-to-more romance?

Read *Time for Me* (A Vacation Sweethearts Prequel) for FREE at the link below. This story starts thirteen months before *Smile for Me* (Vacation Sweethearts Book 1).

Download the FREE prequel here:
JanThompson.com/time-free

Sign up for Jan Thompson's mailing list to keep up with her book news. She writes Christian beach romance, romantic suspense, and suspense thrillers.

Subscribe to Jan's book news:
JanThompson.com/newsletter

# ABOUT SMILE FOR ME

## VACATION SWEETHEARTS BOOK 1

*She is laid-back.*
*He is uptight.*
*Never the twain shall...kiss?*

A deadline-driven workaholic assistant school principal who meticulously plans his schedule months in advance meets an easygoing art teacher and studio potter with no sense of time, living her life as the seasons come and go. When they cross paths again at the Summer by the Sea Day Camp sponsored by his church in Nassau, Bahamas, how can they get along if they cannot see eye to eye?

From *USA Today* bestselling author Jan Thompson comes *Smile for Me*, book 1 in the **Vacation Sweethearts** collection of wholesome, sweet and inspirational Christian romance novels set in some of Jan's favorite vacation places around the world.

**Vacation Sweethearts** is a spin-off of Jan's **Savannah Sweethearts** Christian beach romance series, and we might travel back to Savannah and Tybée Island to meet friends, old and new.

To start off the **Vacation Sweethearts** series, we travel to the Bahamas in the Caribbean, where the waters are clear, skies are blue, hammocks sway under coconut trees, and hearts are in love...

TINA MACFARLAND IS LAID-BACK...

When invited back to the Bahamas for a second time two years after a disastrous mission trip there, potter and art teacher Tina MacFarland isn't sure she wants to face the obnoxious assistant principal of the Chapel by the Sea Christian School again. The last time she encountered Byron Moss, he found fault in everything she did. It seems that nothing she ever does is good enough for Mr. Uptight, as attractive as he may be to her.

Regardless of her personal concerns, they need art teachers at the Summer by the Sea Day Camp, and Tina answers the call to go. Surely God will help her last for four short weeks. What can possibly happen in a month? Nothing she can think of.

## BYRON MOSS IS UPTIGHT...

Assistant Headmaster Byron Moss is at a crossroad in his career. On the one hand, he has worked very hard to get to this position at the Chapel by the Sea Christian School. One more step up from this assistant principal position, and he'd be in charge of the entire school.

On the other hand, when Tina returns to Nassau, Byron suddenly feels hemmed in by his career choice. He is restricted from showing his transforming feelings for Tina. He fears he has taken a wrong turn in his career, and that if he keeps going on that route, he may lose his chances with Tina. More importantly, what is God's will for his life? Somehow, he knows that Tina is part of all that. But she's so...chaotic! And it drives him nuts. For the first time in his life, Byron is confused about what he needs to do.

## NEVER THE TWAIN SHALL...KISS?

Ah, Byron and Tina... How will they navigate the super-conservative work environment where office romance is frowned upon? Can they change the old rules? Or will the old rules change them?

Smile for Me (Vacation Sweethearts Book 1): JanThompson.com/smile

Vacation Sweethearts: JanThompson.com/vacation

Subscribe to Jan's book news mailing list: JanThompson.com/newsletter

# SMILE FOR ME

# CHAPTER ONE

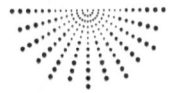

yron Moss had called that woman *Veronique* in a singsong fashion, and that had rubbed Tina MacFarland the wrong way.

She would have to admit that Veronique was a pretty French name—too French for this ex-British colony, but then again, nobody had asked her.

She watched both of them whisper to each other at the front of the long school bus, identical iPads hanging off their necks like some sort of Horn books from the nineteenth century.

At first Tina had thought that Veronique was taller than Byron, but that idea went away when Tina saw the day camp assistant director's five-inch stilettos.

Try walking on Bahamian sands with those—

*Lord, forgive me.*

*Thank You, Jesus.*

Tina didn't know what had overcome her, but every time she had been with Byron, she only thought of the worst of him.

Meticulously overbearing was the last double adjective she had used for him.

Uptight.

A pain in the neck.

The moment the volunteers from Riverside Chapel, Savannah, and a couple of other churches had disembarked from the airplane, Byron was at baggage claim waiting for them.

The way he had checked off their names as if they were school children had bothered Tina.

Then he had herded them into this non-air-conditioned school bus. Everyone just cracked jokes and laughed with him as he checked off their names one more time.

However, when Tina passed by him, he didn't say anything, except to call her name.

The way Byron had said her name was very unlike how he had called Veronique's name. Veronique's name rolled off Byron's tongue in a smoother way than when he had snapped out Tina's name.

"Ti-nah!"

It was curtly British, clipped at the end of the second syllable, as if his disgust of her had taken its toll and he couldn't bear to say her name at all this time around.

Two years ago they had butted heads like two rams or goats. Horns locked as Byron had hissed out her name and stretched it in the air as though he was mentally wringing her neck every single time.

"Tee-yee-yee-nah! Teeenaaah!" Byron would yell at her in disgust because she hadn't done things the way he had wanted.

Well, sure, there was the bell before and after class, but she hadn't finished teaching, and besides, the kindergarteners were having fun, weren't they?

After all, it was Vacation Bible School, not a bar exam.

*Come on!*

In any case, her name sounded awful when Byron had said it aloud.

Well, it wasn't her fault she was named after a citrus fruit. A tangerine, to be exact.

Clementine Gracielle MacFarland.

No one ever called her Clementine, not since birth, according to everyone. It had always been Tina, as if Clementine was a shame of a first name.

Her brother had the better name, Martinelli, though everyone called him Martin.

But Tina.

"Tee-yee-yee-nah! Nah! Nah! Nah!"

"Stop," Tina muttered. "Stop it..."

A nudge and a couple of hard jabs on her shoulder made her jerk straight up and open her eyes.

"Oww... Who did that?"

Two brown eyes, eyebrows raised, edged by a smile, were in her face.

Tina recoiled, but there was nowhere to go. The seat back was stiff. She bumped her head on the metal bar that went all the way across the top of the seat.

"Ouch." She rubbed the back of her head.

Byron Moss straightened up, looming over her. Byron with the lovely brown eyes that kept her out of focus whenever she remembered them—

She cleared her throat.

"You fell asleep. Had a tiring flight?"

His voice was somewhat gentle and quiet, and Tina was beginning to think she had been dreaming that his tone had a sharp edge to it.

*Yeah, must be having a nightmare.*

She yawned and rubbed her eyes.

"We got off the plane?" As soon as she had said it, Tina felt dumb, like she had just given Byron one more "scatterbrained" remark for him to pick on later.

"You got off the plane. We loaded your luggage —all five pieces—onto this bus. We drove all the way from the Lynden Pindling International Airport to Montagu Bay, taking thirty-one minutes due to traffic. And we are now parked outside the Nassau Island Breeze Resort."

Byron waved toward the window. "We unloaded your luggage—three heavy, hard case luggage, two soft sides, but equally heavy—what in the world did you bring?"

Tina didn't feel obligated to answer him.

"Everyone is checking in at the front desk."

"Now?" Tina tried to get up, but her head spun.

"Yes, dear. Did you take Dramamine or some air-sickness meds, perchance?"

*Dear?*

*Perchance?*

Yep. That was Byron for her. He'd say strange literary things like that.

Byron stretched out his hand to help Tina to her feet.

She felt groggy. "Sorry. I stayed up all night to pack my art supplies. Then I couldn't sleep on the flight. Turbulence or something."

"We can get art supplies in Nassau, you know." Byron smiled with his eyes.

He was the only man Tina knew who could smile with his eyes.

"Well, I thought that—I mean, the last time I was here..." Tina wasn't sure how much she should remind Byron of what had happened two years ago when she had come to the Bahamas on her first mission trip outside the United States.

"Yes. Two years ago." Byron stepped back between two seats to let Tina go first toward the exit at the front of the bus. "You forgot all your brushes and canvases."

"You don't miss a thing, do you?"

"I missed you last summer," Byron said. "Why didn't you come?"

*Missed?*

*Did he just say he missed me?*

Tina tried not to read too much into it.

Byron was the last person on earth who would miss Tina.

"The kids at day camp asked for you by name. Where's Miss Tina? Why isn't she here? Doesn't she love us anymore?"

*Love?*

Tina stumbled out of the bus into eighty-something-degree heat. The June sunshine was bright, bright, bright. The sky was clear and blue, and Tina wanted to go for a swim.

Behind her, Byron was on his iPhone.

Tina shed her cardigan she had worn since she sat

down in the cold cabin on the tarmac at the Savannah / Hilton Head International Airport. She was always cold in an airplane cabin, even when the flight was full and the passengers were packed in like paint tubes.

But now she was hot.

"What time is it?" Tina rolled up her cardigan and stuffed it into her worn, oversized zippered tote bag she had been using as her purse for over a year now.

"Two o'clock. Actually, six minutes after two."

"Are you sure it's not six minutes and fourteen seconds after two?"

Byron frowned at his watch. "Well, I don't know..."

Tina gently punched his arm. "Lighten up."

"Did they give you lunch on board?" Byron stood there a minute.

"I guess. I slept through."

"Why didn't they wake you up? You paid for the meal."

"Why are you asking me all these questions, Byron?"

"Because I don't want you to be hungry. Everyone else said they've eaten." Byron stepped toward her. "If you haven't, I'll take you to lunch."

"You'll take me out to lunch?"

Byron nodded. "Yes. Is that a problem?"

"No." Tina wondered why they were standing on the sidewalk. Shouldn't she be checking in?

Then she saw her.

Veronique and her five-inch stilettos, walking briskly toward them as if she were strutting on a catwalk.

She was amazingly graceful.

*Clumsy me, I can't compare.*

Tina watched as Byron dangled the bus keys in front of Veronique. "Thank you for taking the bus back to the school."

Tina wondered how Veronique was going to drive this mammoth of a bus in those heels. Then again, it wasn't her problem, was it?

"How are you going to get home?" Tina asked Byron.

"I left my car in the hotel car park."

*Car park? His way of saying parking lot.*

"You thought of everything." Tina started walking.

"Not everything. You still haven't eaten lunch."

"Don't worry about me. I'll just eat in the hotel restaurant. Surely they have a café of some sort."

Byron stopped at the lobby, and so did Tina. She turned to see what the matter was.

"We need to learn to get along, Tina. Otherwise the Lord's work is not going to happen the next few weeks you're here, or two months, if you decide to stay for the entire camp."

"What does that have to do with where I eat lunch?"

"I get along with everyone else."

"So do I."

"But you and I don't get along with each other."

"Maybe it's best if we stay out of each other's hair," Tina said.

"Or we can have lunch and do things together to break down this wall of ice between us."

"Do things?" Tina widened her eyes. "Like what kind of things?"

"Like maybe we could work in the same class-room and be on the same field trips this summer."

"No. We'd drive each other insane."

Tina went to the end of the shortest line. There were gobs of people in the lobby, checking in. Summer vacationers, possibly. She waved to her teammates and the other fellow volunteers, some of whom were in the front of their lines while others were done and wheeling their bags to the elevator.

"Not if you try to be on time—for once," Byron said.

"Whoa. You just insulted me, and I haven't even checked in."

Byron stared at her.

"Go away, Byron."

"Can't. I'm in charge of the Summer by the Sea Day Camp, remember?"

"Well, bummer. I'm not going to congratulate you for being promoted to assistant headmaster." Even though he probably deserved it. Byron Moss, in spite of his many flaws, was one of the most hard-working men Tina had ever known.

"Can we still do lunch?" Byron's voice was almost pleading. "We have to make the day camp succeed."

Tina's tummy growled.

"Your stomach is begging you on my behalf," Byron said.

Tina burst out laughing. "All right. I'll have to give it to you. You're not only stubborn, but you're also persistent."

"I think those two words mean about the same thing."

"Just say thank you, Byron."

"Thank you, ma'am." Byron glanced at his watch. "I'll help you take your bags to your room after you check in, and we should be on our way by three o'clock."

"You'll help me with my luggage because you don't want me to be late coming back down here to meet you for our already late lunch?"

"No, because your bags are heavy."

"Oh." *How considerate.*

"While you check in, I'll get you a Fanta Grape."

Tina froze. It had been two years since she last had that soda. "You remember."

"I remember everything about you, Clementine Gracielle MacFarland." And off he went.

# CHAPTER TWO

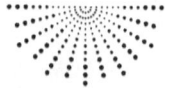

*S*he has baggage.
*Of all kinds.*

Byron Moss flexed his shoulders. He felt a muscle strain from all that baggage handling earlier.

Her baggage.

He reached the cabana on the other side of the outdoor pool and bought a can of ice-cold Fanta Grape. It had to be grape. That was the only Fanta Tina would drink.

Byron didn't know why he would remember such things about her. But he did.

*And one more thing.*

His step had an extra bounce as he recalled Tina's naked ring finger. It had meant that her near engagement to whatshisname had fallen through.

Heaven forbid it had been an annulment or a divorce.

Byron quickly prayed that Tina was still unwed. Otherwise, his mother would not approve—

*Whoa.*

*Mother?*

He tripped up the steps back to the vast indoor-outdoor lobby of the plush Nassau Island Breeze Resort.

He had gotten a great discount at this hotel for the visiting teams. There were ten American Christians altogether serving in various capacities at Chapel by the Sea this summer. Some were teaching at the Vacation Bible School, some at the day camp. Among those teaching at the day camp were three people from Riverside Chapel in Savannah.

The Riverside Chapel team had started out with five people but had dwindled down to three when the wife of the team leader had to be on bed rest due to pregnancy complications. Of course, Byron had not expected the team leader to leave his wife by herself in Savannah.

Ah, Savannah. He had been there some years ago—before Tina—and loved the historic town.

Someday, Byron would like to take another trip to the United States and have a look around. Go on a tour of some coastal cities or take a road trip around the country. Visit Riverside Chapel again. Have lunch with his friend Pastor Diego Flores. See where these people lived in a different type of coastal town than Nassau.

And where Tina lived.

There she was, standing at the check-in counter, rummaging through her giant, shapeless tote bag, looking for something.

Before Byron could reach her, she lost hold of her tote bag, its contents tumbling out to the marble floor, scattering about, making a funny combination of noises—plastic and metal and scrap paper and leather.

Byron braced himself and glanced at his watch.

They weren't going to make it to lunch by three o'clock. After that, he wouldn't make it back to dinner with his mother, brother, and sisters at six o'clock sharp. He wouldn't get to bed by nine o'clock.

*And tomorrow morning, I need to get up early for church—*

*Forget it.*

He had no choice.

Without a word, Byron squatted next to Tina. He picked up the lipstick, lip balm, lip gloss, another tube of lipstick, a container of lip—

*Is she kidding me?*

*How many lips does a woman have?*

He scooped up her heavy coin purse, her passport folder, a spiral-bound notebook that was frayed at the edges, about five pens of various colors, crumpled receipts that looked faded in some parts, and whatever else Tina had in that bag that had probably not been cleaned out in a while.

When he lifted the tote bag to her, he was surprised.

No, shocked.

She had tears in her eyes as she clutched her cardigan against her chest.

"Hey..." Byron dared not touch her.

She looked too fragile, as though if he reached for her, she would simply crumble into a heap on that floor the same way her stuff—there was no other way to describe the pile of things—had done.

Her lips were quivering.

"Are you cold?" Byron asked, realizing that he was still holding the can of Fanta Grape in one hand. It could be turning lukewarm by now, judging from the waft of warm Nassau Bay breeze that came and went through this open space.

The fans were spinning above them, sure, and ventilation was happening around them.

But he felt warm.

*No, hot.*

He frowned. *Why don't I know how I feel?*

He often knew exactly how he felt.

Well, not around Tina, he didn't.

Tina MacFarland would be his downfall, as his prayer partners had warned him. That pretty lady had made him lose his cool too many times the last time she came to town.

*It's that bad.*

But right now, this moment, this very minute, that lady needed his help. And if helping her would break their impasse and enable them to work together as a team, then Byron was willing to swallow his pride and humble himself, no matter how right he was.

Tina sniffed and took her tote bag from Byron. "Thank you. Sorry about that, but I'll be done in a minute, okay? Then we'll go for lunch as we planned, and you can tell me all about Veronique."

*A minute?*

Byron doubted she'd be done in a minute. More like an hour, the way it usually went with this woman.

And what about Veronique?

Why did she want to know about Veronique?

Byron seriously doubted there was anything to tell. Veronique was his assistant at the Chapel by the Sea Christian School, and that was all there was to it.

Well, he was to train her to take over the Summer by the Sea Day Camp.

Yes, what else? That was about it.

Well, Veronique sure gave him the once-over about five times today on their way to the airport, while they were at the airport, and on the drive to the hotel. Byron didn't think anyone had noticed—

Oh. Tina had.

"S-s-sure." He could barely get the word out.

*Look, I can't think.*

*What is this woman doing to me?*

But.

But Tina was single—still single, from the looks of it. Byron had waited for two years for an opportunity to get her on the same page with him.

And he had just begun the process, maybe fifteen—make that twenty—minutes ago, when he had asked her to go to lunch with him, just the two of them, to talk things through.

Now that he thought about it more, Byron began to think it had been a bad idea to ask Tina out. He couldn't recall his rationale for it.

How could he have been forgetful all of a sudden?

He wondered what the team members would

say about his inviting Tina to lunch on the first day she had arrived for the mission work.

What would his church, his school, his teachers, his staff say?

More critically, what would God say?

*Lord Jesus, I pray this is not a fatal error in my judgement.*

# CHAPTER THREE

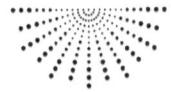

*E*ither Byron had worried too much or God had prevented any disaster from happening, because Tina had begged off lunch, saying that she was not hungry, too tired, and needed to rest after the long flight.

Byron was relieved until he arrived at his mother's beach estate on Paradise Island.

The gnawing feeling of impending disaster didn't go away after dinner with his family. He ate quietly, said little, and basically went through the motion of being among family, and yet his mind was elsewhere.

He realized that he still had a problem. He had to make sure he could work with all of the people who had come a long way to help him run the

Summer by the Sea Day Camp. This was his first year at the helm—previously he had only assisted someone else—and his reputation as the assistant headmaster of the Chapel by the Sea Christian School was at stake.

"Something bothering you, dear?" Mother brought him a bowl of fried plantain chips, only his favorite thing in the world to eat any time of the day.

He shook his head.

"No? Then I know something's bothering you." Mother dug into the chips herself.

"Nothing prayer can't handle." Byron watched Mother nibble at the chips.

She was almost sixty now, her once light-brown hair going silver in places, and yet she still worked a hundred hours a week. The way she spoke gently to her two sons and two daughters belied the fact that she was a fierce CEO at work, managing her chain of five-star Caribbean hotels.

"Let's take a walk?" Mother asked.

"Only if we bring that bowl with us."

"I'll bring it if you tell me what's on your mind."

"Girl problem." Byron's younger brother Donovan waltzed past him without waiting for any replies. He weaved through the family room to the outside veranda and dived into the infinity pool under the moonlight.

Byron sighed.

If Mother wanted to talk to him, Byron knew they had to find another place. He didn't want Donovan to hear anything about Tina, or he'd tease Byron endlessly about it.

The two brothers were three years apart, but Donovan was much taller than Byron for some reason. Byron had inherited Mother's shorter stature, even though he was pushing six feet.

He wondered how tall Tina was without her sandals.

Ah, why did everything have to revolve around the last person in the whole world he could not even begin to understand?

*What makes Tina click?*

*Well, if she clicks at all.*

From the afternoon, her dropped bag, her quickness to change her mind, her curiosity about Veronique, and her general disposition had told Byron that Tina was unfocused and mentally disorganized.

*Did I say that?*

*Oh boy.*

Surely there was something good about her that he could compliment.

Byron ushered Mother toward the side door to the courtyard garden. There they could talk in private.

Outside the property lines, the ocean

surrounding Paradise Island came to life in the night, its waves lapping the sandy shores stretching beyond the Moss family home.

It was here that Byron had grown up, and he had been so used to it that it hadn't occurred to him that this was a life of luxury, until he went to college and switched his major from business to education.

Father had frowned on it, but the fact that Byron would graduate from Brown University, anyway, had allayed Father's fear that Byron would lead a life of poverty.

Teaching school was a noble and altruistic profession and had led Byron into the poorer sections of Nassau. Six years later, he had earned his master's in education while teaching during the day.

Yep, he had worked like a dog to finish his degree.

And it had paid off. He had been promoted to assistant headmaster.

Mother and son sat down on a bench in the side garden, eating chips as they listened to the sounds of the night.

Somewhere in the distance, Donovan was laughing loudly with their sisters, who apparently had joined him in the pool.

"Mother, have you ever worked with amazingly disorganized people?" Byron finally asked.

"Yes, all the time. Have a problem at the school?"

"No, at the day camp."

"Which hasn't started, dear."

"Right. We'll start a week from Monday."

"And the problem is?"

"Tina. She is a problem."

"Ah, Tina. Same woman from two years ago who nearly made you quit the whole educational system and come work for me?" Mother chuckled.

"That Tina."

"If she keeps at it, when can you start work?"

"I'm not going to work for you, Mother."

"Then you'd better solve this Tina problem."

"There is no way—"

Mother raised a palm. "With God, there's always a way."

Byron nodded.

"Who knows why God has brought her back to the Bahamas? Ever wonder what God is up to?"

"All the time." Byron hung his head.

"Sometimes it's more important to trust God without knowing what's going to happen than to try planning it all out ahead of time."

"But doesn't the Bible say that we plan our ways, but God directs our steps?" Byron asked.

"You know, dear, that might be where you need to camp out this entire summer."

"Proverbs 16?" Byron raised an eyebrow.

"Yes, the entire chapter." Mother stopped Byron from reaching into his pocket for his iPhone. "Do you remember your father's last heart attack?"

Byron nodded. He recalled that day too well.

Father had just finished swimming in that pool. He was walking about the grounds when his portrait artist delivered the painting.

"He was so mad at that artist." Mom wiped her eyes.

"All because he'd refused to put a fake smile on Father's face."

"Your father never smiled. But in the portrait for posterity, he wanted a smile, like it or not."

Byron didn't say anything. In many ways, he had inherited his father's eye for details. Good or bad, he had it, together with his angst and impatience with others who couldn't keep up with—

Perfection?

*Sorry, Lord. Only You are perfect.*

"That night, he had a heart attack."

"The doctors couldn't say if it was related to the painting, Mother." But Byron knew. Father had often been stressed out, one way or another, and having one more thing not going his way took him over the edge. Maybe?

"I know it was," Mother said. "So my advice to you, Son, is not to be angry with the artist."

"Don't be angry with the artist." Byron stretched his legs. "I've told you too much about Tina, haven't I?"

"Two years ago now. Let it go, dear. Your father was fifty-seven when he passed away. Don't die young, dear. Live a little." Mother patted Byron's knee. "You know, you've always been the most academic of all my children. In order to run a school, you'll need to be super organized."

Something in her smile told Byron that she was on to something. "But not everyone else I lead is organized."

"Right. It can be like herding cats sometimes." Mother got up with her empty glass bowl. "I'm going to bed. Don't forget to study Proverbs 16."

"About that—I've already prepared other Scripture passages for the day camp staff and teachers to study."

"Not for them, dear. For *you* as you deal with that difficult woman."

"She's not difficult. She's just scatterbrained."

"Ah. An opinion."

"She is!" Byron protested. "And very disorganized."

"Then pray."

"For her to be organized?"

"For God to give you the grace to deal with her."

"Grace. Hmm... And Gracielle is her middle name."

"Isn't that interesting?" Mother asked.

"Indeed." *Very interesting.*

# CHAPTER FOUR

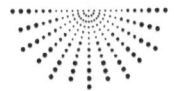

$S$he knew how to make an entrance on Sunday morning at church. That bubblegum-pink floral skirt contrasted wildly with her flaming red hair.

Well, not exactly *flaming*. It was more straw-berry orange. Or something.

And why it mattered to Byron, he couldn't explain to himself.

*Tina, oh Tina.*

He stared—no, watched!—as Tina chattered with Veronique before she sat down on a long pew across the aisle from where the Moss family was sitting.

Somehow Veronique managed to wedge herself into the same pew, and she seemed to be making herself right at home with the American volunteers—some sports coaches, some teachers, some going into ministry, and one befuddling artist.

Yes, *that* artist.

First, she hadn't wanted to eat lunch with him. Then she had said okay. That was before she changed her mind again.

Should he feel embarrassed or what?

The only good thing that had come out of Tina's Saturday indecision was Byron's talk with Mother, now sitting down next to him.

Mother gave him a knowing smile.

*Knowing?*

What did it mean?

Byron stared straight ahead as the choir filled the loft under a bay of stained-glass windows. Chapel by the Sea had owned this building for decades, and a number of churches around the world had copied the design of it.

It would make a lovely wedding chapel—

Someone cleared his throat into Byron's left ear.

*Donovan.*

"I see the redhead is in town." Byron's brother sat down and elbowed him. "Did she say why she didn't come last summer?"

Byron shrugged. Noncommittal.

"I bet it's your fault." Donovan knitted his eyebrows together.

At that moment, Byron saw Father in Donovan's face and eyes and gestures.

And the next moment, Byron felt the weight of his responsibility as the oldest son in the family, holding down the fort now that Father had passed way.

Not that Mother or Donovan needed his help.

No, sir. They seemed to be fine on their own.

"My fault?" Byron asked just as a soft hymn medley started playing.

More people filled the pews. The place was getting stuffy even with the fans at full blast and the windows opened.

"You were too hard on her. Do it again, and she may never come back. I'd have to fly to the US just to ask her out. What's her name again?"

"What did you say?" Byron's iPad slid off his hands and yanked the cord around his neck.

"Never mind. It's coming back to me. Tina Somebody." Donovan adjusted his tie as one of the assistant pastors tapped the lectern microphone and began his long list of announcements.

Byron had no idea why Donovan's words irritated him.

*This is ridiculous!*

Byron kept his eyes looking ahead of him, over the wooden pews and the sea of heads. He didn't hear a single word of the announcements. No matter. The assistant pastor had basically read off the morning service program.

The sun rose up the tall French doors to his left, casting a mosaic of filtered stained-glass colors from the transom windows above the doors onto the wooden floors and pews. Blue from the Caribbean Sea, yellow from those pretty allamanda petals, green from Tina's eyes, pink from her skirt—

*Wait a minute!*

Byron closed his eyes and prayed away this distraction.

A thwack-thwack sound to his right made Byron open his eyes to see Mother fanning herself with the program. The trifold paper looked like it was about to rip.

Suddenly, a freckled hand holding an open fan with Japanese inscription on it appeared in front of Mother.

Byron flicked up his eyes and met Tina's green eyes, glorious in the sunlight.

"Thank you, Tina," Mother said.

Byron nodded to Tina, who swiftly returned to her seat.

Mother relaxed, clearly savoring the artificial wind on her face and neck.

She leaned toward Byron. "Your father and I were going to donate an air conditioner but Pastor

Dixon said it would make our congregation too comfortable in church. This is not a club, he said."

Was Byron seeing things, or were those tears in Mother's eyes?

"We all miss him," Byron said softly as the church service began with a call to prayer.

When Father had been alive, he loved this part of the service best of all. Sometimes Pastor Dixon would ask him to pray.

"Mr. Moss!" he'd say in his deep, pastoral voice. "Would you do us the honor and pray to God in heaven for us, pray that He would rain down His blessings from above, pray that He would bless our congregation?"

And Father would say, "To God be the glory!"

He would stand up and pray so loudly that he didn't need a microphone to reach the corners of this little church by the sea.

Byron missed that.

When Father had passed away suddenly, the whole family—in fact, the whole church—was devastated. The outpouring of support had been tremendous.

Yet the inward grief Byron and his family had felt had been overwhelming as well.

It had hit Byron the hardest.

Father had always expected that Byron, as the

firstborn son, would take over their family business. The chain of beach hotels wasn't going to run itself.

Well, Byron had said no.

In Father's face.

For one, Byron felt a strong conviction against running casinos, which usually took up an entire floor at Moss Resorts. To him, gambling was a sin, and he wanted no part of it.

Secondly, he wanted to teach. Teaching students in a classroom and administrating a school were fun for him. He had worked very hard to get to the position of assistant headmaster. If he kept working hard, he could become the headmaster of Chapel by the Sea Christian School when Gowan Clarke retired in five years—

*Let's not plan too far ahead.*

That was what Mother had said when Father was in his last days in the ICU.

"Let God deal with the future," Mother had added. "Today has enough troubles of its own."

*Today.*

"Mr. Moss!"

Next to Byron, Donovan rose.

"I meant the other one, but you're Mr. Moss too." Pastor Dixon pointed to Byron.

The laughter of the entire congregation hit Byron like a hot noonday sun. He couldn't slink farther down his pew seat. He closed his eyes in great shame.

*Pay attention in class—I mean, church!*

*What is going on with my head?*

*Can't I think straight?*

He willed himself to be silent and pray along with Donovan, who said a heartfelt prayer before he sat down.

"Stop daydreaming, big Brother," Donovan whispered.

The congregation rose and sang a harmonious *Jesus Loves Me* as Pastor Dixon waved for the little children of the church to go forward down the aisle, led by their Sunday School teachers. The little ones dressed so smartly and nicely that everyone oohed and ahhed.

"Someday you'll have little ones of your own," Mother whispered to Byron.

All Byron could see were redheaded toddlers.

*It's not going to happen.*

*After all, red hair is a recessive gene—*

Byron cleared his throat.

Pastor Dixon gave a short sermonette about how God cared for everyone, including little babies and toddlers and preschoolers. The children listened with such sweet innocence and rapt attention that Byron was impressed.

He couldn't remember when he and Donovan

were ever totally still in church, except when they had fallen asleep on their parents' laps during a sermon.

"God is love." Pastor Dixon read the end of 1 John 4:8. "Jesus loves you, little children. Always. No matter what. Can you remember that? Say it with me. Jesus loves me!"

A little kid broke into song.

And the whole congregation joined in to sing the refrain again.

"When you skin your knees or catch a cold, when you are happily playing in the playground, remember that Jesus loves you all the time," Pastor Dixon concluded. "How many of you are going to be five years old next year?"

Several hands shot up.

"Well, next year you'll be promoted to big church, and you can sit with your mothers and fathers in this sacred place we call the sanctuary. Wouldn't you love that?"

"Yay!" The four-year-olds clapped.

Pastor Dixon prayed for the children and dismissed them to their Sunday School.

As they filed past Byron, he waved to the kids, some of whom had attended Chapel by the Sea Preschool the year before. Several of them were entering kindergarten next year.

Byron was glad that his church didn't send the

children away to their own children's church somewhere at the back of the building, away from the
main sanctuary.

He had nothing against Bible studies and arts
and crafts during church time, but his own parents
had brought his siblings and him to the sanctuary
since he had been four years old, learning to sit
quietly, pay attention, sing what he could read from
the hymnal, and take notes when God's preacher
preached.

*Whoa. I sure am opinionated. Is that why Tina
thinks ill of me?*

Still, he remembered holding Mother's hand
one Sunday at church so long ago. She had been so
pregnant that she went into labor right before lunch.
Out popped his twin sisters, Claire and Selena.

When they had turned four, they sat in the
pews during the Sunday morning church service,
and did so through their entire primary and
secondary school years until they went to university.

*That's how I want my family to be.*

*I want my wife and kids to sit together with me
in church every Sunday to listen to God's Word.*

Wife?

Kids?

He was trying to think through a knot, when
next thing he knew, the congregation was clapping,
and he looked up to find the volunteers from the

United States standing at the lectern. Some had song books in front of them, some carried guitars, and Tina held a flute.

Backtracking, Byron figured the pastor had introduced the group. And he had missed the introduction.

What was said about them? Was Byron mentioned? Was he supposed to wave to the crowd or respond somehow?

He had missed it all.

And he knew why.

*That woman is going to be the end of me.*

# CHAPTER FIVE

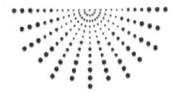

 fter church, Tina was still humming Fanny Crosby's "O Love Divine" hymn that the visiting volunteers had sung before Pastor Dixon preached his long sermon, when Byron's mom appeared in front of her.

"I'm Nancy Moss, Byron's mother."

"And you know my name." Tina shook Nancy's extended hand. It was soft. "Nice to meet you, Byron's mother."

"Thank you for letting me borrow your fan." Nancy handed the fan back to Tina.

"Oh, you keep it," Tina said. "I bought a dozen of those at the Narita airport."

"Really?"

"Yeah, it was an impulse buy. Terrible, I know."

"I know how that is." Nancy smiled. "Except I might have bought more than fans."

"Like islands, for example," someone said from behind Nancy.

*Islands?*

Tina turned toward the voice that sounded like Byron's, but she knew it wasn't his voice, not exactly.

He towered over Tina. Before she could recall his name, he gave her a hug.

"Remember me? Donovan?"

"Ah yes." Byron's younger brother. "Good to see you again."

*Speaking of Byron...*

Tina scanned the sanctuary. No Byron.

*Where did he go?*

Donovan turned to everyone. "Friends, lunch on me back at the Nassau Island Breeze Resort."

Tina wondered why he had to say the entire name of the hotel, but then she remembered Donovan, the walking advertisement, from two years ago.

Donovan had one arm over Tina's shoulders and the other arm over Veronique's shoulders. Tina turned her neck and spotted Byron.

She slid out of Donovan's elbow and made a beeline for Byron.

"Coming?" she asked.

Byron hesitated. His lips were moving.

"It can wait," Tina added.

"What?" Byron picked up a couple of programs off the floor. Some church members had dropped them on their way out, it seemed.

"The planning meeting with yourself." Tina pointed to Byron's head. "That can wait until after lunch."

"We have an evening service tonight, so this is a short day."

"It's Sunday, Byron. Come to lunch with us."

"Us? You and my brother?"

"Us. A dozen people."

Byron reached for Tina's face, and his thumb gently flicked off something from her right cheek. "Clay. Stuck to your cheek and dried there. What did you do before church?"

Tina laughed. "You mean I had that on my face the entire service?"

"Even while you were up there singing... I love that hymn."

"Me too. I mean, I like a lot of hymns."

"Yeah, that's what I meant too." Byron tossed the programs into a nearby recycle bin. "Now I know why your five-piece luggage was heavy."

"Why, Detective Moss? Pray tell." Tina put her hand around Byron's arm and ushered him out of the sanctuary.

"You brought clay. I told you we have clay in Nassau."

"I forgot." Tina's voice was low. Her hand slipped from Byron's arm. "Don't call me a scatterbrain."

Byron stopped. He breathed deeply. Sighed. "About that."

Tina waited.

"That was two years ago, Tina."

Tina tried to hold it in. But her eyes stung. It must be the sun.

Byron looked startled. "Tina?"

~

*A*nyone *knows that words can hurt. But woe is me. She still feels it two years later.*

Those tears weren't there because the sun shone into Tina's liquid green eyes. Such pretty eyes.

"Please don't," Byron whispered. "I didn't mean... I might have meant it at that time, but it was spoken in sincerity."

"You insult people sincerely?" Tina's voice broke.

It had always been important to Byron that his school staff, day camp volunteers, and team members got things done in any projects he led. They reached their goals. Met their objectives.

That was all that had mattered to him two summers ago at the Vacation Bible School and summer outreach.

But.

One of Pastor Dixon's past sermons came to mind. He had quoted 1 Corinthians 13:13.

*And now abide faith, hope, love, these three; but the greatest of these is love.*

Byron's shoulders slacked as his pastor's voice ricocheted in his head.

*Love! The greatest of these is love!*

Byron's thumbs wiped away tiny trickles of tears on Tina's face. "Stop, Tina. Please."

She didn't, and neither did Pastor Dixon's words running in Byron's head.

*Love, brothers and sisters in Christ! Love! If all you have are faith and hope, and you have no love, you are nothing more than noisy, clanging cymbals.*

Byron gulped. The indictment was severe.

*Noisy cymbals.*

Were those all that Byron had been to Tina two years ago?

Another verse from 1 Corinthians 13:1 rang in his head.

*Though I speak with the tongues of men and of angels, but have not love, I have become sounding brass or a clanging cymbal.*

Byron wanted to say something repentant. He wasn't sure how to word it. He decided that being frank was best. "Please forgive me, Tina. I was wrong."

Before Tina could reply, someone honked at them.

It was Donovan driving his red-hot Humvee. "You two coming?"

# CHAPTER SIX

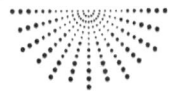

"Feeling better?" That was the first thing Byron said to Tina when he came to her as she stood in the shade of the awning by the juice bar.

Well, she wasn't exactly standing alone, since there were many people around her this side of the pool. She had to get out of the hot Caribbean afternoon sun after that full lunch. And she could not get into the water today.

Around them, Summer by the Sea Day Camp volunteers milled about the hotel cabana, jumping in the pool with other hotel guests.

Tina nodded. "I didn't mean to be weepy, okay? Sorry. Just having my monthlies—oops."

Her face reddened.

"I know what monthlies are," Byron said quietly. "I have two sisters."

"Well, it's still no excuse, I know. I'm sorry—"

"Tina, don't say sorry again. I don't want to hear it."

"Every time I'm around you, I don't know how to..."

"Behave?" Byron smiled. "That makes two of us. Maybe we should have had that lunch to clear the air and get on the same page."

"We just had lunch."

"I meant the lunch you canceled yesterday."

Tina sighed. Her first day on the ground on Saturday probably hadn't given Byron a good second impression of her after the fiasco two years ago. To be sure, she had been exhausted after a sleepless night and the flight to Nassau. She had every good reason to cancel their Saturday lunch.

"In a way, I'm glad we didn't have the lunch." Tina kept her voice down. She didn't want to make a scene. "It's not a very good idea, if you don't mind me saying it."

"You can tell me anything as frankly as you want."

"What will your staff think if they see you and me at lunch?"

"It would be a business lunch."

"If Lucy and Keith came along, it would make it less questionable."

"Well, sure. I didn't think of them, because I don't have a problem with them. Oh sorry. It came out all wrong."

"Or you meant it," Tina said. "I am a *problem* to you, am I not, Byron Moss?"

"You are not a problem to me." Byron stepped closer. "You're a paradox."

*A paradox?*

As Tina wondered about that, she smelled Byron's aftershave, and all thoughts were lost. She didn't know he had any beard to shave.

She chuckled.

"You read my mind and found something funny?" Byron asked.

"It's nothing. Just...nothing."

"We have a meeting tomorrow morning at nine o'clock sharp." Byron lifted the empty Fanta bottle from Tina's hand. "Want another?"

Tina frowned. "And you're telling me the time because..."

"Just a gentle reminder. That's all."

"So I shouldn't take it seriously?"

"You should take it very seriously. I want to see you at nine."

"You *want* to see me."

"Poor choice of word. I *must* see you at nine."

"Even worse." Tina smiled and walked toward the pool café.

Byron followed after her. "I can't get my words right when I'm with you."

"That wasn't the case two years ago when I was here."

"No, it wasn't. Things have changed."

"Have they?" Tina ordered another Fanta. She paid for it, then turned toward Byron. "I'll see you tomorrow, all right? I'm going to get some prep work done. Can't wait for summer camp to start."

"It's a week away from tomorrow."

"I'll be early. You would be happy about that, wouldn't you?" Out of the corner of Tina's eye, she spotted Veronique coming over in her surprisingly modest swimsuit. Not a two-piece, but a neon-orange one-piece with a skirt.

And heels.

She had on heels.

Again.

Tina waited. Veronique was showing off her outfit, bright in the sun, and made the entire poolside look like a catwalk.

Suddenly, Tina feared she herself would slip and trip on her cheap flip-flops.

Byron held her elbow. "Whoa. You okay?"

"What happened?"

"You lost your balance."

"I did?" Tina looked down. One of her flip-flops was off her foot. Her toes scooted toward it and nabbed it. She slid it back on.

"Go get some rest," Byron said quietly. "I'll see you tonight at the evening service, right?"

"Byron! Byronnnn!" Veronique screeched.

"All right. You talk to your girlfriend." Tina peeled away.

"She's not..."

Tina didn't hear the rest of it. Veronique's voice masked whatever it was Byron was saying.

# CHAPTER SEVEN

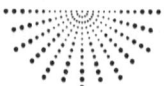

"**W**hat do you mean she missed the bus?" Byron stood at the door and stared at the empty seat he had expected Tina to sit in at this all-important mandatory Summer by the Sea Day Camp staff meeting.

"She was late." Veronique tapped her watch. "I told everybody. Eight twenty-five. On the minute."

"So you left her behind?" Byron's fingers rolled into fists in his khaki pants pockets.

"Yeaaahhh." Veronique drew out the word. She sat down, crossed her legs, and inspected her coral-pink fingernails.

"At the hotel?"

"Wherever she is. Eight twenty-five. Nassau time."

Lucy Khoo, one of the volunteers and Tina's

roommate at the hotel, raised her hand. "Byron, I'm sorry. I was downstairs eating breakfast. I should have gone upstairs to get her."

"Was she sleeping?" Byron cringed at his own question. Too personal.

"She was in the shower when I left to meet the others," Lucy replied. "It's my fault. Don't blame her."

Byron wasn't sure how to respond.

*Okay. Pray first.*

*Dear Lord, that woman is the end of me!*

Maybe that wasn't a prayer.

"Is she taking a jitney here?" Byron asked as calmly as he could. "Or maybe a taxi?"

"I don't think she'll walk." Veronique shrugged.

Lucy shrugged.

Everyone shrugged.

Byron drew a deep breath and counted to ten. Then twenty. Then five more, for good measure.

He paced. "This is a mandatory planning meeting. I don't have to remind everyone."

"She knew." Veronique waved her nails in the air in a geometric formation. Byron knew she did that when she lost her patience. "Everybody knew."

Another volunteer stood up. Keith Medford, the leader of the Savannah team. "I'll go back to get her."

Byron wasn't sure why he didn't like the idea of

Keith going back to the hotel to pick up Tina. Not that a team couldn't have two leaders, especially a proactive leader such as Keith, but not in front of Tina.

*Huh? Whatever did I mean?*

"Why in the world didn't you wait for her?" Byron felt the frustration in his own voice, but he couldn't hold it in.

"Then we'll *all* be late." Veronique's voice was dismissive. "You said the meeting is at nine sharp, and here we are."

Byron glanced at the clock. It was five minutes after nine o'clock.

"Give me a minute." He stepped outside the door, closed it, and leaned against the painted walls. He pinched his nose bridge.

*What do I do, Lord?*

His iPhone pinged several times, telling him he had email.

*Okay. That's it.*

Byron called Tina. No answer.

He decided against leaving her a message.

He dragged himself back to the meeting room where volunteers from all over the hemisphere and his own day camp staffers were waiting for him to tell them what to do the next two months.

He handed Keith his iPhone. And tried to keep

his voice low. "Could you record our meeting? I'll email it to Tina."

"Sure thing. Good idea, man."

"But this shall not happen again," Byron said.

Yet he didn't believe it himself.

Anything could happen with Tina.

# CHAPTER EIGHT

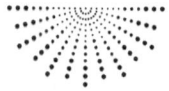

ina was hiding under the covers when Lucy walked into their hotel room. She could sense that Lucy was standing over her bed. She slid the comforter down from her face.

Lucy put down her folder on the round table in the small room. She sat down at the end of Tina's bed.

"Little did I know that when I signed up for day camp, it would be day cramps," Tina said feebly.

By the time she had reached the lobby earlier this morning, Veronique's bus had left, the end of its tail pipe only a whiff of exhaust as it exited the hotel gate.

So she had gone back to bed, her hair all wet from the shower.

"I hate it when that happens," Lucy said. "Do

you want me to get something for you from the pharmacy?"

"Already done that. The concierge was very helpful." Tina closed her eyes. "This, too, shall pass."

"Well, at least it's not food poisoning. I was concerned about that feast that Donovan threw yesterday."

"It was just lunch, Lucy."

"Yeah. I've never seen so much seafood in my life."

"It was a buffet."

"You're in a bad mood."

"Sorry. I am." Tina's lips trembled again. She sniffled.

"I'm praying for you." Then Lucy laughed. "You should have seen Byron. He was bent out of shape over your absence at the meeting."

*Poor Byron.*

"Maybe you should call him to let him know."

"He's been calling. Repeatedly. I turned off my phone."

Lucy raised her eyebrows.

"I don't know what to tell him," Tina explained. "It's none of his business."

"You could say you're not feeling well, and that would be the truth."

"It won't come out right." Tina tried to sit up.

"Every time I'm with him I'm a giddy schoolgirl, and I say and do all the wrong things."

"Avoid him then," Lucy said.

"Easier said than done. He's in charge of day camp, remember?"

"We'll pray."

Tina chuckled. "That he'll get fired?"

"That's an option. Veronique can handle everything."

"Oy, that's even worse." Tina's head fell back on the plush pillow. "Lots of women have this, and they can handle it better. I feel like I'm the least of all the women."

"No, Tina. Don't think that way." Lucy went to the window and drew the blinds open.

Tina squinted at the bright late-morning sunshine.

*I should get out of bed.* "Maybe walking around a bit could help."

"We'll google and see if we can find some remedies to help you."

"Google this away, please."

"In all things, give thanks, remember?" Lucy leaned against the windowsill.

Tina nodded.

"You'd better get well soon, is all I can say. We're checking out tomorrow morning."

"I forgot about that." Slowly, Tina sat up. "I wonder who's hosting us."

"You and I are staying with Veronique—"

"No!" Tina's cramps worsened at that very second.

"It'll be okay. We'll room together. Help each other."

"You mean you'll help me?" Tina asked. "You don't need any help."

"Tina, my friend, you're humble, but there's a difference between humbling ourselves and humiliating ourselves. Let's find our self-worth in Christ alone, shall we? In Him we're worth more than sparrow or gold. We're worth so much that God's Son Himself died on the cross for us. Now stop debasing yourself and thinking of how helpless you are."

"Byron thinks—"

"Byron is human. Don't put stock in what people think. Focus on what God thinks of you. He who has begun a good work in you will complete it."

"Philippians 1:6," Tina said. She had memorized the verse years ago in children's Sunday School. "'...being confident of this very thing, that He who has begun a good work in you will complete it until the day of Jesus Christ.'"

"There you go. Keep your eyes on Jesus, not on Byron or on Veronique."

*Veronique.*

Tina drew a breath. "How did we end up with her? What happened to Mrs. Clarke?"

"She bailed out. Her husband—you know Gowan Clarke, the school principal?—has multiple doctor visits this summer, and their grandchildren are coming to town all of a sudden."

Headmaster Gowan Clarke. Byron's boss. "What's going on with him?"

Lucy shrugged. "Byron didn't say, but I'll be praying for his health problems, whatever they are."

"You're terrific. You're always praying for someone."

"Anyone can pray." Lucy pointed to Tina. "And I'm praying for you too."

"I know. I need a better head. Be less scatterbrained."

"Stop it."

"Byron said I was—oh." Tina felt ashamed. "He has apologized."

"When?"

"Yesterday after lunch."

"When you two were lovey-dovey at the cabana?"

"We were not!"

"Whatever. So if he has apologized, don't bring it up again."

"I know. I forget."

Lucy was going to say something, but her phone rang. She fished it out of her skirt pocket. "Hey, Byron. Yeah, she's here. She's not feeling well... No need to panic. It's not food poisoning... Not infectious... Thanks. I'll tell her. I'm sure... Yes. Bye."

"Tell me what?" Feeling better now, Tina slipped into her flip-flops.

"He says he has a good family doctor."

"How thoughtful."

"Isn't he? He's also praying for you."

Tina stopped. "Uh-oh."

"Uh-oh what? It's good for him to pray instead of worrying about you."

"We don't know what Byron is asking God for."

"But God will only give you what is good," Lucy countered. "If you ask for bread, will your heavenly Father give you a stone? Besides, God will not go against His own will, and there is no evil in Him to give you."

"That's a good reminder." Tina reached for her iPhone. She queried her online Bible and found the passage. "It says, 'If a son asks for bread from any father among you, will he give him a stone? Or if he asks for a fish, will he give him a serpent instead of a fish? Or if he asks for an egg, will he offer him a scorpion?' Luke 11:11-12."

"That's right." Lucy also read from her phone. "Luke 11: 13 says, 'If you then, being evil, know how to give good gifts to your children, how much more will your heavenly Father give the Holy Spirit to those who ask Him!' Is that a good passage or what?"

"That's amazing, Lucy. You should teach Bible."

"You think? I'm writing a devotional book, actually, that I hope will encourage other Christian women."

"Just don't mention me and all my problems."

"Which Jesus has nailed to the cross! Problems solved."

"Amen," Tina said, and she began to believe it.

# CHAPTER NINE

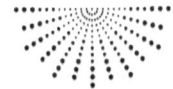

yron was reading his morning email as
he walked along the edges of a quadrangle between two wings of the Chapel by the Sea
Christian School, when he heard the prettiest
whistling this side of heaven.

It perked his interest because the whistling tried
to match the morning chirps of the birds.

His legs took him around a corner and across a
carpet of green grass and fallen red poinciana petals
directly to the siren song.

And there she was.

In a bright green tee-shirt.

Byron took a deep breath and steadied himself.

At the wooden picnic table on the veranda
outside the art room, Tina MacFarland was sitting

pretty, playing with scissors and colorful construction paper.

And whistling in the direction of the poinciana trees.

Byron stepped into the morning sunshine, conscious that she could see him crossing the grass toward her.

Tina stopped whistling and waved to him. "Good morning!"

She looked well. She hadn't returned any of his calls from Monday, but he had simply chalked it all up to her monthly moodiness.

Usually, he would feel invasive for knowing about such things, but as he had told Tina, he had two sisters, and they had given him all the information there was to know about "women things" ever since they had been twelve years old.

*So there. Nothing new under the sun.*

"Morning. It's eight o'clock," Byron said.

Tina smiled. "Thank you for letting me know the time. When it's nine o'clock, you may tell me again."

"Huh?" *What is wrong with this woman?*

Eccentric came to mind, but Byron did not want to call Tina eccentric. In fact, she was intriguing.

*Yes, intriguing is a better word.*

"What brings you here?" Tina asked.

"I'm passing through on my way to a meeting

and to check on the science wing renovations on the other side of the campus." Byron didn't know why he had explained in great detail, but this was Tina, and he felt a need to tell her everything.

*Well, not everything.*

There were things—feelings—he could not explain even to himself.

"I called a meeting at nine o'clock, and you failed to show up," Byron said. "I moved today's meeting to eleven, and here you are at eight in the morning."

"Today is a workday." Tina waved her scissors about.

"So was yesterday."

"I was unwell yesterday, as you know."

"You seem to be better today. I'm glad."

"And you're also glad that I'm not infectious." Tina squinted at Byron.

"Sorry. I was thinking of the other teachers and the kids." Byron sighed. "How did you get here?"

"Your brother's driver picked up Lucy and me," Tina said nonchalantly.

Byron could not believe what he was hearing. "Donovan?"

"You only have one brother."

"How did he—Did you call him?" Byron had to sit down. So he did. Right on the bench across from the pile of colorful construction paper between him and Tina. It wasn't much of a barrier.

"No. He called last evening to say hello, and we chatted, and he couldn't believe I missed the bus. He offered to always provide his driver free of charge."

*Always? Always?* Byron grunted.

"Did you have a comment?" Tina asked. "Or is that just guttural noise?"

Byron didn't know how to respond to that. Donovan had always been competitive, but Byron didn't think for a moment that Tina was their competition.

*No, it can't be.*

*Tina isn't even Donovan's type.*

"Thank you for recording the meeting for me," Tina said. "That was considerate of you."

"I'll make sure you won't be late for any meeting or class the next three weeks."

Tina put down her scissors. "Not to worry. Donovan says his driver will pick me up anytime."

"There's no need to get Donovan involved." Byron bristled. He hoped it wasn't obvious.

"He says he doesn't mind. He found it amusing that Veronique left me behind. I did explain it was my fault."

"Yes, it was."

"Snappy this morning, aren't we? Did you

spend time with God when you got up?" Tina asked, returning to her paper cutouts.

Byron saw then that she was making name tags. Next to the stack of shaped cutouts was a printout of day camper names he had prepared for the teachers. That meant Tina had to have logged on to the teacher's website somewhere between yesterday and this morning to make the printout at a location where she had access to a printer.

"Where did you print that?" Byron asked.

"Veronique did it for me from her office. Why?"

*Ah, Veronique.*

Byron sighed. He'd been thinking too much.

"Earth to Byron," Tina said in a singsong voice.

"You know, you won't be late if you leave with Veronique every morning. She's always on time."

"As opposed to being always late?" Tina's voice didn't sound emotional. It was as if she was stating facts that she had always known and accepted as part of her life.

"You don't have to be *always* late. If Veronique leaves without you, text me, and I'll come pick you up."

"Didn't I just say that Donovan's driver—"

"I don't want his driver to pick you up."

"Why?" Tina straightened up.

The sun rising into the Bahamian sky brought

out orange and red sparkles in her hair. Byron realized he was staring.

"Maybe if you moved your clock one hour forward, you won't ever be late." Byron didn't know how that idea rolled out of his mouth. It sounded indicting.

"You mean live in my own little time zone?" Tina's voice was perturbed now.

"Aren't you already?" *Uh-oh. Fighting words.*

Tina's green eyes flared. In the morning light, they looked altogether lovely. Byron could stare into them forever, but she snapped them closed. Then she clamped her mouth—her pretty mouth—got off the bench, and walked away.

"I was joking!" Byron followed her through the open double doors into the art room and nearly tripped on a row of suitcases. "Whoa! What are these things doing here?"

Tina spun around. "The hotel checkout is at eleven o'clock, did you realize that?"

"So?"

"You scheduled our meeting at the same time, so I had to pack up early and bring all my luggage here. Maybe you can organize better schedules," Tina snapped. "And use your eyes when you walk."

"I did!" *On you.*

Byron quickened his pace and stepped in front of Tina. "I'm sorry. Forgive me?"

Chuckles behind him made him turn around. Two secondary school students and an adult volunteer—the mother of one of the teenagers—were standing at the door connecting the art room to the interior hallway.

"We've never heard Mr. Moss apologize like that," one of the teenagers said.

"And we've never seen him clumsy, tripping over things," the other chimed.

"Hush, girls," the adult said.

"My helpers!" Tina ducked around Byron, spread out her arms, and embraced her visitors.

"So nice of you to come early to help me today. I'm sorry I wasn't here yesterday afternoon. Had the cramps..." Tina glanced over at Byron standing there by himself. "Not infectious!"

The teens sympathized with her, all chatting at the same time.

Byron decided to let it go. He had a meeting with the headmaster at—

*Oh no!*

His eyes dipped toward his watch. "In twelve seconds!"

As Byron ran out of the room, he could hear the teens say loudly, "Mr. Moss is never late!"

And then he heard Tina say, "There's always a first time."

*That's it. My reputation is ruined.*

# CHAPTER TEN

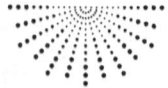

"Stage four?" Byron shook his head slowly at Headmaster Gowan Clarke. "I'm sorry, sir. So, so sorry."

"I knew I had some kind of it, so it's not totally unexpected." The headmaster spoke those words so calmly that it put Byron to shame. "More test results are coming in tomorrow, and then we'll set the course for treatment."

*Treatment? There might not be a cure for him.*

Byron could not reel back his shock. Gowan Clarke was only fifty-four years old, a few years younger than when Byron's own father had passed away. Why did all the good people—

"Take heart, son. God is in control."

"Yes, He is always sovereign."

"Even over such a disease as cancer." Clarke

pointed a finger at Byron. "Never, ever, ever forget that."

"Yes, sir."

"Even in the day-to-day operations of this very small school, we have to depend on almighty God to carry us through. Like Pastor Dixon says all the time, be thankful."

Byron nodded. Inside, his heart dropped to his stomach like an anvil.

"The question is whether you're ready to keep up with God, Byron."

*Am I?* Byron didn't have an answer.

"We are a very small educational establishment, as you know, and the responsibilities of one headmaster spans all the way from preschool and kindergarten to primary and secondary schools. Are you ready for this?"

*Am I?*

"I can take your hesitation to mean one of two things. Either you're thinking about this seriously or you're unprepared."

"I'm prepared, sir."

"But?"

"Your shoes are very big, sir."

"I do wear a size fourteen."

Byron laughed so hard that tears welled in his eyes.

"Now, Byron, it's only an interim position. The

school board has been informed, and they will be interviewing for a new headmaster. It is my hope that, as my protégé, you will earn this position. There's no need to find someone from the outside when you're already here."

"But you could—I mean, with the proper treatment, cancers can be in remission," Byron said.

"Not always for pancreatic cancer, son." Clarke smiled. "Don't worry. I will see you again in heaven. And when I get there, I will play a couple of rounds of golf with your father. I am assuming there will be no fishing in heaven, since we're not killing any fish."

"I don't know about that, sir, since we're feasting in heaven."

"I'm of the belief that we are all vegetarians in heaven."

"You mean we won't have steak?"

"Look at us." Clarke shook his head. "We're off topic."

"And we pride ourselves as being meticulous."

"Indeed. Good thing nobody else is listening in to our rabbit trails." Clarke rose from his chair and walked to the window.

Byron stared at that chair, soon to be his, but only for a short time if the board did not approve his application for the headmaster position.

Why would they not approve him?

Byron could think of many things, but one of them was what Tina had said this morning.

*Maybe you can organize better schedules...*

Byron had prided himself at being the most organized person he ever knew now that Father had passed away. Not even Donovan and Mother came close to his ability to organize.

And yet he had gotten the hotel checkout time and the second staff meeting crisscrossed.

*Not good at all.*

He felt inadequate to fill that seat.

"Sir, I will do everything I can to help you through this transition period. When the new head-master comes, I will do my best to help him or her."

Clarke seemed to study him. A little smile edged his lips. "If I didn't know you any better, I'd say you're a humble man."

*What?*

"But since we have worked together these four or five years, I've gotten to know you more. I suspect you had a mishap recently that has shaken your confidence." Clarke returned to his seat.

"A mishap?"

"Yes. Did something happen at the day camp I need to know about?"

"Like what?"

"People management, for example?"

"People management?"

"Anyone giving you trouble?"

*Tina!* "No."

"Are you getting along with everyone?"

*Gulp.* "Trying to."

"Good answer, Byron. A leader should not be a people pleaser. Yet a leader should not be so assertive that he earns the name of a dictator."

Byron nodded.

*Tina thinks I'm...*

"I'm starting chemo next week."

Byron snapped back into the conversation. "Whoa. Same week as the start of day camp."

"Fortunately, for you and me both, our faculty meeting isn't until the tenth of August, and school doesn't begin until the seventeenth. That gives us about seven to eight weeks to transition. We have a bit of time, except for a few things."

Byron nodded. "Yes, the delay in the science lab expansion."

"That's one. Once they fix the water drainage problem, we'll have a new science wing." Clarke tapped the window pane with his fingers. "But it's going to take a few more weeks. After that we might not have enough money or time to build new kinder-garten classrooms."

Byron wasn't sure why Clarke was repeating what he had told him the week before. Yes, he had cancer, but his mind wasn't going, was it? It seemed

that the headmaster was rehashing things unnec-
essarily.

Okay. Clarke had a lot going on right now. Like
incurable pancreatic cancer, for example.

*Give the man some grace.*

At the back of Byron's mind, another note-to-
self popped into his head.

*Give Tina grace too. God's grace. She needs a lot
of it.*

*Did I say a lot?*

# CHAPTER ELEVEN

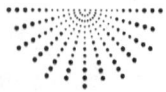

ina wandered off the beaten path, looking for outdoor painting spots she could safely take her day campers to in the next few weeks. Between hedges of dark-green bushes, she found the lovely garden she had visited two years ago.

This time the bougainvilleas seemed so much brighter and taller. The mauve and dark rosy petals of one tree contrasted with the white flowers of the tree next to it.

No one else was around. She heard birds in the air, distant vehicles, a bit of the ocean, and an occasional airplane overhead. Otherwise it was peaceful and quiet.

The bougainvilleas had little fragrance, if at all, but she loved the colors. She hadn't been much of a watercolorist, but her artist friend from Savannah, Abilene Dupree-Cargill, was one.

"I bet she could paint this scene," Tina said aloud.

"What scene?"

Tina jumped about five inches into the air. She spun around and grasped the collar of her tee shirt. The fabric wrinkled under her clenched fingers.

"Gus!" She greeted her old friend. Augustus "Gus" Moss was one of Byron's cousins, as Tina recalled. "You still doing landscaping?"

"Indeed. I must've made a terribly good impression on you when I last saw you." Gus dropped his rake on the ground, took off his gloves, and hugged Tina.

"How can one forget a gentleman who brings a lady flowers?"

"Hibiscus, your favorite. And frangipani, not your favorite."

"You do remember," Tina said. "How have you been?"

Weatherworn, Augustus looked older than his thirty-something years of age. He still didn't have a ring on his finger. Poor guy had been trying to get married for years.

Tina had reminded him that not any woman would do for him. She had to be God's chosen woman for him. A lady for a gentleman. No one less would suffice.

"Never better," Augustus said. "Say, you cut your hair. It used to be all the way down to your waist."

"I'm glad you noticed. My curls were getting heavy and too thick for hot weather."

"Love it at shoulder length. You look good, Tina."

"Thank you. And you do too."

"Now, what are you doing here, wandering around this morning?"

"I have a meeting at eleven o'clock. I have a bit of time to spare." Tina leaned toward Augustus's wristwatch. "Oh no. I had no idea. Is your watch accurate?"

"Yes." Augustus wagged a finger at her. "You're ten minutes late already."

"I thought this would be a short stroll."

"Strolls are never short. Otherwise, it's not a stroll."

"True. And you promised me a stroll through your tamarind tree grove."

"I did, didn't I? Let's do that soon. How long are you in town this time?"

"Three weeks."

"I thought the day camp is for seven weeks."

"Yes, but another art teacher is handling the

other four weeks. I'll stay for an extra few days just for my own personal time off, and then I'll have to go back to my pottery studio, you know. Can't leave the business to my brother the entire summer."

"Your brother, Martin?"

"Yes. You met him two years ago when he was here teaching VBS."

"How is he doing?"

"He's doing well, but he's holding down two to three jobs to make ends meet. He's my office manager at the moment, but he wants a pay raise."

Augustus laughed. "Ah, I have it better, don't I? I get paid for doing what I love: gardening."

"You do. And I look forward to our next garden tours."

"We'll be able to do a lot of tours in three weeks." Augustus picked up his rake and gloves. "Let me walk you to your meeting, and you can blame me for being late, late, late."

"I can't do that to you, but you may walk me to the quadrangle. That's where our pre-lunch meeting is. Would you like to join us for lunch? Our Savannah team is buying."

"Well, if you're paying, sure." He laughed. "When is lunch?"

"Noon. Come back then, or stay to hear Byron dissect details for forty-five minutes."

In no time, they drew closer to the crescendo of

voices and laughter coming from the rectangular patch of grass under the vermillion flowers that covered almost all of the half dozen or so royal poinciana trees.

In an old conversation, Augustus had told Tina that those trees were also called *flamboyant* in the Bahamas. In some other parts of the world, they might be referred to as the *flame of the forest*.

Regardless of their regional names, Tina found the trees altogether lovely.

Augustus promised to return for lunch at noon, and then Tina was left standing at the edge of the quadrangle, facing a veritably angry-looking Byron Moss, who made a show of stopping everything he was doing—including whatever speech he was in the middle of making—all to give her one of his signature stares.

Tina felt self-conscious.

Bravely, she ignored his stare and walked nonchalantly toward Lucy and Keith. Lucy patted the picnic blanket they were sitting on, and Tina sat down without a word.

# CHAPTER TWELVE

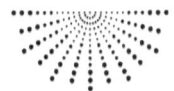

t precisely noon on Byron's iPad, he ended their day camp staff meeting, said a blessing, and they began to serve the food. Tina wondered if Byron did this all through the school year: lived by his iPad.

Tina, Lucy, and Keith spread out to mingle so they could get to know some of the other day camp workers and school staff members. The Savannah team served the fried chicken they had paid for, and everyone had double servings of desserts that Chapel by the Sea staffers brought.

As far as Tina was concerned, she had successfully avoided Byron throughout lunch. In fact, she hadn't seen him since he disappeared through the art room into the hallway on the other side of the room. Wasn't he going to eat?

Gus had arrived, ate quickly with people he knew, and then left after promising Tina that he'd bring her flowers to decorate her art room.

Somehow, even after eating and chatting and mingling, Tina ended up back on Lucy's blanket on the grass. Lucy and Keith were nowhere to be found, but Tina's art room assistants and helpers joined her.

All four were digging into their chocolate mousse cake, when Tina spotted a visitor coming across the lawn.

In one hand, Veronique carried a slice of cake. In the other hand was the backrest of a camp chair she was dragging toward them. She stopped at the edge of the blanket.

"I've been told—no, ordered—to socialize with you," Veronique said.

"By?" Tina wiped her lips with a napkin.

"Who else?" Veronique rolled her eyes.

"He has no right." *What in the world was Byron up to?*

"He's in charge."

"He can't force behavior on people," Tina said. "He can't make you sit here if you don't want to."

"That's right!" Veronique said, the hand that had held the camp chair now turned into a fist. "I'll go tell him."

"No, no. You can't." Tina shook her head.

"Why not?"

"He's going to be mad at both of us. Maybe he wants us to speak with each other because we have to work together for the next three weeks."

"And you're staying with me."

"About that, let me guess." Tina feared the worst. "He volunteered you."

Veronique nodded. "Your host bailed out."

"I could stay at the hotel."

"Byron wants it, and Byron gets it. Nothing we can do but get along."

Tina sensed a break in the ice. "Well, I'm glad you brought your own chair, because we don't have a lot of room on the blanket."

Veronique looked startled. "Are you calling me fat?"

"I didn't!"

"You said I can't fit onto that blanket."

Tina sighed. She really wanted to be nice to Veronique. "Come sit with us, please?"

Everyone scooted around on the blanket to make room.

"I can't," Veronique said, patting her hips. "This skirt has no give."

Tina could agree that Veronique's skirt looked tight, but she had thought it was stretchable. *Guess not.* "When we go shopping later this week, we'll look for a stretchable skirt for you."

"Or maybe some stretchable fabric. I can make my own skirt."

"You can?" Tina was on her feet. "Could you teach me how to sew?"

"You don't know how to sew?"

"I can make pottery." Tina wondered why she had never learned to sew.

"You can't wear dishes."

"You can wear ceramic beads."

"No. They're not shiny enough for me," Veronique said.

"Well, maybe we can barter something." Tina thought for a quick second. "Is there anything you need? Maybe someone to clean your house?"

"Are you offering to trade services?"

"Why not? You teach me to sew, and I'll clean your house."

*How hard can cleaning a house be?*

Tina had hired a maid service for her own house in Savannah, but that was only because she was a busy businesswoman running a pottery studio. If she had time, she'd clean her own house.

Then again, she almost wanted Veronique to turn her down.

Veronique seemed to be taking a long time to think about this. Then: "What do you want to sew?"

"A skirt," Tina said. "It would be fun to make my own skirts."

"Elastic waist?"

"Sure. Why not?"

"That's too easy. Maybe I'll teach you to sew several different types of skirts. Like this one." She spun around.

*Maybe not that one.* "We'll see how fast—or slowly—I learn and go from there. How about that?"

Veronique nodded. "Shall we set a time frame? How about a week? Try to learn as much as you can in a week."

"One week sounds good. I'll clean your house for one week, then. Deal?"

"Deal!"

# CHAPTER THIRTEEN

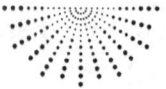

*V*eronique's house was on the other side of New Providence in a sprawling property that stretched to the coast of the island. The grounds were dotted with swaying green casuarina trees anchored into sandy soil that poured into Tina's flip-flops and between her toes as she and Lucy followed Veronique through the yard toward the ocean.

"You have your own beach?" Tina asked, suitably impressed, as they stood facing the vast ocean.

Veronique shrugged it off. "Not as pretty as Byron's family estate, but it is nice, I must say."

*Byron's family estate? What is she talking about?*

Tina brushed it off. She lifted the edge of her palm to her forehead, providing shade for her eyes from the bright afternoon sun. She had left her sunglasses in her luggage somewhere. "How far does this ocean go?"

"Well, if you keep going that way, you'll reach Cuba, Jamaica, Haiti, and then South America."

"Wow. Now I feel like I'm really on vacation," Tina announced.

Tina looked for Lucy. She seemed pretty quiet today. There she was, behind her and Veronique.

Lucy was thumbing her iPhone. Texting?

"Lucy, come see," Tina called. Lucy simply waved. Her eyes never left her iPhone.

"You're missing it," Tina whimpered into the wind.

When she returned to gaze at the blue skies, she found Veronique at the verge of speaking. She waited.

"I must apologize," Veronique said.

"Everyone is apologizing. We've all been apologetic this week."

"Have we?"

"Apology accepted, whatever it is that bothers you. Don't worry about it. We carry on. Today is a brand-new day in the Lord, right?" Tina kicked off her flip-flops and stepped onto the sand.

Her tee shirt fluttered in the wind. Her linen capri pants felt hot. She'd have to wear her shorts henceforth. The island had called for them.

"Tina?"

Tina turned around. "Yes?"

"If I had known you were having menstrual cramps on Monday morning, I would have waited for you," Veronique said.

Tina's eyes darted back and forth. "Why are we talking about this in public?"

"Don't worry." Veronique waved her long nails in the air. "Nobody can hear us. And we're all women here. I left you behind, Miss MacFarland."

"Tina."

"Tina, I'm sorry."

"All forgotten."

"Is it?"

"What do you mean?" Tina's toes dug into the warm sand.

"Now Donovan's driver is chauffeuring you about. Is that to get back at me?"

"No, ma'am. Far from it." Tina wondered how to put it. "He's a kind man, and he's being helpful because I don't have a local driving license."

"And because he knows that his brother is a stickler for people being on time."

"I haven't been late since."

"You walked in late to the eleven o'clock meeting."

*Everyone noticed?*

"I was on the school grounds," Tina protested.

"Chatting with Gus, I saw."

"But in my defense, I was in the art room before eight o'clock." Tina chuckled. "Thanks to Byron, I haven't had much sleep at night. I feared missing my ride so much that I set my alarm for every hour from four in the morning onwards."

"You're kidding me."

"Nope. Don't tell Byron that I was losing sleep over this, okay? I don't want to cause more trouble." Tina lifted her face to the sun and closed her eyes.

She knew she would have to go inside or under the shade soon. Staying too long outside would burn her.

"Besides, Lucy and I are lodging with you now, and we can all ride together," Tina added.

"Speaking of Byron..." Veronique's face grew serious. "The other reason I didn't care if I left you behind was that he was paying too much attention to you."

"Nah. Don't let that bother you. He's only picking on me. You remember two years ago?" Tina walked back to where she had left Lucy. She picked up her flip-flips on the way, shaking off the sand from them.

"He gave you a hard time." Veronique giggled. "All right. I won't worry about it. Now let's go back to the house, and I'll show you my sewing room. Aunt Edna should be starting dinner soon."

Quietly, Tina thanked God for the breakthrough. Little did she know that skirts and sewing machines and house cleaning could bring her and Veronique to amicable terms.

She prayed that their friendship would last and that they would stop being jealous of each other.

*Jealous? Of what?*

*Or of whom?*

*It's Byron's fault.*

Tina cringed. Was it really Byron's fault?

She wasn't sure anymore.

# CHAPTER FOURTEEN

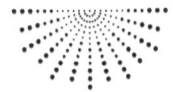

yron arrived at Chapel by the Sea too early for his Bible study on Wednesday evening and decided to peek into the sanctuary to watch the choir practice. He knew that the Savannah team had decided to sing with the choir while they were in town, and he was curious to see how their first practice went.

Before he reached the back entrance to the sanctuary, he could hear the piano and organ through the closed door, and the choir director starting and stopping the singers every few minutes.

He spotted Donovan coming down the rotunda toward him. His brother never came to church on Wednesdays. "What are you doing here?"

"I'm auditioning for the choir," Donovan announced.

Byron frowned. "Don't you have a new cruise line to run or something?"

"That's still in negotiations."

"Why the choir?"

"Contrary to popular belief, I can hum quite well."

"They *sing* in the choir."

"That too." Donovan rolled up his light-yellow shirtsleeves. "You think they'd let me stand behind Tina?"

"This is a house of God, not a dating service," Byron snapped.

"Ah. Gotcha." Donovan laughed. "You got a thing for her, don't you?"

Byron cringed. "Stay away from Tina. It can only end badly for you."

"No need to be that dramatic, Brother."

"I wasn't."

"Was too." Donovan raised a finger to stop Byron from speaking further. "If you're interested in her, you'd better act fast. I see that Keith dude is single, and our cousin Gus is single. So are a bunch of choir members."

"I'm not..." *Am I interested in her?* "In any case, she's only here for three more weeks, and then she goes home to her business in Savannah, and that's the way life is."

"That so?" Donovan opened the sanctuary door. "After you."

Byron glanced at his watch. "No time. Bible study. See you later."

He went down the hallway toward the men's Sunday School class, where the Wednesday evening Bible study would be held. He had taken over teaching the evening class since the previous Bible study teacher had moved to another church in Freeport, Grand Bahama.

His mind should be on the Scripture passages he was to teach tonight, but at this moment, this minute, it had wandered back to the choir.

*Three more weeks.*

He had waited two years for Tina to return to Nassau. Now she was here. Soon she would be gone again.

It seemed to him that if God had wanted them to have anything to do with each other that He would make her stay put.

Yet he knew that God wouldn't *make* people do things. He had given His children the freedom to do the right thing.

*What is the right thing for Tina and me?*

He caught himself.

*There is no "Tina and me."*

Byron could not imagine how they were going to

get along, if ever. Sure, they tried, but he couldn't stand Tina's tardiness.

He was quite sure Tina didn't like him all that much. She seemed to tolerate him, but that was all.

He bet that if he went to Tina's home, he would see big messes everywhere.

There was no way he was going to let Tina touch his stuff when he had worked so hard to keep everything in meticulous order.

*There is just no way.*

*So here we go. We just need to put up with each other for three weeks.*

And yet, somewhere in Byron's heart, he did not want Tina to leave.

# CHAPTER FIFTEEN

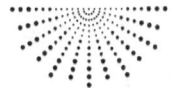

"*I* thought I saw your brother at the door," Tina said to Donovan after choir practice.

"He was on his way to his Bible study. I can tell you where the room is, if you need to talk to him."

"Oh, I don't *need* to talk to him." Tina reached toward the pew for her tote bag and Bible. "I was only wondering. That's all."

"He was wondering about you too."

Tina's hand froze in midair. "Why? Am I in trouble again?"

"Are you always in trouble?"

"With him, yes. It seems I can't do anything *just so*."

Donovan placed a hand on Tina's shoulder. "If

anybody is the matter, it's Byron. Don't worry about it."

"It's not him. It's me." Tina moved away.

"Don't play victim. He's very much like my father. Uptight. Hard to get along with."

Tina didn't say anything.

"Say, I'm having a dinner party on Friday night. Would you like to come?"

Tina wasn't sure how to reply.

"I'm inviting Lucy and Veronique—they've already said yes—so I'll have Trey pick up everyone."

*Trey the driver. Again.*

Was Donovan looking for compensation for his generosity?

When Tina hesitated again, Donovan said, "It'll be on my new yacht."

"Wow. I've never been on a yacht."

"Not ever?"

"Ever."

"It'll be docked, so we're not sailing, I'm afraid. Will you come?"

Well, it wouldn't hurt, would it? Tina was single, unattached, and Donovan had said Lucy and Veronique were going.

When did he ask them? Why hadn't they said anything to her?

*Oh yes.*

Donovan had talked to them minutes before he had approached her. Tina had been busy chatting with the pianist.

"Sure. I don't see why not. Do I have to dress up?"

"It's not a formal black-tie dinner. It'll be on the top deck in the open air so we can see the stars. Just wear something semicasual."

"Sounds lovely. Okay. I'll go." Just for the experience, Tina told herself.

She wondered what Donovan was up to.

Then she wondered what Byron would say about it.

At the front entrance to the church, Tina and Lucy waited for Veronique to finish chatting, and drive them home.

Tina was feeling sleepy. She knew she had to get back to her art room the next day. Fortunately, she had scheduled her meeting with her helpers after lunch. There was no reason to make everyone get up early the day after these evening church activities.

Lucy was busy on her smartphone again. She had been on that thing almost every day.

"Whatcha doing?" Tina asked. "Texting your boyfriend?"

Lucy looked up. Giggled. "Nope. I'm writing that devotional we talked about."

"Seriously?" Tina couldn't believe it. "How can you write on that thing?"

Lucy wiggled her thumbs.

"You're going to get deep-vein *thumbosis!*"

They couldn't stop laughing.

"What's so funny, ladies?"

Tina turned toward the voice. "Hey, Donovan."

Right behind him was Byron.

Tina didn't say anything to him. He didn't say a word to her either.

Interesting. They talked at the school, at meetings, and even before and after meetings, but not casually. The last time they had an exchange at church was the first Sunday Tina had arrived in town. That was when past hurts had surfaced, thanks to her lack of control over her emotions.

Well, she got over that, and she wasn't going to let her emotions get the better of her around Byron anymore.

Byron stood next to Donovan.

What a contrast these two brothers were. Tina tried to gauge the height difference between the two men. She figured Byron was about four or five inches shorter than Donovan, making the latter about six five.

Byron was only a few inches taller than Tina, and truly, that was how she liked her men.

*Her men?*

She chuckled. *Yeah, so we could see eye to eye!*

"What's so funny?" Byron asked.

"Nothing," Tina said.

"It was something."

"No, Byron. It was nothing at all."

"At all?"

"Why are you picking on me?" Tina asked.

"I'm not picking on you."

"You're in a bad mood."

"I'm not."

"Is something the matter?" Tina stepped closer to Byron as Donovan faced Lucy. They were chatting about something.

"Like what?" Byron looked puzzled.

"Like what your face is telling me. You're worried about something."

"You can tell?"

"I'm guessing." Tina didn't mean to stand this close to Byron. They weren't touching each other, but she didn't want to step back now, in case he thought he repelled her.

"Well, okay," Byron admitted. "We had more news tonight about Headmaster Clarke."

"You mentioned at the lunch meeting yesterday that he was stepping back due to his cancer." It was one of the things Tina did remember. The rest of it... Well, she should have taken notes.

"You were paying attention at the meeting." Byron's eyes brightened.

"I heard what's important."

"Uh-oh."

"I figured you'd send a memo out if there's anything else that we needed to know before Monday."

"You know I would."

"What's the situation with Clarke?" Tina genuinely wanted to know. It could affect how Byron ran the day camp.

"His new biopsy results were bad."

"How bad?"

"They're giving him months."

"Oh... I'm so sorry. But with chemo..."

"He's in God's hands," Byron said.

"We'll pray."

"Thank you."

"Now," Tina said.

"What?"

"We'll pray now," she repeated. She bowed her head, closed her eyes, and waited.

She couldn't hear anything. "Go on."

"You want me to pray?" Byron asked.

"God is waiting."

Byron prayed. He seemed to unload his heart right there at the front of the church. When he said "amen," Tina didn't.

"Father God, I agree with Byron's prayer for Headmaster Clarke," Tina prayed. "I ask that You comfort him and his family and show them Your peace, mercy, and grace in this terrible situation. Nothing is impossible for You. If You so choose to heal him this side of heaven, we rejoice. If You choose to heal him in heaven, we accept Your sovereignty. May Your perfect will be done, Lord. In Jesus' Name I pray. Amen."

"Amen," Byron echoed.

"Keep me posted," Tina said when Byron looked up.

"I will." His face was weary.

"Go home and get some sleep. I know you work hard. You need to rest also."

"Now you sound like my mother," Byron said.

"I don't want to sound like your mother."

"I don't want you to either."

# CHAPTER SIXTEEN

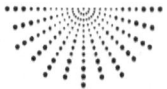

"My clay is still missing." Tina was standing in Byron's office doorway.

He looked up from what he was doing at his desk. To be sure, his door was open, and his assistant wasn't at her desk outside the door. No one had stopped Tina from barging into his office. It was too late to tell her to make an appointment.

"What clay?" Byron raised his eyebrows.

"You do that a lot."

"Do what?"

"Wiggle your eyebrows." Tina pointed.

"I'm not wiggling."

"Your eyebrows have a mind of their own then."

"Whatever. What was it, Tina?" Byron paused. Suddenly, he sprung up from his seat, rushed to the other side of his desk, and held a chair. "I'm sorry. Please have a seat. May I help you?"

"Thank you." As Tina sat down, a light, floral perfume floated into his nostrils.

Byron's mind went to places—

"About my clay," Tina said. "I ordered them two weeks ago. I don't see them anywhere in my art room. I waited all morning. I waited through lunch."

"I'll check on it for you." Byron folded his arms and leaned against his metal desk.

"Three boxes to last three weeks."

"Okay. Noted."

"I need them pronto. It's Thursday."

"I know what day it is."

"Day camp starts in four days."

"No need to panic."

"You said y'all have clay." Tina's bangles jingled on her wrists.

Byron hadn't noticed the bangles before. Maybe she had gone shopping. The colorful bangles matched her floral summer dress. It looked pretty on her.

"My clay?" Tina waved her hands at him.

"Yes. I'm sure there's a tracking number," he said.

"You'll take care of it, right?" Tina asked.

"Yes, I will."

"Now you can thank me."

Byron tried not to raise his eyebrows. "For?"

"For bringing extra clay in my suitcase."

"Ah, that."

"Still, it won't be enough. We're going to make some samples this afternoon at my art meeting. Right off the bat on Monday, we'll be teaching twenty-plus kids how to make coil and free-form pottery. Whatever I brought won't last past next week."

"So we have a week. Good."

"We don't have a week, Byron. Days. We have days."

Oddly enough, Byron had never seen this side of Tina, the side where schedule was suddenly important to her.

Was she turning from Tardy Tina to Timely Tina?

Tina wasn't finished. "Will the clay arrive on time? Will it be before midweek? We don't know."

More bangles jangled.

Byron tried to remain serious. He liked this new Tina—or the Tina he hadn't known—but her worries were making her unhappy.

*I don't want to see Tina unhappy.*

"I'll look into it," he said. "Anything else?"

"May I use your phone? It'll save me roaming charges. I have to speak with the local potter whose kiln we're using. Get some directions to his studio."

"Raymond Fordham? I know where his studio is. We can take the school van if we need to transport pottery there next week."

"We could, but you're a busy man. Are you sure you want to take the time?"

"No problem. I'll drive you there."

"Sometimes you also drive me up the wall." Tina laughed.

Byron did not.

"It was a joke."

"Uh-huh. When do you want to visit Ray?" Byron asked.

"Anytime you're available."

"When does your art meeting finish today?"

"Three-thirty or thereabouts."

"We can leave at four."

"Don't you have any plans for tonight?" Tina asked.

"Plans? What do you mean?" Byron didn't want to speculate, but Tina was onto something he wasn't.

"Like a date night?"

"On a work night? No. Besides, I don't have a girlfriend." *Not yet, anyway.* "Look, let's get back to work. As for the phone, you can use my phone here or in the waiting area anytime."

Tina got up from her seat.

"I'll make some calls to track down your cartons

of clay," Byron said. "Meanwhile, keep busy, and you won't worry about it. I suppose you have a lot of work to do, like setting up a schedule."

"Oh, that's already done." Tina produced a folded stack of paper from her skirt pocket.

Byron watched her unfold it. There were several staples in one corner. Some of the paper had been torn and taped back together with scotch tape.

"Is that it?" Byron reached for the stack. He lifted it—as carefully as he could as if it were an ancient parchment—to his eyes.

He couldn't believe it. At first he thought the calligraphy was printed from a laser printer. But no. It had been handwritten in ink. It was the most beautiful piece of penmanship he had ever seen. "This is amazing."

"Thank you. I'm glad you like my plan. I had some help from a friend of mine. Do you know Abilene Dupree-Cargill? She's a watercolorist. Goes to the same church I attend."

"No. Haven't had the honor of meeting her. I'd like to visit Riverside again sometimes. Diego has invited me, but I've been busy." Byron was still staring at Tina's handwriting. "Amazing."

"You keep saying that. Yes, I think we can do a lot in three weeks. We could replicate this plan for the rest of the summer, I suppose, but your incoming art teacher might want to do his own planning."

"I meant your handwriting."

"That's nothing."

"You're extremely artistic."

Tina was silent.

Byron looked up from the paper. Tina was staring at him, a puzzling demeanor on her face.

"That's the nicest thing you've said to me in two years," she said softly.

Byron felt bad. Half the time, he could not remember what he had said to Tina that had been so bad it had hurt her. Apart from his calling her a scatterbrain—to which he had apologized on Sunday—he truly had no idea.

He could ask her for a list, but that would dig up her past hurts he'd rather not be aware of.

"Is there a way you could forgive me for everything I've ever said to you in our past?" Byron asked. "I was probably a fool two years ago, but I'm not one now."

"You mean like a blanket forgiveness?" Tina asked.

"Something like that. Please?"

"What are you confessing, exactly?"

"I don't even know. Just forgive me for whatever it is, and we can move on."

"I thought I forgave you Sunday after church."

"Well, I didn't actually, technically, literally hear it."

Tina chuckled. "You talk funny."

"Besides, if you did, you took it back."

"I did not." Tina straightened up in the chair.

"You remember things. You bring it up. You recall what I said. You choose to relive the pain and hurt."

"It just happens. You trigger it."

"All right, how about this. Whenever I trigger a memory, you tell me, and I will apologize if it was my fault. Does that sound fair?"

"We can do that."

Byron reached for Tina's hand. "Let's shake on this."

They did.

When Byron let go of her hand, he said something he himself did not expect. "Look past my words, Tina. See my heart."

"Your heart?"

Byron didn't acknowledge what he had said. Neither did he take back his words.

"Oh, I see." Tina nodded. "Your heart for the kids. An educator's heart. You're so sweet, Byron."

*That's not what I meant at all.*

But Byron couldn't explain otherwise. Wrong place. Wrong time.

He let it go.

For now.

# CHAPTER SEVENTEEN

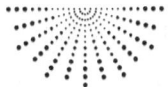

"I'm home! I'm home!" Tina felt silly saying it, but she truly felt at home among the shelves of drying clay plates and cups and jugs surrounding several old pottery wheels.

Raymond Fordham, the potter and studio owner, and Byron simply waited on the side for Tina to enjoy herself. She felt self-conscious then and turned serious.

"We'll have twenty bowls in the first week, and possibly twenty plates in the second week. Will your kiln be able to handle them all?" she asked.

Raymond checked his tablet. "I have other things to fire in the same kiln, but I think I can fit you in if you bring them here a week in advance."

Tina ticked off the days in her mind. "We start

day camp on Monday. If the kids make the pieces then, we could bring them here Monday afternoon. We'll have to glaze them and then refire."

"I'll have them done for you by the next Monday."

"One week. I guess that'll work." Tina turned to Byron. "It would be easier if I brought the art students here that day to glaze their pieces. Then Raymond can put them back into the kiln."

"That makes sense. I'll see if I can arrange for the church bus to take the kids." Byron checked his iPad. "Well, the sports camp needs the bus on Mondays to go to the pool. How about Tuesday?"

"Tuesday morning sounds good," Raymond said.

"Great." She looked around the studio again and felt sorry she had to leave.

"You're welcome to stop in anytime to make your own pottery," Raymond said to Tina.

"I wish I could, but I can't. I'm busy the next three weeks. I'm staying for just a few more days after that for some personal time, and then I have to get home to my own studio."

"You're staying a few more days after the art camp?" Byron asked.

Tina nodded. She had forgotten to tell him, but then it was none of his business what she was doing after the day camp was over.

Raymond ushered them out the door toward the outer gallery. "The offer still stands, Tina. Anytime."

"Thank you. Maybe I'll stop by after the camp is over. I'm looking for new potters to add to my studio, and I like what I've seen." She pointed to some teapots by the window.

"They're very colorful," Byron said. "Like your skirt there."

"I do like colorful things."

"I noticed."

Minutes later, they were back on the road, a bubble-wrapped handmade teapot on Tina's lap.

Byron drove them through downtown Nassau, heading for Veronique's house where he was supposed to drop off Tina for the evening.

Tina looked out the window at the tourist traps lining both sides of the road when she spotted the most gorgeous displays of fabric fluttering in the late-afternoon wind.

"Look at those pretty colors!" she exclaimed.

She must have startled Byron, because he slammed on the brakes. The vehicles behind them honked loudly.

"I'm sorry," Tina said.

"Do you want to have a look at the shop?" Byron asked, his face serious.

"Do you always look this serious?"

"We almost got into an accident."

"My fault."

"No, no. I was... Never mind. Do you want to shop?" Byron asked again.

Tina nodded.

# CHAPTER EIGHTEEN

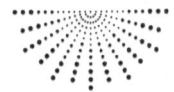

*B*yron parked outside a coffee shop a few doors away from the fabric and dress shop that had almost caused a traffic accident minutes ago. He turned off the ignition.

"I'll wait in there. How long do you need?" He picked up his iPad and power supply cord from his car door pocket.

"Twenty minutes," Tina said.

"Precisely?" Byron wondered if he should double or triple that time. He wasn't sure how long it would take Tina to shop. He had never shopped with her before.

Well, he wasn't going to shop with her now. He was going to sit in the coffee shop and work on his schedules until she was ready.

As he got out of the car, he decided to get his laptop from the backseat. Knowing Tina and her sense of time—or lack thereof—he could be waiting awhile.

Still, he had the evening off.

He could wait.

"Let's not take too long, all right?" Byron said.

"Do you want me to find you at the coffee shop when I'm done?"

"That sounds good."

"Okay." She was off, bouncing down the sidewalk in her floral dress.

In the coffee shop, Byron found a spot by the window. He did not order any coffee. It was twenty to five, and he made it a point not to drink anything with caffeine after four o'clock. He preferred to go to bed early and then get up early in the morning to read his Bible, walk on his treadmill, and start working.

Clarke's medical situation weighed heavily on his mind. He was glad that Tina had prayed with him on Wednesday evening at church. While it was God who healed, Byron felt the support that Tina had given him. It made his day go better when he knew that he had the support of people he cared about.

*Cared?*

Well, sure. He cared about all his teachers, staff, and volunteers.

Tina, particularly.

He hadn't realized he had been sitting at the table for a while until his computer announced that it was six o'clock.

*Six o'clock? No way!*

That meant Tina had been gone for an hour and twenty minutes. He looked out the window. He could see his car from here. But there was no Tina.

A sense of panic rose in his throat.

*What if she couldn't find this coffee shop?*

Byron packed up his iPad, laptop, cable, shoulder bag, and doubled out of the coffee shop. He'd come back another day and buy a meal to make up for not being a customer today.

When he reached the fabric and dress shop, there was a commotion inside.

"Let's look here," someone said.

"Miss, are you sure you dropped it in our shop?" another said.

Several sales clerks were gathered around—

Tina.

Always Tina.

*What now?*

Byron went to her side. "What's going on?"

"I can't find my debit card." Her voice was not calm.

Byron wanted to wrap his arms around her and tell her everything would be fine.

Yet it wouldn't be true.

This was Tina. Something always went wrong with Tina.

"Where did you see it last?" Byron asked, his arms folded across his chest.

"I don't remember."

"Did you leave it at Raymond's studio?"

"I didn't buy anything there. He gave me the teapot, remember?"

"Yes, he did. At the school then?"

"I don't know."

"Okay. Let's pray."

Tina nodded. She extended her hands.

Byron didn't know what else to do than to hold them. "Father God, Tina has lost her debit card. Please show us where it is. I pray this in the strong name of Jesus, who knows and sees all things. Amen."

A chorus of *amen* went around the store.

Byron wasn't sure if they were all Christians. He didn't want to think too much into the reasons people said *amen*. Right now, in front of him was a befuddled woman he was falling in love with.

"Let's look again," said someone who looked like the floor manager.

Ten or fifteen minutes later, Byron couldn't take

it anymore. He went to Tina, who was wringing her hands. Surely she was not this confused, this disorganized?

Someone with an MFA?

Something was up.

Meanwhile, he had to take care of this matter with the lost card.

"Tina, we can keep looking, but I think you should call your bank and cancel the card," he said quietly. "This is a tourist area, and anybody could've walked out with your card."

Tina nodded. She blinked. Then she turned toward the floor manager. "I can't pay for the dress and fabric now. I'll come back later to buy—never mind. Sorry for the trouble."

Byron saw Tina's eyes on the multiple bolts of fabric on the table and the pile of colorful clothes in a basket, also on the table. In between the fabric and the basket were a few packets of sewing patterns. The top packet showed a photograph of a long, flowing skirt on the cover.

"Cut the fabric," Byron said. "I'll pay for it."

"Oh, Byron. I do not expect you to do that."

"I want to. Get whatever you want."

"I'll pay you back."

"No need." Then and there, Byron realized that to keep up with Tina, he had to learn to expect the unexpected. Good or bad? He wasn't sure. With Tina, he had to take it one day at a time.

Perhaps even one hour at a time.

While Tina discussed with the sales associate how much fabric to cut, Byron called Raymond. The potter was still in his studio, but he had not seen her debit card. Byron believed him because he was the father of one of his staffers. Byron knew him a little and had no reason not to believe him.

It was likely that Tina had simply misplaced her card.

He could tell her that it would have been safer had she brought a disposable, reloadable temporary credit card when going overseas to travel. Cash would have been okay too. To bring a card that was connected to her primary checking account was inviting disaster.

But this was not the time to lecture her.

He followed Tina to the cash register.

*Yikes.*

*No way.*

He could not believe how expensive—

Too late.

He had given his word, and now he must follow through. Still, what was the fabric made of? Gold threads?

He swiped his credit card through the reader

and felt dollars drain out of his checking account. Then he followed a happy Tina out of the store.

"Let's get back to the school to see if you left your card in the art room, before you call your bank to cancel it," Byron suggested.

"Good idea." Tina climbed into the passenger side, fastened her seat belt, and dozed off.

# CHAPTER NINETEEN

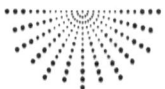

"**Y**ou must think the worst of me, Byron," Tina said as they drove across the island toward Veronique's house.

Byron hadn't spoken a word to her in the last ten minutes. He had kept his eyes on the road and his hands on the wheel.

"We found your credit card." His voice seemed calm.

"Debit card."

"Right. I'm glad it was in your art room rather than downtown, where anybody can steal it."

Tina was embarrassed beyond belief. "I do have some things together, you know."

"We won't mention it anymore." Byron didn't look at her even at the stop light. "You're in a different country, that's all. It's a lot to take in while trying to be yourself."

"I'm not always like this."

"I believe you. You didn't go to grad school for nothing."

"Actually, that was fun."

"What were you planning on doing with your MFA in ceramics?"

Tina shrugged. "I was thinking of teaching, but I found that I'd prefer to open my own studio and run a business."

"See. You own a business."

"Meaning what?"

"If you can run a business, you're not as useless as you might think you are." Byron followed the flow of traffic out of Nassau. The GPS told him where to go. He had mentioned that he'd never been to Veronique's house before.

"I do have a lot of help," Tina said.

"You hire the right people. That's smart."

Tina laughed. "Actually, I might have made a mistake. I hired my brother to manage my office, and I don't think I can ever fire him, or he'll get back at me at Christmas."

"That could be a problem. Still, it's good to have people you trust around you."

"God provides."

"Yes. He always provides. See how He answered our prayer?"

Tina nodded and turned away from Byron so that he didn't see her blush.

She remembered being so glad to have found her debit card that she had hugged Byron in the art room. It would have been all right had they been in public, but it was in the evening, and there was nobody else around in the art room, or the entire school, for that matter.

Well, God was there, and they hadn't done anything untoward.

It had been an innocent hug of happiness.

"Are you still tired?" Byron asked.

"A little."

"And still not hungry?"

"Don't worry about it. I'm sorry you missed your dinner."

"I'll eat when I get home." Byron put his blinker on and turned into the street that his GPS showed him. "Why don't you take tomorrow off? Sleep in. Rest."

"Are you trying to get rid of me?" Tina asked. "Or keep me from further trouble?"

"No. Just that I think you look tired. You fell asleep on the way from the shop to the school, remember? Did you get enough sleep last night?"

"I went straight to bed after choir practice."

"And you got up at?" Byron pressed.

"I don't know. Maybe three."

"Three in the morning?"

"Maybe twoish."

"That's even worse, Tina."

"I woke up worried that the clay hadn't arrived." To be fair, she should have asked about it as soon as she had arrived in town, and should not have waited until four days before day camp started.

And Byron had been right—she had some clay, and she could stretch it to last the entire next week if she had to. Perhaps the kids wouldn't be making bowls. Perhaps they could make smaller saucers.

"If you don't get enough sleep, it could cause you to be forgetful," Byron added.

"You mean that's why I misplaced my debit card?"

"I'm not sure what I'm saying. But I know that if you—speaking in general terms—don't get enough sleep, you can't function during the day. You're going to be forgetful, clumsy, irritable, and generally...generally...whatever. Tell you what. Take the day off tomorrow."

Tina wasn't going to tell him that she had hardly slept since she arrived in Nassau. She was happy to help out with the day camp, but at the back of her mind, she wasn't sure if she should be gone from her Savannah studio this many days.

Leaving the Tina's Turn Pottery Studio in the hands of her nonpotter, nonartistic brother was probably not a good idea.

But she was committed now.

Perhaps next weekend she could make a quick trip back to Savannah to see if all was well.

No.

It would be a vote of no confidence on Martin, and Tina had to give her brother some respect. After all, he wasn't a business major and a part-time virtual assistant for nothing. He had an eye for details, was good with bookkeeping, and should be trustworthy enough to run her studio for three weeks.

Only three weeks.

Plenty of time for her to show Byron that she was not a chicken running around without a head.

*Ewww.* She cringed at her own thoughts.

"What?" Byron asked.

"Nothing. Just thinking about all the things going on in my life right now."

"Maybe you can simplify some?"

"Can't. I have lots of things to do. Besides, there's Donovan's dinner party."

Byron's eyes widened. "What dinner party?"

"Tomorrow night on his new yacht."

"And he invited you?" Byron parked in

Veronique's driveway in front of the psychedelic orange-and-pink cottage by the sea.

"It was probably a last-minute thing," Tina explained. "He asked Veronique, Lucy, and me last night after choir practice."

"Ah."

"He said I could bring someone." Tina decided to go for it. "Would you come?"

"Me? You're asking me to accompany you?"

"Bad idea, I know. Sorry. Forget I even mentioned it." Tina opened the car door.

"No, no. I'll go with you."

"Because I asked?"

"Because I have to protect you from my brother."

Tina didn't know what to think of that. "I thought you got along with your brother."

"Yes, I do, but not when he wants to steal my—uh..."

"Steal your thunder?" Tina felt she had to give him a way out.

Byron cleared his throat. "Something like that."

Tina was confident that it wasn't *something like that* at all.

ina had missed dinner, but she wasn't concerned. Somehow, she was still not hungry. And she was eternally grateful to God for helping her recover her debit card. God had given Byron a clear mind to help her backtrack until they found it in the art room.

It had fallen out of her tote bag somehow—probably when she had been looking for her lip gloss sometime in the afternoon—and had ended up kicked into a corner, possibly by one of her helpers or herself.

*Thank you, Lord.*

Veronique eyed Tina suspiciously as she related her adventure of the evening. "He paid for your fabric and bought you a dress? We're talking Byron here? Budget-conscious Byron?"

"Is he?" Tina dumped the fabric and dress on the couch. "Want to see what I got?"

"These are beautiful." Veronique's voice turned solemn. "There has to be something going on for Byron to pay for all this. He's rarely this generous."

"I don't think there's anything more than what I've told you," Tina explained. "I'll reimburse him."

"He wouldn't take it."

"Why not?"

"He doesn't lend money. Say, did he kiss you?"

"What?"

"I hope he didn't kiss you. It would be against school policy." Veronique straightened up. "You don't want to get him fired."

"Oh no. Not at all." Tina felt an alarm bell clanging in her spirit. "However, I'm not on the school payroll."

"No, but you're a volunteer."

"Don't forget that, starting Monday, you're in charge of the day camp," Tina reminded her. "Clarke's cancer changed the leadership."

"True."

"Therefore, I'm not even working for Byron."

"Then as your supervisor, I would advise you to stop flirting with the new interim headmaster."

"What? Did you accuse me of flirting?"

"I guess I did."

"Please take that back."

"Or?"

"Or I'll move out to a hotel tonight. I don't need this."

"You want to get me into trouble with Byron, don't you?" Veronique got off the couch.

"I don't want anyone in trouble. I've explained to you. There's nothing between Byron and me... Uh-oh." Tina's palms flew to her mouth.

"Ha. Just as I suspected. Out with it."

"Donovan's dinner party on his yacht tomorrow night."

"Yes?"

"I asked Byron to go with me."

"He said yes?"

Tina nodded feebly.

Veronique laughed. "He's so fired, sister!"

# CHAPTER TWENTY

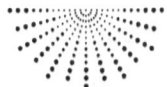

"You did what?" Gus stopped clipping the hedges. He lifted a palm to stop Byron from speaking further. "Step into my office."

Dutifully, Byron followed his cousin and his wheelbarrow down a winding path to a courtyard of frangipanis and green hedges, with a gurgling fountain against a wall. Around the fountain was a low stone wall that was wide enough to sit on.

Byron sat right on the middle of it. The stone felt cool.

"It's just a dress," Byron said.

"It's never *just* a dress." Gus put down his wheelbarrow and sat on the grass near Byron.

"And some fabric." Expensive fabric, but no one else needed to know.

"Fabric too. How does that look?"

"She lost her debit card." Byron shrugged. "Are you saying..."

"I've known her for two years. It's not the money I'm worried about. She can afford it. Did you know her pottery design is award winning and her studio is thriving? I hear she has opened a second gallery in Charleston. I'm sure she's not starving for money. In fact, I'm confident she's here in the Bahamas for charitable reasons."

Byron nodded. He knew about all that. And he knew that Tina's talents had not been what had attracted him to her.

Still...

"I don't know what overcame me, Gus." Byron stretched out on the stone trim. The fountain was noisy and sprayed water at him.

He closed his yes. "Maybe I did it on a whim."

"Byron?"

"Yeah?"

"You never do anything on a whim. You don't even know how to spell that word."

"I do know how to spell it."

"Listen, cousin." Gus kept his voice even, but Byron knew a lecture was coming. "You don't go around buying dresses and fabrics for some random woman."

"Tina is not some random woman."

"Exactly. When was the last time you bought a woman anything?"

"Well, there's...hmm... I guess that ex-girlfriend I had... Well, there's Mother. I buy her gifts every year. Okay, I get your point." Byron sighed. "Anyway, it's moot. Tina texted me this morning to disinvite me to Donovan's boat party tonight."

"She invited you to it?"

"Disinvited."

"That's just proof she had invited you in the first place. You can't disinvite the uninvited."

"Whatever. The point is, she must be thinking I had designs on her."

"Ha-ha. Listen to yourself. Designs. Fabric. Dress. Funny..." Then Gus stopped talking.

Byron knew his cousin had turned serious. He waited. He knew Gus would pray before giving him advice. That might be why a lot of what Gus had advised him over the years had been wise counsel.

And as far as Byron was concerned, he needed a lot of wisdom right now.

"It's a good thing that she disinvited you," Gus resumed. "Office romance can happen, but I'm not sure if that's a good thing at this time for our school when the board members are looking to raise funds to renovate some of the old buildings on campus."

"Technically, she's not an employee of the school or the church, for that matter."

"But she's working at the school, even as a volunteer."

"Yes."

"So if you two have something going on—even off hours—wouldn't that be a distraction from your job when you see—literally—each other on campus?"

"I suppose."

"The Bible advises us to avoid all appearances of evil." Gus produced his smartphone and found the verse online. "Here it is in 1 Thessalonians 5:22. 'Abstain from every form of evil.' That's the New King James Version. In the old King James, it said this: 'Abstain from all appearance of evil.' That's even more severe."

"I hear you, but—"

"But you two are not *evil* per se? Sure, but what about the perception of other staffers and teachers and the parents of students? They'll think something is going on, something distracting, something that could cause someone out there to misunderstand or to stumble."

"Are you just saying it, Gus, or is that really what you think?"

"Look, Byron. I like Tina. If you weren't interested in her, I would have dated her myself."

"Take a number. Donovan's ahead of you. But

think about what you just said. If it were you and Tina, would that be okay?"

"We don't work with each other," Gus said.

"You're on the same campus."

"True."

"So what do I do? I'm not in charge of day camp anymore. Yet..." The whole idea of perception bothered Byron. Why couldn't people see his heart?

Wasn't that what he had asked Tina to do?

*Look past my words, Tina. See my heart.*

He cringed. What had he started?

"That woman is going to be the end of me. When I'm with her, I forget what I'm supposed to do. I was late to meetings—with Headmaster Clarke, for example. I lost track of my entire day."

"Bring every knot to God, and He will unravel it for you." Gus stood up, brushed grass off his shorts, and pushed his wheelbarrow toward a nearby hedge.

"I'm losing it, Gus," Byron said. "What to do?"

"Pray, Cousin."

"Done that."

"Pray again. Nothing God can't handle." Gus picked up a clipper and began trimming some tiny leaves that stuck out of the lush green hedge nearby. "If you're meant to be together, then God will work it out in His timing."

*In His timing.*

"Good reminder, Gus."

"On the other hand, if you're not meant to be together, then you'll part ways in three weeks and never see each other again."

Somehow, Gus's words hurt.

Byron didn't know why. Women had not been an issue for him before. He had dated in the past—not this year—but no one had stayed in his heart as long as Tina.

Byron closed his eyes to the morning sun. He put his forearm over his forehead.

*I should get back to the office.*

But his heart was not in his office this morning. His heart wondered where Tina could be today—assuming she had accepted his advice to take the day off.

His heart wanted to be with Tina.

*Only Tina.*

"Like right now. I know I have work to do, but look where I am, Gus." Byron heard the noise of clippers and assumed Gus was still listening.

Byron thought of what had been happening to him, to his summer schedule, to his system—

His system?

Well, he'd like to think he owned it.

Every Friday morning he would compare what he had done all week with what he had planned on doing. Throughout the week—and the weekend—he thought of work.

*So, yeah, I own it.*

"Go on," Gus said as he continued working. *Clip. Clip.*

"This week I've only managed to get a third of my stuff done," Byron complained.

All because he was distracted.

*Clip. Clip.*

"The two-thirds I didn't get done will be carried over to next week. I have a boatload of things I already need to do next week." Byron groaned. "My system is being poisoned."

*Clip. Clip.*

Then: "Poisoned?"

It wasn't Gus's voice.

Byron leapt straight up into the air.

# CHAPTER TWENTY-ONE

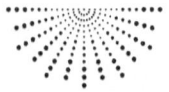

"*T*ina!" Byron sat back down on the stone. It was hard.

"Yes, that's my name."

In front of Byron, ethereal Tina stood. She was wearing the multicolored dress he had purchased for her. He recognized the colors but didn't realize it was such a feminine dress. Cottony, the long skirt made flapping sounds in the sudden gust of wind through the courtyard.

Around them, the frangipani and the green bushes shook. Above them, the sun in the sky brightened the colors of Tina's hair, eyes, face, dress, all the way down to her—

*Bare feet.*

"You're not wearing any shoes," Byron said.

Tina wiggled her toes. Her pink toenails seemed

to sparkle in the sun. "Left them in the art room. I love the feel of grass beneath my feet. Now, Byron, tell me about this poison."

"What poison?"

"You said your system is being poisoned."

"I did?"

Tina smiled. "The Byron Moss I know doesn't forget things."

"He doesn't?"

"Nope. If you don't want to talk about it, we can drop it." She produced an apple from her skirt pocket. "Want it?"

It was a red apple.

All Byron could think of was one word: poison.

He inhaled, exhaled, and tried to count to twenty but lost count somewhere between nine and seventeen.

"Why are you here?" Byron asked as calmly as he could. "Didn't I ask you to take the day off?"

"Yes, you did, but I don't have to listen. Besides, I asked Veronique—my direct supervisor—and she said I could come in if I want to."

"Why?"

"Why not? I don't have to explain everything I do."

"I guess not."

"Why are you lying around doing nothing,

Byron? Isn't this a workday for you? Shouldn't you be in your office?"

Byron was silent. What could he say?

"And why is your system poisoned? By what? By whom?"

Byron raised his eyebrows. "Did you have too much sugar at breakfast?"

"What kind of a question is that?"

"You're talking a mile a minute. Hyper—"

"I'm not."

"You didn't even wait for me to respond to one question before you went to the next."

"You don't answer most of my questions, Byron. I should just give up."

Byron left his stone bench and stood in front of Tina. "I'll prove you wrong. Try me. Ask me a question."

Tina seemed amused. She opened her palm. The apple sat on it. "Would you like an apple?"

"Where did you get that apple?" Byron asked, suddenly curious.

"At breakfast."

"With Veronique?"

"She was there too. So was Lucy. Donovan wanted to cook us an American break—"

"Donovan!" Again.

Byron's heart sank. Sank like a stone bench in mud.

Tina laughed, and the apple slipped out of her hand and dropped onto the grass. "Oops."

She retrieved the apple and wiped the skin on her dress.

"It probably has weed killer on it now," Byron said. "And who knows what else."

"Only you would say something like that."

"What do you mean? Are you picking on me?"

"Tit for tat, Byron."

"I don't pick on you."

"Yes, you do. I'm always in trouble with you. You rarely smile when you see me, except when you're amused by some silly thing I do."

"I do not—"

"I irritate you, don't I?" Tina's arms dropped to the side.

"No, Tina."

*I'm attracted to you more than I can tell you.*

*More than I'm supposed to be.*

Well, all he had to do was suppress it for a few weeks, and then Tina would be gone and he could get back to his normal life.

*Normal life of what?*

Work, work, and more work?

Was that all he wanted out of life? He had worked so hard all these years with his eyes on the headmaster's office. Now that it was one step away, he couldn't possibly lose it all to a woman.

*No way.*

He felt her warm fingers on his arm. He looked down to see Tina lifting his wrist with one hand and placing the apple into his palm with her other hand.

"You don't have to worry about Donovan," Tina said quietly.

"I don't?" Byron searched her eyes.

"No. He knows I'm giving this apple to you. He's fine with it."

"We—I don't need his approval."

"There are many other apples," Tina said. "He has plenty."

"Sometimes there's just one."

"Perhaps." Tina didn't say more. She simply walked away.

Byron watched her go, but every bit of him wanted to go after her to—

*No.*

Yet, as she disappeared around the corner toward the royal poinciana quadrangle, she took something of his with her, something he couldn't put a finger on.

Something heartfelt.

# CHAPTER TWENTY-TWO

When Veronique, Tina, and Lucy arrived at Veronique's house after school that Friday afternoon, Tina changed into her favorite cotton pajamas, old and faded, but oh so comfortable.

She was sitting by an open window listening to the ocean and reading a book when Veronique strutted into the living room in a glorious sparkly gown and twirled in front of her.

"What do you think?" Veronique asked.

Tina didn't have the heart to tell her that Donovan had specifically said it was a semiformal dinner. It was on a boat, after all.

"It's lovely," Tina said sincerely.

"I wish you could come with us, sister."

Veronique twirled again and then held her forehead. She sat down on an armchair. "Ooh. Dizzy."

"That's a lovely gown." Tina put the bookmark back into her book and closed it.

"You like it? I made it."

"You did?" Tina crossed the tile floor in her flip-flops to have a closer look at the gown. "It's very nice. You're talented."

"I think so too. But"—Veronique pointed a finger toward the ceiling—"God made me that way. All credits to Him."

"Certainly. God is always good, my pastor says."

"Someday, I'll visit your church." Veronique got up and adjusted the straps over her shoulder. "Can't believe it's on a riverboat."

"You're welcome anytime, and please stay at my house." Tina meant it.

She had Byron to thank for this new friendship with Veronique. If he hadn't forced Veronique to host her, they would not be having this conversation.

*Byron.*

*He's in the middle of everything, isn't he?*

Lucy came out of the guest bedroom looking lovely in a blouse and a pair of pants. She stopped and stared at Veronique. "Are we supposed to dress up?"

"Only Veronique," Tina said. "Isn't she lovely? She's going to light up the party!"

Veronique stopped smiling. "Do you think I'm overdressed?"

"No," Tina and Lucy said in unison.

"I think the most important thing here is to be yourself," Tina said.

"This is me!" Veronique spun around again.

"This is me." Lucy smiled.

"And this is me." Tina curtsied in her pajamas.

"Yes, that is you, Tina," Lucy said.

"Oh, I'm so hungry," Veronique said, checking her watch. "I hope we get to eat right away when we get on board."

For some reason, Tina was not hungry at all. All day long, since her encounter with Byron by the fountain, she had been wondering what his rambling was all about.

Byron seemed to be a man of fewer words than Tina had thought. It made it harder for her to understand what he was communicating, if he was at all.

It had been a strange week, this. On the one hand, Byron had been trying to lead the team—up until Headmaster Clarke had made the announcement that changed the leadership of the Summer by the Sea Day Camp.

On the other hand, Tina wasn't sure if he had been much of a leader.

She'd have to wait until Monday to see if Veronique did better than Byron with the day camp.

Several honks outside the front door freaked out Veronique and Lucy.

"We're going! We're going!" Veronique squealed. "Hope I don't get seasick!"

"I brought some motion sickness tablets," Lucy said. "We'll be okay."

"Then let's go!"

"I'll leave the lights on for you," Tina called out, but they were gone, the door slamming shut in their wake.

Tina ambled to the window to look outside. It was Donovan in a bright-blue convertible. No chauffeur tonight. Tina waited for them to leave before she locked the door.

Veronique's aunt was gone for the weekend, visiting her sister in Freeport, Grand Bahama.

Tina was alone now.

Suddenly hungry, Tina went to the kitchen to find some leftover food. Aunt Edna—*bless her heart!* —had cooked enough food to last the entire next week.

Munching on fried chicken and plantain chips— not necessarily at the same time—Tina booted up her laptop to Skype Martin.

She had to check on him, but she had to prepare herself not to sound like she didn't trust her brother to run her pottery studio.

Martin picked up on the fifth ring. The video image was jiggly because Martin couldn't hold his iPhone steady.

"Whatcha doing?" Tina asked.

"Hey, sis. Eating some ice cream and talking to you."

"What flavor?"

"Vanilla. What else? Why? You checking on me?" He laughed.

"Yes and no. I need someone to talk to."

"Ah. Boyfriend trouble."

"No!" Tina snapped. It was too late. The fact that she had said it that quickly only added to Martin's suspicion.

"Name?"

On Tina's screen, Martin leaned back into his recliner.

"Nothing happened."

"Name."

"I don't know if something is going on."

"Okay. Then nothing is happening. You're just speculating. Guessing. Making things up?"

"No."

"Then there's evidence something is going on."

"Maybe."

"Ah." Martin nodded like he knew what to do.

*Good.* Tina sure didn't know what to do.

"Let's pray, sis," Martin said.

*Oh, he does know what to do. Talking to God is always the right first move.*

"You've been paying attention when Pastor Flores preaches."

"For sure. He gives pop quizzes, and I don't need to be embarrassed in front of—"

Martin clammed up.

Tina chuckled. "Name?"

"Nothing is going on."

"Okay. Speculating? Making it all up?"

"Touché. I guess we're in the same boat."

"I agree. So that's a good idea—the best idea—for us to pray." Tina settled down on an armchair. "Let's pray then."

"What shall we pray for?"

"Wisdom from God," Tina said and realized then she hadn't prayed enough for wisdom. She decided that she would pray for not only herself and her brother but also for Byron.

For her brother, she would pray that God would enable him to run his businesses—and hers—wisely.

For Byron, that God would show him the right decisions to make regarding the school and the day camp.

And for herself, Tina decided to pray that God would give her wisdom to *not* be a stumbling block

to Byron, to *not* be in his way, to *not* cause him problems, and to *not* be a problem for him.

*Whoa. A whole lot of nots.*

*Yes, I've been a problem for him all week.*

It had to end.

# CHAPTER TWENTY-THREE

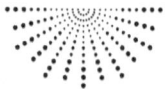

*H*e could barely speak.

Called to fill in at the last minute for his Sunday school teacher who was down with laryngitis, Byron found it impossible to form his rehearsed words, even while looking at the notes on his iPad and the underlined Bible next to it on the lectern in the increasingly stuffy Sunday school classroom at Chapel by the Sea.

When he looked up from his notes, his eyes met those of a concerned—almost panicky—Tina.

*Tina MacFarland, my undoing.*

*My unraveling.*

Byron cleared his throat. "Let's pray before we continue where Benedict stopped last week."

As he bowed his head and closed his eyes, he

heard rustling noises. Fabric, chairs, footsteps, door gently closing.

And he knew what Tina had done.

"Father God, forgive us when we sin against You in ways we cannot explain ourselves. May the light of Your holiness shine into our hearts and expose our wickedness. Lead us in Your everlasting way, and straighten out the path You have before us so that we will do Your will in Your way and according to Your timing. May Your Name be glorified forever and ever. Amen."

Sure enough, when Byron opened his eyes again, Tina's seat was empty.

He wondered where she had gone, whether she had decided to attend another Sunday school class, or if she would be back.

She did not return.

Sunday school was only an hour long, and by the grace of God, Byron was able to stay focused on his talking points. He led a productive discussion among the Sunday school class members.

All went well until he crossed the hallway to get to the sanctuary, and passed the nursery, and spotted Tina changing diapers while another nursery worker sat on a mat and cooed at a crying infant.

He stood to one side of the hallway, hoping the ladies didn't see him.

Tina finished changing diapers, cleaned the changing table, tossed her gloves into the trash can, and stretched her arms toward the wailing baby on the other woman's lap. She lifted the baby, and he stopped crying.

*Instantly.*

The scene emblazoned in Byron's mind all the way to the sanctuary.

He sat down at his usual pew. Well, the Moss family didn't own the pew, but they liked to sit in this row, or the rows in front or behind this one, depending on whether it was occupied before they arrived for the service.

As if on cue, another thought popped into Byron's mind.

*Poison.*

He wondered whether the enemy of God was trying to nudge him out of God's will by putting temptations in front of him. Or was it the will of God for him to have a wife, and that the enemy was trying to dissuade him from the path.

It was hard to tell in the fog of love.

*The fog of what?*

He could ask his Sunday School teacher about it, but the man was single. He could ask Pastor Dixon about it, but the man was older. He could ask his cousin Gus about it, but the man couldn't get a girlfriend himself.

Whom could he ask?

*What about God?*

Byron chided himself for skirting the issue. Quietly, he prayed, asking God to show him what to do. When his friend Pastor Flores of Savannah had sought God's will about his love life, God had answered his prayers.

"Will You answer my prayer, Father God? Will You help me see through this fog?" Byron felt the peace of God as soon as he placed the burden of his heart at the foot of the cross.

He could go on his knees right now right here, but it would be overly dramatic and would draw attention where it needed not be.

He sat there, eyes closed, waiting for the service to begin.

He recalled how he had been startled on Friday morning when Tina had walked into his *session* with Gus. He wasn't too happy with his cousin for wandering off with his hedge clipper while Byron was yammering away about poison.

*Poison.*

Byron opened his eyes and knew what he must do.

# CHAPTER TWENTY-FOUR

*B*yron squatted at the edge of the hot tub and ran his hand in the water. The churning water was warm. He supposed that his brother could put a tub on the deck of a yacht this long, but why bother? Such a luxury item he could have done without.

But then he wasn't Donovan.

"Join me?" Donovan lifted his flute of champagne at him.

"Thanks, but no," Byron said. He didn't drink, and his brother knew that. That wasn't what Donovan had asked, actually.

*Join me in my luxurious living?*

All Byron wanted to do now was get away from this yacht, go back to his office at the school, and do some work before the evening church service began.

He didn't have all the time in the world like Donovan had. Donovan only went to church on Sunday mornings—when he felt like it. He had only recently started showing up on Wednesday nights due to the Savannah team.

*Ah yes, the Savannah team.*

"How was your dinner party here Friday night?" Byron sat cross-legged on the teak deck, facing his brother.

"Splendid. Too bad you missed it, Brother." He chuckled. "You look worried."

"Am I?" Byron turned his face toward the sun above. The noonday heat was beating down on him. He had rolled up his sleeves, but his linen pants would be soaked through soon.

"May I ask you something?" Donovan put his drink down on the side of the tub.

"Sure."

"Is it okay with you if I date someone from your Savannah team?"

"They're technically not *my* Savannah team," Byron said. "They came here on their own accord."

"Then it's not a problem to you?"

"Who do you have in mind?" Byron asked too quickly.

"Ah. It is a problem for you."

"No. I'm just curious."

"Aren't we all?"

Byron waited. Gulls flew overhead. The sun hid behind some floating clouds, but that was no respite for him.

"Guess?"

Byron humored his brother. "Veronique?"

Donovan laughed with the gulls above. "And get raked over by Gus? I'm not stupid."

There were only two other women left. "Tina?"

"She's nice, isn't she?"

*Oh no.* Byron braced himself.

"There's a problem with Tina." Donovan put his hands in the air to make his point. "I don't get her. A bit weird, I think."

"Weird?" *This, I have to hear.* "What do you mean?"

"I told her plus-one for dinner. If she didn't have anyone to ask, come alone. Does that sound logical to you?"

Byron nodded. *I was her plus-one.*

"So what did she do? Can you guess?"

"She came alone?" Byron asked.

"She didn't show up."

"No?" Interesting. Byron had expected Tina to come here alone after she had rescinded her invitation to him. *Guess that didn't happen.*

"Veronique said she stayed at home reading a book in her pajamas."

*Oh.*

"And she looked very sad, they said."

*Double oh.*

Donovan sat up. "What did you do to that poor lady, Byron?"

# CHAPTER TWENTY-FIVE

*K*icking off each week with a Bible study at six o'clock on Monday morning had been Byron's idea, but the idea didn't seem brilliant anymore as he stood in the near-empty break room.

Even Veronique wasn't there.

Neither were Tina, Lucy, the other volunteers, and most of the Summer by the Sea Day Camp teachers. Only Gus and Keith showed up.

Byron glanced at his watch twice, iPad five times or more.

"Maybe we need more coffee," Keith volunteered.

Keith Medford, who had stayed with Gus at his house across the street from the Chapel by the Sea church and school campus, had shown up because Gus had shown up.

"I second that," Gus chimed, getting up noisily from his chair, making a show of dragging himself to the coffeemaker on the countertop near the sink and dishwasher.

"Where two or three are gathered..." Byron didn't finish the sentence.

"Amen," Gus said. He lifted his mug to Byron. "Go on. Start the Bible study, Cousin."

Byron nodded, turning to Proverbs 16.

Sure, Mother had suggested it for his personal Bible study time, but why not make it count double? This way, he didn't have to prepare twice.

"Let's take some prayer requests. Then we pray and dive into verse one," Byron said, his enthusiasm returning.

He couldn't wait to get to it. He had prepared his notes, his talking points, his questions to ask the group. If there was any subject he'd rather teach more than any other subjects, it was the Bible.

He should have gone to seminary.

Keith raised his hand. "This prayer request is not for me, and I would rather you keep it confidential since she's not here."

*She?*

Byron opened his notepad on his iPad and waited.

"Tina's brother just bought a new Ducati, and he hasn't told her."

"And?" Gus asked.

"He has wrecked three bikes in five years, and he's just super uncoordinated on two wheels."

"Okay. Martin is concerned his sister will freak out," Byron typed.

"How did you know his name?" Keith asked.

"I know her brother's name too," Gus said before Byron could answer. "We knew Tina from two years ago."

"I see. Well, I wasn't even a member of Riverside Chapel when they took their first trip here," Keith said. "But Martin and I sometimes ride together on our bikes."

"Bet Tina loves you for that," Gus said.

*Love?* Byron didn't want to hear that word.

"She and I have not totally gotten along," Keith explained. "She thinks I'm a bad influence on her brother."

Gus laughed. "That was an interesting mission trip two years ago."

Keith raised his hand. "If it involves Tina, I don't want to know."

"Remember when she had food poisoning, Byron?"

"Gus, I said I don't want to know." Keith groaned.

Byron looked at the two men. "Moving on, we need to pray for the children who are attending the day camp. We have two hundred and twenty-five kids this year."

"That many?" Gus whistled.

"We don't know how many of them are Christians," Byron added. "Pray that the teachers and staffers would show the love of Christ and point to Jesus."

*Point to Jesus.*

That was what Byron wanted to do the rest of his life.

He could do it here at the Chapel by the Sea Christian School. He was the assistant headmaster because he was good at it. Now he was heading toward being the headmaster of the entire school—primary and secondary—because he was made for this.

Or was he?

He had always wanted to be a teacher.

It was a noble profession.

But what kind of teacher?

So far he had been academic.

Yet as the Bible study progressed that morning and seven o'clock came around, one of the verses he had read kept resounding in his mind.

Proverbs 16:9 seemed to have jumped out of the page of his Bible and latched itself to his heart.

*A man's heart plans his way, but the Lord directs his steps.*

What was God trying to say to him?
What?
Byron couldn't put his finger on it.

# CHAPTER TWENTY-SIX

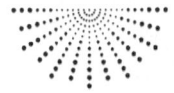

$\mathcal{B}$y Monday afternoon, Byron was worn out. He could barely drag himself down the hallway as Veronique chattered incessantly next to him about her plans to make the Summer by the Sea Day Camp "the most successful ever" in the history of the school.

He was sure her words—her high pitch—were more for the consumption of the people around them, the teachers and staffers now answering to Veronique, rather than for his benefit.

Byron felt a slight strain in his calf muscles. He reminded himself to get back to running soon. For years he had been running around the track on the secondary school field, but this year had been quite a crazy year, beginning with his promotion to assistant headmaster, and now with his being the interim headmaster in light of Headmaster Clarke's cancer treatment taking up the rest of summer.

There wasn't supposed to be much to do for the next couple of months besides the Summer by the Sea Day Camp, but the science wing renovation had been finally underway, but the plans for the kindergarten additions had to be finalized.

For all practical purposes, Headmaster Clarke had dropped everything on Byron's lap.

It didn't always pay to be trustworthy.

Byron wished he had gotten more sleep. He had tossed and turned all night. He had gotten up at the crack of dawn, but didn't feel hungry enough to eat breakfast.

What seemed like gallons of coffee later, Byron had made it to the school feeling like he had been carrying a ton of bricks on his shoulders.

Peels of laugher broke out of the art room.

*Tina.*

Then they were singing.

Curious, Byron walked that way.

He stood at the door. The art room was bright and sunshiny and warm and all things Bahamian. Across the art room, all the windows and doors were open to the grass and trees and sky outside.

The tables were teeming with students—happy students—playing with clay.

Right in the middle of it all, Tina was going from table to table, singing "Jesus Loves Me."

Suddenly the room went silent.

Tina spun around.

"Byron—ah, Mr. Moss." Tina walked toward him, a lump of clay in one hand, and bits of clay on her face and hair.

He couldn't help himself. He reached up to pick away the clay in her hair. The clay had fused to a clump of hair.

"Ouch!" Tina flinched, reaching up with her clay-smeared free hand.

"Sorry. You have clay in your hair," Byron explained. "I was trying to help."

"Thank you." Her eyes sparkled. "You're so kind."

"Am I? Wasn't I trying to pull your hair out?"

Veronique cleared her throat. "We've got work to do, Mr. Moss."

"Ah, yes. Carry on, Tina. Sorry to interrupt," Byron said.

"Don't worry about it. Byron?"

"Yes?"

"Remember our discussion about transporting clay pieces to Ray's kiln?" Tina asked.

"When do you want it done?"

"We're finishing up faster than expected, so tomorrow after day camp."

"Tuesday." Byron swiped his iPad to check his schedule. He had to fit her in. "I'll come back tomorrow afternoon to help you load up the van after the class is dismissed."

"Works for me. Thanks."

"Don't mention it." Byron felt the heaviness of one more thing he had to do to his already over-loaded list. And yet...

Yet he knew he would do whatever Tina asked of him.

*But why?*

He didn't understand it himself.

All he knew was that he wanted to be with Tina.

How could he stay away from her for three weeks?

Someone called Veronique's name, and she strutted toward the classroom door to speak with the teacher. Byron was about to follow her when he felt Tina right behind her outside the classroom.

"Is everything okay?" Tina asked in a whisper.

"Yes," Byron whispered back.

"You look exhausted."

"I am." *Why would I be telling her?*

Somehow Byron felt that her presence comforted him, as if whenever he was with her, he was in a retreat from the busy world.

Tina pressed a gentle finger on his bare arm near his oxford short sleeves.

"What was that?" Byron asked.

"A mini hug."

*A mini hug.*

Byron wanted more than that. But he could not ask for more. Not here at this place, at this time. He wasn't sure when he could ever ask for more from Tina.

Tina smiled and walked back to her classroom of students who had now resumed singing in merriment.

Byron watched her go, his heart feeling the same loss he had felt by the fountain on Friday morning when Tina walked away after she had given him an apple.

A small gift.

A mini hug.

Simple gestures that meant so much.

Byron knew then that he loved her.

He didn't know how he knew, but he just knew.

# CHAPTER TWENTY-SEVEN

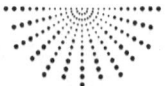

*a*fter day camp on Tuesday, Byron and Tina carried the trays of twenty-seven free-form saucers and small bowls from the art room to the school van.

The twenty-five-minute drive from Chapel by the Sea Christian School to Raymond's pottery studio turned into a fifty-minute snarl in rush-hour traffic through Nassau's busiest time of day.

"Thank God for the AC." Tina turned it up. She checked her safety belt for the tenth time.

"Why are you doing that?" Byron asked as he pulled up at the pottery studio.

"Doing what?"

"Checking your safety belt. You don't trust my driving?"

Tina wondered what to say. Truly. "Well, come to think if it, I have no idea why I did that."

"Nervous about something?"

"When I'm with you, maybe."

"With me?"

"You're perfect. I feel like a big pile of mess when I'm around you."

*Yikes. There went the words.*

Tina waited to see what Byron would say to that.

There was a long pause between them.

*Oh, well.* Tina put her hand on the passenger side door to open it.

"Me too," Byron finally said.

"You too? As in, you agree that I'm a mess around you?"

"No, no." His eyes searched hers. "As in, I'm a mess around you."

"Ha! I don't believe that for a second." As soon as she said it, Sunday morning came to her mind. "Well, I take that back. You were very nervous in Sunday School."

"Ah, yes. I'd rather you not bring it up."

"I've never seen you so unsure of yourself, Byron."

"You were in the room."

"That's why I left." Tina remembered walking down the hallway to find a bench to sit down until the church service began, when she had heard cries from the nursery.

One of the workers had called in sick, and the baby room was short of people. She volunteered on the spot.

"You didn't have to leave," Byron said. "It made me feel even worse."

Tina faced him. "If you're nervous when someone is in the room, it's a weakness that the devil can exploit."

"I believe it," Byron said.

"Maybe you could pretend I'm not in the room next time."

"I can't. You're always on my mind—oops. I didn't mean to tell you that."

Still, he didn't apologize.

Tina searched his eyes. He seemed to have said what was in his heart.

It scared her a little bit. She fumbled with the door and could not get it to open. Next thing she knew, Byron was opening the door for her from the outside.

"After you, Lady MacFarland," he said.

"Thank you, Sir Moss." Tina chuckled.

The awkwardness broke.

She followed Byron to the back of the van, where they unloaded the trays.

Raymond didn't come out to help them, so they

carried the five stacked trays, two in Tina's arms and three in Byron's.

"Clay can be heavy," Tina said.

"Yep!" Byron said, pushing the front door open with his shoulder and side.

The chime went off, and Raymond sprung up from his easel to tell them where to go. The whole process took ten minutes, and they were back in the van for the long drive back to the school, where Tina would catch a ride with Veronique back to the latter's house. Byron had work to do, apparently.

"Is your studio in Savannah similar to Ray's?" Byron asked as he put the school van in gear.

"You mean in size?"

Byron nodded.

"Possibly. I do love my studio." In fact, she missed it. She missed her pottery wheels and the half-glazed washbowl she had left in the studio. "If you ever go back to Savannah, look me up, and I'll give you a tour of my studio."

"I've been there once, but it's been a few years."

"That's what Pastor Flores said." It was interesting to Tina how everything connected, how God worked all things together for the good of His children.

Pastor Flores had come to the Bahamas, attended Chapel by the Sea services, met Pastor Dixon, was introduced to Headmaster Clarke, and next thing Riverside Chapel knew, they had been sending mission teams to Nassau.

This year was different though. This year, Riverside Chapel went on mission trips elsewhere, but a small teaching team had decided to continue their yearly volunteering services at the Summer by the Sea Day Camp. Lucy had asked Tina to join them, and she had said yes long before she found out Byron was the day camp director—before he wasn't anymore.

"I do like it here." Tina looked out the window. The afternoon sun reminded her of Tybee Island and coastal Florida, only there was more water here in the Bahamas.

Could she live here? She wasn't sure.

"You do?"

Tina nodded. "But I must go home."

And there she was, fiddling with her safety belt again.

"Give me a vote of confidence," Byron said. "Stop fidgeting with the safety belt."

Tina lifted her hands off the belt. "Sorry."

"Nothing to be sorry about." Byron's iPhone chimed. He checked it at the next red light. "Your new clay will arrive Wednesday. Soon enough for you?"

"Yes! Thank you, Lord!" Tina cheered. Then she turned to Byron. "Wish I could be helpful to you in return."

"It was nothing." Byron drove the van toward town. "You could pray that God's perfect will would cover our school and day camp."

"I can do that."

"We need His provision, protection, purpose, plan."

Tina nodded. "Yep. Certainly not man's plans, of which there are many, but God's plan."

"Proverbs 16." Byron smiled. "You didn't talk to my mother, did you?"

"No. Why?"

"She has suggested I study Proverbs 16."

"There's some good advice in that chapter for running a business," Tina said. "Some of the verses guide me at Tina's Turn."

"Tina's Turn," Byron repeated. "Nice name for a pottery studio."

"Thank you." Tina tried to recall a verse, but she could not. She checked her phone. "For example, Proverbs 16:3. 'Commit your works to the Lord, and your thoughts will be established.'"

"That's a good one. I guess I should commit the school to the Lord, and He will establish my modus operandi."

"Yes, God will guide you always." Tina turned toward Byron. "I will pray for you, Byron."

"For me?"

"You're taking on such a heavy task. The entire school, not just elementary but also high school."

"Elementary? Ah yes, you meant primary. And secondary."

"Whatever you call them around here." Tina waved her hands about. "The whole school."

"Thank you, Tina. I need all the prayer I can get."

"Anything specific I should focus on?"

Byron breathed in deeply as he parked the van outside the front door of the Summer by the Sea Day Camp. "The science wing renovation is behind the timetable, and spending is going off the charts. If spending keeps going up, we'll never get to add those new kindergarten classrooms."

"That sounds like a good thing—more kindergarten space."

"Yes. In the last few years there has been a waiting list."

"How about fundraising?" Tina asked.

"Tapped out. The new science labs are costly, and our sponsors have given more to that than to the kindergarten project."

"We'll pray about that," Tina said. "Anything else? How's Mr. Clarke doing?"

"Not good. Truthfully, I want him to get well and take his job back, but the prognosis is grim. It's probably the end of the road for him." His voice cracked a bit. "The transition has come too suddenly when...when I have other plans for the summer."

Tina started praying in her heart. "You were in charge of the day camp."

"Yes, until last week, but that wasn't it."

Tina nodded. "You don't have to tell me."

"Someday I might."

"But not today."

"No. Not today." Byron started to get out of the van.

"No need to open the door for me. I can get out on my own."

Byron shut his door and remained seated on the driver side.

Tina was about to exit the vehicle, when she remembered something. "Oh, about my class field trip to Ray's studio next Monday..."

"Tuesday, remember? The sports campers need the bus on Monday."

"Ah yes."

"Already arranged. Gus is going to drive you all in a big old school bus for the field trip. He said he'll hang around for two hours and then drive everyone back here."

"Wow. Thank you." Tina grabbed her tote bag and slid out of the passenger side. "Appreciate it."

"Don't mention it."

Tina came around to the driver side. "You're very organized."

"Just another day's work."

Tina nodded. "It seems to come so easily to you."

"God gifts us in different ways."

"And we give glory to Him no matter what." Tina waved and entered the school building.

"No matter what," Byron echoed.

# CHAPTER TWENTY-EIGHT

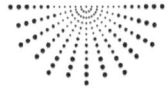

*O*utside Byron's office was another garden that his cousin had planted. It was small and didn't have a fountain but was covered with rows of hibiscus, all flowering in different shades of white and pink and purple.

Of all the spots on the Chapel by the Sea Christian School campus, Tina and her assistants had to choose this area for their outdoor painting project this morning.

Byron did not want to be distracted.

But there she was, in a flowing floral dress, pretty flowers and leaves draping her. She was Miss Summer.

And Byron's heart ached.

He tried to concentrate on his paperwork.

But distraction got the better of his eyes as he watched the teachers and their enthusiastic, loud, boisterous students oohing over flowers and leaves and stems and bees.

He wanted to leave his desk and see what it was really about, until he spotted his cousin Gus walking toward the outdoor classroom, fresh-cut flowers in his hands.

Byron watched Tina receive the bouquet of flowers, and felt jealousy. Gus went on to give each of Tina's helpers a bouquet of flowers too.

The anguish remained in Byron's heart as he watched Tina lift the flowers to her nose and close her eyes.

Byron put down his iPad.

*Why this pain, Lord?*

Perhaps it was his feelings unfulfilled. Perhaps it was the archaic school staff policies that had been crafted so many years ago, back in the dark days of yore.

No romance on campus—unless you were already previously engaged or married before you came to work here.

It had made sense, for all practical purposes.

Until now.

Now it made no sense.

Now it was personal.

There was no way Byron could follow his heart and keep his job, unless, of course, the school policies changed.

It could change.

Sometime.

# CHAPTER TWENTY-NINE

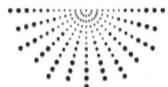

$\mathcal{T}$he angst remained in Byron all the way after school and stuck to him like chewing gum on a shoe sole on a hot Bahamian day, even as he arrived at church for the Wednesday night Bible study.

He felt terrible that his thoughts were occluded with feelings of jealousy toward his cousin and brother for their friendship with Tina, knowing that nothing could happen between himself and Tina, regardless of that pain in his chest.

How could he walk into his Bible study class-room with such feelings in his heart? They were not impure, not precisely, and to be sure, even God Himself had been said to be a jealous God. Yet God's jealousy was pure and holy.

Byron's jealousy was one of possessiveness.

As if Tina were his.

And as if no one else could have her but him.

He reminded himself that there was no "Tina and me."

*But could there be?*

Just as the question began to form into a petition to God above, Byron spotted Tina and Donovan walking together toward him, speaking to each other in low voices, apparently not being aware that he was standing in their path as they approached the entrance to the sanctuary.

It was not a sight he wanted to see while dealing with his internal issues.

Byron turned to leave.

"Byron!" Tina's voice reached him.

Byron quickened his pace and then realized how juvenile that was. He stopped, spun around—

"Ooomph!" Tina smacked into him.

He held her arms and pushed her back as gently as he could. "Seriously, Tina."

Tina's face reddened. "I was going after you. You were running away."

"I was not."

"You were too."

Donovan came up to them, laughing all the way. "You two are killing me."

Byron ignored his brother. "What do you want, Tina?"

"Just to ask you to come sing with us," Tina said, joy in her voice.

"Sing with you?"

"In the choir."

"I can't. I have Bible study tonight."

"Oh, I forgot." Tina looked dejected.

Byron softened his voice. "I'm probably already late."

Standing next to Tina, Donovan waved his wristwatch at Byron. "Not even seven o'clock yet."

"Okay, I'll be on time then." Byron started moving away.

"Ask him," Donovan said to Tina.

Byron stopped. He watched Donovan wave and disappear through the sanctuary doors. "Ask me what?"

"Donovan's having a dinner party at his beach house this Friday night," Tina said slowly.

"Another one?" Byron frowned.

"He wants us to go."

"Us?"

"Us—day camp teachers, staffers, volunteers."

"Oh."

"Will you come?"

"He could have asked me personally." Byron didn't know why he said that.

"It's not a formal dinner, Byron. Anyone can go. He just needs a head count ASAP."

Byron breathed in deeply. "And why are *you* the one to ask me?"

"Don't read too much into it. We're all going—well, except Veronique and Lucy. Veronique and her aunt are going to visit another aunt in Lucaya for the weekend. Lucy has never been to Grand Bahama, so she's going to tag along."

"Meaning what?"

"Meaning Donovan is going to pick me up from Veronique's house."

Byron's eyebrows rose. "He offered to pick you up?"

"Well, his driver could, I suppose."

"So if I go..."

"Then *you* pick me up," Tina said. "It doesn't look good for him or his driver to keep coming around to get me."

"No."

"I'm more familiar with you than I am with your brother."

"Familiar? That's not a good word. We have school policies."

"Oh. I forgot. I totally forgot. I'm sorry. I didn't mean..." Tina backed away. "Veronique told me—I should've remembered. I put you in a bad spot. Forgive me."

"Nothing to forgive. If it weren't for school policies I would..." Byron's fingers reached Tina's chin. He kept his eyes on her lips—

And blinked.

He sighed as his fingers dropped away from Tina's face.

"Better run to your Bible study," Tina said softly. "You're late."

Byron nodded.

# CHAPTER THIRTY

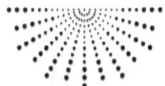

*H*eadmaster Clarke lived in one of those candy-colored houses over-looking the marina and Nassau's many yachts, one of which was Donovan's new seventy-five-foot women magnet.

On Clarke's second-floor balcony, Byron sipped more mineral water from the cold bottle as the salty wind twirled his hair, whipping it here and there. His sunglasses blocked the noonday sun from his eyes.

Byron had come here a few times a week for lunch since Clarke's cancer news had broken last week. Sometimes he had brought takeout lunches from the school cafeteria for him and Clarke to eat, but other times he had picked up something from restaurants on the way.

Frankly, he didn't care how much he spent. All he wanted was to buy more time with his mentor.

His sandwich done, Byron crumpled the paper wrapper into a ball and put it back into the paper sack. When he looked up, Clarke was looking at him.

None the worse for wear, Clarke had weathered the chemotherapy well, though it had only been a week. If he was awfully sick from it, Byron couldn't tell. Clarke had a high tolerance for pain, it seemed.

"Something on your mind, son?" Clarke asked. He was in tee shirt and shorts. That had been as dressed down as Byron had ever seen his mentor.

"I'm not sure, exactly." Byron didn't know what to say nor how to say it.

"Yep. Sounds like a problem."

"Because I can't define it?" Byron knew the answer to his own question.

"Because you have the same look since Tuesday in my office when we discussed our transition." Clarke sat back. "Tell me what's bothering you."

"Our school policies."

"Ah. We did a major revision some four or five years ago."

"We kept most of the original. Almost a hundred percent." Even archaic policies from the fifties.

"And? We liked it. The school board liked it."

Clarke folded his arms gingerly around his chest. "Nobody complained."

"I was in my twenties when I went with it." *Yeah, blame youth. Young and single youth.*

"What does age have anything to do with it?"

"How many people whom God was bringing together have we separated?" Byron cringed. He hadn't expected his words to roll out like that, but it was done now.

Clarke was silent for a moment.

Then he broke into a guffaw.

Then he laughed so hard, so loud, so long that tears come out of his eyes.

*This cannot be good for me.*

Byron was stunned into silence. He tried to recall what he had said, but he couldn't repeat his own exact words. Somehow he had brought God into the equation, and it might have been a mistake.

God was sovereign, yes, but never had Byron dared to use the name of God to get his own way.

*Get my way? What way?*

When Clarke had somewhat calmed down, he began to speak. "We evaluate our school policies every few years, don't we? Are you saying it's time for us to see whether they still work?"

"I don't know what I'm saying, sir."

"Our school policies are not the commandments of God. We sat down, in our flawed thinking and finite reasoning, and we made a list of rules to help us keep the school functional."

"They've been prayed over," Byron said.

"Yes, but they're not set in stone. If we try to change the Word of God—adding or subtracting from it—then we're in deep trouble. But school policies are not written on stone tablets. Which rule do you have a problem with?"

"Dating."

"Ah, I can see that could be a problem for single teachers and staffers on campus."

"I know we're trying to prevent office romance—"

Clarke lifted a palm. "No. You forgot. We're trying to keep the team together. If two members of a team are in love with each other, that's one sort of distraction. What if they fought and broke up? That could fracture our team."

Byron nodded.

*I don't want to ever break up with Tina.*

Ha! First he had to begin something with Tina before they could even have something to break up.

"We can get down to the technicality of it—that is, paid staffers versus volunteers—but the bottom line is team unity," Clarke said. "What if the team members were already engaged or married to each other prior to joining the team? And here they are, fighting."

"Our school policy for that situation says they would agree to resolve it outside of school or get some counseling at Chapel by the Sea or at their own churches." It was all spelled out.

"Then what's the problem, son? Do you have an issue I need to know about?"

Byron knew he'd ask that. "Hypothetically, if one of my paid staffers wants to date one of the unpaid short-term day camp volunteers, can they?"

"It would be best if they wait until after the day camp ends."

*But she's going home after the day camp ends.*

Clarke leaned forward. "The question is one of focus. We are here to make the day camp successful. We have a mission. We owe it to the children to give them their most fun summer ever. We owe it to God to do the job to the best of our abilities."

"And not be distracted," Byron added.

"Exactly. And who is this staffer we're talking about?"

"I'd rather not say, sir."

"Well, then, please give this person my advice on this."

"Yes, sir?"

"Tell the staffer that timing is in God's hands. If this volunteer is meant to be with him, then nothing can stop the purpose and plan of God. Patience is required in all matters of the heart."

*Patience?*

"Patience to wait on God, wait for Him to carry out His will, wait for the day camp to finish. Patience to focus on the task at hand, to complete the work of the Lord. Patience to know that God works out all things for our good. Do you understand, Byron?"

"Yes, sir."

"Patience, Byron. God will bring it to pass."

# CHAPTER THIRTY-ONE

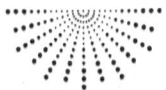

*B*yron wasn't sure if it was the works of man or the mercy of God that had caused Donovan to call him on his way back to his office after lunch with Headmaster Clarke.

"He's got a bad cold, and I don't feel like playing chauffeur tonight." Donovan's voice came though the phone along with the sounds of the waterfall at the edge of his infinity pool.

"I thought you told Tina you'd pick her up."

"Yeah, I was going to show off my new Royce, but then I decided to ask Trey to drive it instead, but he called in sick. He caught a cold from his wife, and now all four of them are sick puppies at home. You don't want your volunteers to catch his cold, do you?"

"Not with two hundred kids at stake."

"Exactly. So could you do me a favor and pick up Keith, Gus, and Tina?"

Byron shook his head. "I'm not going tonight. Gus has a truck. He can drive."

"I thought Tina asked you."

"I told her no."

"You're breaking her heart."

"She understood. We discussed it."

"It's not a date night. I've catered enough food for a hundred people. You'll be lost in the crowd. Nobody would notice you. Besides, we're brothers. We eat together all the time."

It seemed silly for Byron to fret over such little things. He wondered if he had been overly worried for nothing.

"All right. What time?" Byron asked.

"Whenever. I did tell Tina to be ready by 5:45."

It meant Byron had to pick up Gus and Keith at five o'clock. The details ran though his mind.

"I hope Tina wears something pretty," Donovan said. "I think she has a beautiful figure underneath those flowing dresses. I hope she wears something stretchy and fitting—"

"Shut up, Donovan," Byron snapped.

# CHAPTER THIRTY-TWO

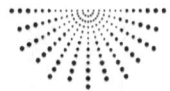

*S*omewhere in the middle of the outdoor dinner party surrounded by candles and sand and surf and live Caribbean music, Tina MacFarland felt she owned Donovan Moss a huge apology.

She had misread him.

The gentleman had been polite, kind, and generous to almost everyone. It was obvious to her now that Donovan liked women and enjoyed the attention that came with his popularity and good looks.

That was to say, he had not singled out Tina for any reason.

Sure, he was not her type by any means, for Tina preferred a less flashy, less flamboyant man.

Still, she was sorry she had misread Donovan's intentions.

Perception.

Funny how things were.

Just like the glazes that Tina used in her pottery studio back in Savannah.

When first applied to the unfired pottery, the glazes were still wet and looked dull and common. Fired in the kiln, the colors intensified, changed into glossy permanence. In the sunlight, all the colors would come out.

If leaves were adhered to the pottery surface, the high temperature would burn away those organics, leaving imprints on the mug or bowl or platter or whatever she had made.

Which was Donovan? Unglazed or glazed?

And for that matter, which was Byron?

Two brothers, so unlike each other. One sought the stage. The other stayed in the shadows. One flashed his wealth. The other—well, Tina had never thought of Byron as more than an educator, with an educator's salary. It seemed to her now that the Moss family was fairly wealthy, but none of that was of any interest to her.

Sure, Donovan's house here was even bigger than her own house on Tybee Island, but so what?

It was the heart that mattered to God, and so would it matter to Tina also.

Did Donovan have a heart of gold? Perhaps. But all this wealth, this opulence...

She looked back at the Moss Mansion lit up with strategically placed outdoor lighting. The massive structure rose into the Bahamian night sky like a veritable tower of means.

Yet.

Tina remembered a Bible passage, those verses that spoke of gold, silver, and precious stones versus wood, hay, and stubble.

What was that verse?

She reached for her iPhone, when someone touched her hand.

"No, no." It was Donovan. "It's after hours. No work allowed."

"I just want to look up a verse," Tina said.

"Oh, that's allowed." Donovan lifted a glass at her. "A pity you don't drink."

"I don't count it as pity."

"But we can still work together, can't we?" Donovan was unsteady on his feet.

*Now that's pitiful.*

"Thank you for inviting us," Tina said. "You have been very generous."

She meant it. Before the new school year would begin in August, everyone would know how generous this man was. But that was news for another day. She only hoped Byron wouldn't take it in the wrong way.

"Hope you get some sort of tax write-off," Tina added.

"None whatsoever."

"Sorry."

Donovan inched closer. "I went to your website, Tina Faromacland."

Tina didn't correct him.

"Those ceramic platters you make for restaurants are very nice."

"Thank you." Tina smiled. "I have a wonderful team of potters."

"But the design is yours."

"Yes. As are most of the signature pieces that Tina's Turn produces."

"I'm opening a new hotel with a restaurant and a casino at Lucaya," Donovan said. "I'd like to commission you to design some unique platters for me. Can you do that?"

"Let's talk. When do you open the hotel?"

"Next February, before the spring and summer vacationers arrive."

Tina thought for a bit. It was the end of June now. February wasn't too far away. She had planned on closing the studio for several weeks around Christmas.

"I have a few commissioned works on my

schedule between August and December, so it's going to be a tight fit."

"Tight fit? Yeah, I told Byron that you should wear something tight—"

Someone cleared his throat rather loudly next to Donovan.

"Maybe you had a bit too much to drink." Byron took the glass out of Donovan's hand. "Time to call it a night?"

"The dinner just started."

"We were done with desserts," Byron said.

"Tina and I were talking business."

Tina was amazed how Donovan wasn't slurring his speech. She was pretty sure he was still functional.

"What kind of business?" Byron asked.

It amused Tina that he was curious. One more interesting tidbit to add to Byron's profile.

"Excellent pottery, that's what," Donovan said. "Tina here is going to make me hundreds of platters for Moss Lucaya."

"Ah, your new hotel. Like you need another one."

"I don't need it. The tourists do." Donovan pointed to Tina. "At some point in time, I'm going to make a trip to Savannah to tour her pottery studio. Want to come, big Brother?"

Tina grinned. "It's not a huge studio. I think you can almost see everything in ten minutes."

"Well worth the ten-hour round-trip flight, I'm sure," Donovan said.

"And jet fuel," Byron added.

"You have your own plane?" Tina asked.

"Doesn't everybody?" Donovan spotted someone else. "Ah, I need to talk to Tom What-shisname."

And he walked off without excusing himself, leaving Tina and Byron standing on the sandy beach.

They weren't alone, and yet they were.

"He's really a nice guy," Byron said.

"Brothers. What are we going to do with them?" Tina asked no one.

"Yeah. How's *your* brother doing?"

"I spoke with him a week ago, and we've been texting all week. He's busy keeping my office running and doing some VA work." Tina thought it was odd that Byron would bring up Martin. "Why do you ask?"

"Just making small talk."

Tina pointed to the bottle of mineral water in Byron's hand. "You don't drink?"

"Never had a taste for it. My whole family drinks though."

"I won't hold that against you, but I do prefer teetotalers."

"Prefer?"

Tina didn't answer his question. The music around them seemed to grow louder, giving her a way out. The kettledrums continued their melodies, chatter and laughter filled the harmonic scale, and the crashing ocean waves rounded up the symphony of noise.

# CHAPTER THIRTY-THREE

$\mathcal{T}$he day after Donovan's party, Tina was still on Byron's mind as he lazed around his townhouse on a rainy Saturday.

It was a typical rain these parts of the world. Byron was used to the incessant sprays on his roof sounding like drumbeats.

When he had been a boy, he and Donovan would run outside to play in the rain and mud puddles. Sometimes they had brought their corgi with them, to the chagrin of their parents and the consternation of their maid, who had to give the puppy a bath before it was allowed back into the Moss Mansion.

Moss Mansion.

Mother had sold it to Donovan sometime in the decade before Father passed away. Mother and

Father had wanted to build it as a bigger and better home and retreat. It was unfortunate that Father had only enjoyed several years of their new home next door to the old Moss Mansion before his heart had given out.

Byron had never been into space. He'd rather have his abode small and cozy, thank you very much.

He had lived alone for over ten years now and hadn't found the need to expand this town house at the edge of town, right across the street from the school. He saved on petrol and time going back and forth to work.

He was only a couple of blocks away from his cousin Gus's house. It was ironic that Gus, land-scaper extraordinaire, had only a small yard and preferred container gardening in his own home. It was as if Gus had been preparing to move somewhere.

To where?

Many people had said that Christians were only passing through this world on their way to heaven.

Gus epitomized that by traveling light.

*What about me?*

*Do I travel light?*

Byron got up from his teak writing desk that his grandfather had left him, and stretched by a window.

As the rain came and went, he could see the Chapel by the Sea Christian School from his third-floor window. There were hints of construction vehicles parked between a clump of royal poinciana trees and the school's basketball and tennis courts.

Byron stared outside as he listened to the rain, now getting heavy again. It was a while before he was aware that his phone was ringing, its harp ring tone mostly masked by the pelting rain.

By the time he reached his iPhone sitting on the coffee table, the phone call had gone to voice mail. He picked up his iPhone to read the screen. One missed call.

*Donovan.*

*What does he want?*

Byron grabbed a bag of plantain chips from the pantry before he called Donovan back. He poured a pile of chips into a handmade blown-glass bowl that one of the graduating students' parents had given him some years ago.

Byron returned his brother's call. "What's up?"

"Commiserate with me," Donovan said on the phone.

"Go on."

"I called Tina half an hour ago to apologize for last night."

"You should. You were tipsy."

"But I do want those platters."

"Whatever." Byron walked toward his living room, one hand holding his phone and the other the big bowl of chips.

"So I apologized." Donovan made a show of sighing deeply.

"You said that."

"I asked her to marry me," Donovan said.

The bowl slipped away from Byron's hand.

Oily fried banana pieces and broken shards of local one-of-a-kind glass spread out in a starburst pattern all over the floor in front of him.

He stood rooted to the spot, his flip-flops the only protection for his feet against the broken glass.

*Calm down.*

*Pray.*

Byron decided that Donovan couldn't possibly have meant Tina. He was interested in Lucy, wasn't he?

"Is this Tina we're talking about?" Byron asked. His hands shook.

"Yeah. Didn't I say? Tina MacWhatever."

*Calm down.*

*Kill him.*

"What did she say?" Byron hissed, his teeth clenched.

"She said, 'Get lost!'"

Byron nearly smiled. "Exact words?"

"Yeaahhh. Tell me if that's not rude."

Byron didn't know how to respond.

"Well, if you must know, Brother, she said that she's not marrying anyone."

"Ever?" Byron wondered if she had said it in the heat of the moment.

"Ever."

*Ever.*

Byron's heart fell out of his chest and rolled to the floor where the glass shards were.

# CHAPTER THIRTY-FOUR

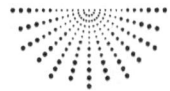

he rain continued through the weekend and into Tuesday, when Tina's art class was supposed to take a field trip to Raymond's pottery studio in the middle of the island on the other side of Nassau.

Raymond had texted Tina the day before, saying that all the pieces but two had come out of the kiln. Tina had prayed for a way to tell the two kids that their bowls had exploded in the kiln, probably because their clay pieces had trapped air in them.

In the end, they didn't cry, and Tina had helped them shape new bowls on Monday, and those bowls were now in the box she carried as she ushered twenty-four kids in wet ponchos into the school bus.

Silently, she prayed for the three kids who didn't show up at day camp this Tuesday.

"Thank you, Gus," Tina said as she brought up the rear, rain dripping off her own poncho.

It was nice of Gus to volunteer to drive the bus. He couldn't work in the school yard on account of the rain anyway, but he could have done some other work in his toolshed.

Instead, here he was, driving Tina's class around.

"No problem." Gus started the ignition. "Better sit down. Don't want you tossing around when I drive."

"Ha-ha." Tina surveyed the bus. All her volunteers were here today, helping out on the field trip. She counted seven adults, including herself, and twenty-four kids. That was a pretty good ratio, considering.

For that, she had Veronique and Byron to thank. They had sent her two more helpers when they realized how big her class enrollment was.

Tina took a seat in the front of the bus, the box safely on her lap.

She closed her eyes.

She had been trying her best to get up at six o'clock every morning so that she wasn't late for day camp, and it had been taking a toll on her. However, the good news was that Veronique had softened and had not left her behind at the house. Still, five days of early rising had slowly transitioned her biological clock to who knew what.

She yawned.

*Need more coffee.*

She glanced at her watch. It was around 9:30 local time. For whatever reason, she wondered what Byron was doing this morning. A chatty Veronique had told her that the science wing renovations at the school were coming along, but the rain hadn't helped.

Tina prayed for Byron and Veronique, that God would give them energy and wisdom to run the school and day camp. Those two worked well together, and she wished God's blessings upon their lives.

Tina was staring at the box in her hand when she realized that her tote bag—with her passports and money and cards—was not on the seat next to her, nor was it slung over her shoulder.

*Uh-oh.*

She must have left it in the art room.

She wanted to call Veronique or Lucy to keep an eye on it for her—

*My cell phone is in my tote bag.*

"Hey, Gus!" Tina wondered if he could hear her.

"Yes?"

"I left my tote bag in the art room. Do you happen to have Veronique's number?"

"It'll be safe there. No worries," Gus said. "Then again, anybody can walk in and out of the school compound at any time."

"Right."

"I'll text Byron."

*Byron. Oh dear.*

*He's going to say this proves yet again that I am scatterbrained.*

"T-thank you." *I guess.*

Tina forgot all about the stigma when Raymond's studio came into view. She couldn't wait to get off the bus and run to a potter's wheel—

*But no. We're glazing today.*

When the bus parked, before the door was opened, Tina stood up.

"All right, students. This is how we're going to do this. Miss Amber is going to stand outside the bus and check off your names one by one as you exit the bus. Then we're going to get inside the building and out of this rain, but we're not going to run, okay? Mr. Raymond has been so kind to let us come here to glaze our pottery pieces, and we don't want to knock anything down entering and exiting his lovely studio, right?"

And so they filed into the studio, shed their rain-coats and umbrellas, and sat down shoulder to shoulder on three long tables, eight to ten artists per table.

In their wake, the cement floor between the tables in the art room and the door to the outside was wet and muddy.

"Raymond, if you have a mop, I'll clean that up." Tina pointed to the streaks and puddles on the floor.

"Sure do." Raymond disappeared through an inside door.

While he was gone, Tina gave her students instructions. "Does everyone have a paint tray? Put up your hand if you don't have one."

Everyone had one.

"Good." Tina walked about. "Each of your paint trays only has six wells, so we're going to have a maximum of six colors, okay? If you want more colors, tell the teachers. It's okay if you only use two or three colors."

The kids nodded.

"The more colors you use, the messier it could be. You'll have to imagine how the colors will come out when fired in the kiln at a very high temperature. The glazes look light, but they will be darker in the end."

The kids nodded again.

Tina wondered how much they understood what she had said.

Raymond returned with a mop and propped it by a wall. He went back to his work.

Tina figured that, with so many kids, she would have to go table by table. She wished she had put more thought into how to organize the class, but she had taught art classes before, and had been banking on her previous knowledge.

In other words, she was somewhat winging it.

Now it made sense to her why Byron planned ahead.

Planning ahead would've been less stressful.

*Stress?*

*This is supposed to be fun!*

Quickly, she prayed for God to give them a day without disasters. A disaster would be if any kid knocked over glazes and she had to pay for them.

Then again, accidents happened.

"Class, before we begin, let's pray." Tina waited for everyone to pay attention. Thirty souls in front of her, plus herself.

"Thank you, Father God, for this beautiful day. You brought the sunshine and the rain, and we thank You for all forms of weather. You brought us here safely. Thank You, Lord, for Mr. Gus and for all the teachers and helpers we have here today." She listed them by name. "Thank You for creating art and colors and for the clay that we could shape into artwork. May all that we do today bring glory to You. In the Name of Your Son, Jesus, I pray. Amen."

Tina felt much better after she prayed.

Her stress of leading such a big group lessened.

Her focus clarified when she saw what she had to do.

"Everyone, stay in your seats. We have seven teachers and helpers, and we're going to bring your pottery pieces to you. Once we've done that, we'll bring the glazes to you as well. You pick the colors, we squirt them into your paint trays, and then you can begin. Yes?"

"Yes!" Everyone said at once.

# CHAPTER THIRTY-FIVE

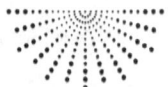

yron came out of the meeting stunned. He still had no idea who had suddenly decided to foot the bill to expand the kindergarten classrooms. Some extremely generous people, yes. But this generous?

Headmaster Clarke followed him.

Byron stopped. "We'll never know?"

"Possibly," Clarke said. "Let's not question God's provision, shall we?"

"Right. But—"

"Our donors have always been compassionate toward the cause of Christ."

Byron nodded. Clarke was right. When the Chapel by the Sea Christian School had needed a new educational building several years ago, donors had stepped up to the plate.

Some of them were still unnamed.

"Aren't you a bit curious about this sudden infusion of cash for our school?" Byron asked.

"We prayed. God answered. We thank Him. Done." Clarke excused himself and left Byron standing there in the hallway.

*Done?*

Somehow it wasn't that easy for Byron. He wanted details. Someone—or a group of people—had found out that the kindergarten additions were delayed due to the cost overrun of the science wing renovations.

*Oh well.*

Byron turned on his iPhone to find that Gus had texted him while he had been in a meeting.

*Here we go again.*

Byron sighed as he made his way to the art room to retrieve Tina's purse. With the doors unlocked during school hours, no one could guarantee that belongings were safe.

Tina should be more careful with her stuff. The other day, she had lost and found her debit card. Had it been only a week?

As he entered the art room, the mystery of the kindergarten donations still bothered him.

Whom had they told about the shortage of funds?

Whom had he told?

The information had been private.

*Until now.*

Byron cringed.

Tina.

He had told Tina. It had come out of his mouth when she asked him what she could pray about. When was that again?

Ah yes, when they had been driving back and forth to Raymond's studio to drop off the pottery pieces last Tuesday.

A week ago.

And right now, Tina was at the same pottery studio with her art class.

He had told her something about donors having given more to the science wing than they had to the kindergarten project.

Kindergarten.

Two years ago, Tina had helped with the kindergarteners when she came here on that Riverside Chapel mission trip to run the Vacation Bible School.

And last Tuesday in the car, she had said something almost in passing.

*That sounds like a good thing—more kindergarten classrooms.*

Could it be her?

Nah.

Byron knew that Tina was a potter. She had a

studio. Gus had said she had won awards. So what? Most artists didn't earn enough to be wealthy. Or did they? Byron knew so little about the art world.

And why had she been whispering to Donovan that Wednesday night at church? Had they been conspiring to do something? Give a sizable donation, perhaps?

He wouldn't put it past Donovan to be persuaded. Singlehandedly, Donovan could have paid for all the school renovations combined.

Well, Byron could too, but he wasn't touching any of his inheritance. He was saving it for...

*Ah, so who's the selfish, stingy one now?*

Byron frowned.

*Oh boy. I sure have a lot going for me. I'm jealous, and I'm stingy too.*

*Two strikes against me compared to my wonderful, amazing baby brother.*

He didn't like it.

At all.

But what did any of this have to do with Tina?

It was only a speculation.

Chapel by the Sea had been a mission church for years. Many supporting churches in the United States and Germany and the Caribbean and elsewhere had always made sure that the school was never in any debt.

What Clarke had said to him minutes ago

returned to Byron's mind.

*Let's not question God's provision, shall we?*

# CHAPTER THIRTY-SIX

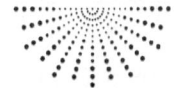

*A*fter a brown-bag lunch at their tables, Tina's art class filed out into the rain again. By now the parking lot and ground was awash with tropical rain, and Tina's sandals were soaked all the way through, such that when she entered the bus, she could hear loud squishing sounds coming out of the soles.

A veritable thunderstorm threatened the bus trip back to the Summer by the Sea Day Camp. Everyone sat quietly in the bus, and Tina prayed for safety.

She was confident Gus could handle the bus. He had driven here twice today, once to drop them off this morning, and now to take them back to the art room at two o'clock.

The kids' parents and guardians would be

picking them up at three, so as soon as they got back to the school, the day was over.

Tina closed her eyes, feeling tired, yet thankful. The field trip had gone without a hitch. Nobody had dropped any of their pottery pieces. No fights had broken out among the nice kids. And they hadn't used up all of Raymond's glazes.

To be sure that he had been properly compensated, Tina bought a few more pieces from his gallery. She wondered how she was going to transport twenty pounds of pottery back to Savannah without having to pay extra fees for overweight carry-ons.

She opened her eyes and looked outside. She couldn't see a thing. Sheets of rain fell around the bus, veiling the surrounding streets and windows from her view. It was as though they were going through a car wash.

She glanced at Gus. He was leaning toward the steering wheel, trying to see what was in front of him. Tina doubted he could see anywhere beyond five or ten feet ahead—

A loud craaaack and several thumps jolted Tina out of her seat, then pushed her back against her seat, amid a sea of screaming kids and adults.

The bus came to a complete stop, its tail end tilted down, as if the road was uneven—

*A sinkhole?*

*A wreck?*

*What?*

Terrified of her own imagination, Tina turned to Gus.

He was out of the driver's seat. "Sit tight. I'll check. Make sure nobody gets out."

The door opened, and Gus was out in the rain that continued to pour. The tropical showers beat down on the bus roof, the rain rhythm sounding like a noisy waterfall.

Tina stood up. "Everyone, stay in your seat for a second."

It was a very long second.

Gus came back in. "People, our axle fell off. Rolled down the road and hit a parked car."

Tina almost laughed, but she wanted to cry also. "So we didn't get into a wreck?"

"The rear end is a wreck, all right."

"No accidents?"

"No, but we're in the middle of a busy road. Right in the middle. I don't want any kid to be run over when we get out."

"So what do we do?" Tina asked.

"I've called the police, and they're on the way. They can block the road so we can get the students safely off the bus."

"We'll have to get the kids home," Tina said.

"Right. Byron is on his way with another school bus."

*Byron.* Tina breathed in deeply. "We're always troubling him."

Gus smiled. "All he wanted to know was if *you* were okay."

"Me? I'm fine."

"That's what I told him. It didn't seem enough for him."

"Meaning what?"

"Until he sees you, he won't be satisfied that you're okay."

"That's a bit silly, don't you think?" Tina asked.

"Silly? Byron? Only when he's in... Never mind."

# CHAPTER THIRTY-SEVEN

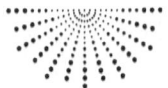

$\mathcal{T}$ina was suitably impressed that the Royal Bahamas Police Force vehicles arrived in no time at all, together with an ambulance and a massive tow truck.

If she were a baker, she'd bake a cake for the police officers for their trouble directing traffic away from the poor school bus with its separated axle and back wheels, and for doing a superb job of it in the heavy downpour.

But she wasn't a baker. Perhaps a donation would suffice.

Tina led her helpers to usher all twenty-four kids in their rain gear into the second school bus that Byron had driven to the accident site.

One of her adult helpers had an apparent kink

in her neck—whiplash?—and she was being examined at the ambulance.

As for the kids, well, they had thought they were at the carnival, going on clunky roller coasters.

"Can we do that again?" One spritely boy said to Tina as she checked off his name at the door of their new bus.

"No." It was all Tina wanted to say.

"Thought I'd ask." He skipped to his seat, rivulets of water rolling off his poncho.

*If we don't clean that up, someone's going to slip and fall.*

"Everyone!" Tina got their attention. "Please walk slowly. The floor is slippery. Don't want you to fall and hurt yourself."

Someone began to cry.

"I want my mommy." And echoes went all around the bus at the power of the suggestion.

"They're waiting for you at the school," Tina said. "As soon as we finish the head count, we can get rolling, boys and girls."

"Rolling?" one little girl asked.

*Oh boy. Bad choice of word.*

"Listen, boys and girls," Tina said. "Don't worry. Okay?"

They quietened.

Tina stretched her neck to look through the

window. Gus was helping the whiplashed adult volunteer to the bus. She seemed to be all right.

*Thank God.*

"Looks like we have everybody." She stepped to the center of the bus. "God has protected all of us. No one is seriously injured."

A kid raised her hand.

"Yes, Lydia?"

"I have a boo-boo."

Alarmed, Tina rushed to her side. "Where?"

The girl pointed to her knee, where a cartoon Band-Aid was falling off, probably losing its stickiness in the rain. "I fell last week."

*Last week. Whew.*

Tina placed a palm on her own chest to calm herself down.

She went back to her spot. "Kids, God was with us and He is still with us. Mr. Moss is going to drive us—safely!—back to the school, where your moms and dads are picking you up."

"My mom is not coming to get me," a kid said, and he began to cry.

"Johnny, your mom just had a new a baby, but your grandpa is picking you up," Tina said gently.

He didn't stop crying.

"Why don't you sit with me over there, and you can tell me about your new baby sister?" Tina pointed to her seat in the front of the bus.

The third-grade boy nodded and slowly got up from his seat. He held Tina's hand as she stood there.

"All right, everyone," Tina said. "Let's pray and thank God for taking care of us."

After she prayed, loud voices said "amen" behind her.

Byron and Gus.

"Ready to go?" Byron asked.

"Yes." Tina nodded. "Let's go home."

# CHAPTER THIRTY-EIGHT

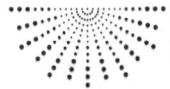

*B*yron kept glancing back at Tina as he drove through the dissipating rain toward the Chapel by the Sea Christian School gate, inside of which were the wings dedicated to the Summer by the Sea Day Camp.

Tina was sitting next to a crying boy. At her feet was her tote bag which he had brought to her. Didn't she realize that the canvas bag would soak up all that water and mud trekked into the bus from the great outdoor rain?

Byron checked his rearview mirror. Gus was sitting one row back behind the driver's side, taking a nap.

The fifteen-minute drive seemed long and slow, but Byron had to be careful. All three school buses had been serviced at the same time, and whether it mattered or not, he couldn't be too sure.

He had already called the service center where the broken bus had been towed. It would be an additional expense to recheck the rest of the buses, but the safety of the students and teachers were paramount. It could be merely a loose bolt, but even that could have caused worse injuries than bumps and bruises.

Byron parked the bus at the entrance to the school. One by one, the kids and volunteers filed out of the bus. A sea of concerned parents and grandparents and guardians stood all around the bus, some still carrying umbrellas, though the rain had somewhat subsided.

"Thank you," Tina said to him as the last kid disembarked into the waiting arms of his grandpa.

"No problem, Tina."

Byron liked saying her name.

*Tina. Lovely Tina.*

An old thought popped into his head. Two years ago, Tina had been nothing but annoying to him, with her inability to get anything right and for her clumsiness. He remembered how he used to say her name.

*Tee-yee-yee-nah!*

That would usually be followed by another pair of words.

*Not again!*

Now, things had changed. He'd like to think that two years had matured them both.

"Is Veronique giving you a lift home?" Byron asked.

"That's so British," Tina said.

"British what?"

"You say *lift*. I say *ride*."

Byron didn't know what to say. At such a moment as this, after a near disaster, wouldn't Tina at least try to be serious? Perhaps she was using humor to lighten up the situation.

*Or perhaps this is just Tina.*

*Just Tina.*

*Lovely Tina.*

Byron decided to try again. "Is Veronique taking you and Lucy home?"

"Ah yes," Tina said. "We'll have to wait though. She has a meeting at four or something. It doesn't matter. We'll still get back to her house in time for dinner."

"I'll drive you if you need to change into dry clothes and rest after that harrowing experience."

"It wasn't *harrowing* per se, Byron. Everyone is alive. Everyone is fine. Thank you anyway. I can wait for Veronique. Save you the trouble." Tina waved as she stepped off the bus—

And disappeared headlong into a scream and a splash.

*What in the world?*

Byron sprung up like a bolt of lightning in a tropical storm, and flew out of the bus.

There she was.

Tina sitting in a pothole, clothes and hair all askew.

Byron hadn't realized he had parked so close to a small pothole on the road. Well, nobody else had said anything. And no one else had an accident. How many people had exited the bus before Tina did? Twenty-four kids and eight adults, including Gus, had stepped across this pothole without incident.

It had to be Tina.

Her skirt, already wet, was all muddy.

Eyes closed, Tina was cringing, making some sort of agonizing moan.

The people still around them—some entering their vehicles with their sons and daughters, some staffers and volunteers from the day camp—seemed to be watching to see what Byron would do.

He didn't care.

He was on his knees. "Tina, are you okay?"

Tina tried to get up. "Owww. I think I sprained my ankle."

Her legs were muddy. Byron wondered about

that water—oily, grimy, probably full of germs. And Tina was sitting in it.

He helped her up as quickly as he could.

Tina tried to stand on both feet. She made a face. "A stupid sprain."

"An accident, Tina."

She tried to hobble to the door.

Byron stopped her. In front of everyone, he swooped her up into his arms and carried her into the building.

He tried to think of where he could put her. The school sick bay was down a second hallway. Nurse Beatrice was probably still there. He made a beeline for it.

Tina wrapped her arms around his neck.

He liked that.

He said nothing and tried not to make eye contact with her, but he knew Tina was looking at his face the entire time.

When he realized she was saying something, his ears perked up.

"Pardon me?" he whispered.

"You frown too much."

"No, I don't." Byron stepped into the sick bay. No one was there.

"You're frowning now."

Byron didn't reply to that.

"Smile for me, Byron," she said softly, for his ears only.

Byron placed Tina on her good foot. She limped a little.

He called out for Nurse Beatrice, but she was nowhere to be found. She had to be here somewhere, because the door was open.

When he looked back at Tina, she was standing close to him.

Very close.

"Maybe you should sit down," Byron said. "I'll go find Nurse Beatrice."

"Thank you." Tina touched his arm.

When she lifted her chin toward Byron's face, she seemed to be trying to plant a kiss on his cheek.

He turned his face just enough so his lips met hers. He didn't know why he did that, but it was done.

Her lips were soft and supple.

Suddenly, Tina gasped and drew back. "Uh-oh."

"Uh-oh," Byron echoed. He ran a gentle hand over her arm. She didn't pull away.

It made Byron's day, and he broke into a smile.

# CHAPTER THIRTY-NINE

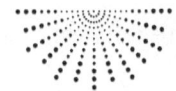

"*B*yron there is never spontaneous." Veronique pointed a fingernail at him sitting at the other edge of the lunch table, away from Tina.

Tina glanced at Veronique directly across the table from her, then at Byron. She waited for him to respond to that indictment.

The couple of staffers who sat between Veronique and Byron seemed to be ignoring their conversation. On Tina's side, the seats were empty. She had saved them for Keith and Lucy, both running late.

All around them, the school cafeteria was noisy. Kids and teachers everywhere.

Tina's own students were sitting with another class of kids somewhere in the same cavernous dining hall. Her helpers plus the teachers from the other class were enough chaperones for the large group of kids. Tina had decided to take a break and eat with Veronique and Lucy.

*Speaking of Lucy, where is she?*

"I can be spontaneous," Byron finally said. His eyes met Tina's. "After the day camp is over."

*What is he telling me?*

Tina wondered if anyone else had seen them together in the sick bay on Tuesday.

Veronique laughed so hard her teeth were showing. "With all due respect, Sir Byron, planning ahead is not being spontaneous."

"Planning ahead is wisdom," Byron countered. "Sometimes it takes only a few seconds to plan."

*A few seconds?*

Tina mulled over the memory of his spontaneous kiss. Had he planned it at the spur of the moment? It had certainly broken all sorts of school policies, for which Byron could pay with his job and any future prospects at the school.

Why had he done that?

Why throw away a career, or at the very least, create a scandal?

Granted, no one had seen them in the sick bay, and as far as Tina was concerned, it had been an accidental kiss. Yes, she had meant to give him a peck on the cheek to thank him for carrying her.

No, she had not expected him to respond in that fashion.

*It's unlike Byron to do things like that.*

Well, accidents happened.

She finished her sandwich and reached for one of the two pineapple upside-down cake slices she had on her lunch tray.

Veronique pointed to them with her fork. "Why do you have two pieces of cake?"

"One is for Gus," Tina said.

"Gus? As in Augustus Moss?"

"I know no other."

"Why?"

Tina was about to answer Veronique when she realized Byron was staring at her too. "Well, I wanted to thank him for taking us to the pottery field trip on Tuesday."

"And how did you know he likes pineapple upside-down cake?" Veronique asked.

"He does? I didn't know that. I just thought he might want some dessert since he doesn't get to eat in here much."

"He brings his own lunch. All organic," Veronique declared. "And did you have a cake for Byron? He drove everyone back to the school after the axle rolled away."

Tina's face felt warm. She wasn't sure if she blushed. She didn't look at Byron, and he didn't look at her. The other two staffers got up to leave. Byron spoke to one of them briefly.

Tina cleared her throat. "Byron can get his own dessert."

"Poor Byron." Veronique laughed. "Tell you what, sister. I'm done here. I'll take that cake to Gus. Save you a trip."

"Sure. Give him my regards."

"You want me to hug him for you?"

"Not that kind of regards," Tina said.

Veronique pouted and left the table noisily with her tray.

Tina ate her cake quietly.

"How's your ankle?" Byron's question reached her ears.

"Hurts a bit, but it'll get better."

"I can't hear you." Byron changed seats. Now he was directly across the table from Tina. "What did you say?"

"My ankle still hurts, but my pride, all the more. I'm so embarrassed."

"Don't worry about it. Accidents happen, as they say." Byron fell silent.

"I hope I wasn't too heavy for you to carry." Tina dug into her cake. It was way too sweet for her, as if someone had poured extra sugar on top of the canned pineapple.

"If you keep eating that sort of dessert, I may not be able to carry you much longer."

Tina straightened up. Put down her fork. "You know, Byron. If you weren't you, I would have felt insulted."

"What do you mean?"

"You've said a lot of things to me about me." Tina waved her hands. "Sticks and stones."

"I'm sorry. Again."

"Apology accepted. Again."

"I do mean well," Byron added. "You can be sure I'm honest with you. No sugarcoating."

"You've been honest with me, yes," Tina agreed. "I'm glad for that. I wish everyone just spoke the truth right away."

"What do you mean? Something happened?" Byron seemed interested. "Someone lied to you? It's not my brother, is it?"

"No, not your brother." Tina wondered how much to tell. But she carried it in her heart and on her shoulders. She felt she could trust Byron with the information. "Mine."

"Your brother?"

Funny how his face looked to Tina. For a moment there, she saw indifference. "You don't seem surprised. Do you know something I don't?"

"About Martin?"

"You know that Keith is a friend of my brother's."

Byron didn't reply.

"Did Keith say anything to you about Martin's new bike?"

Byron didn't reply.

"Am I the last to know?" Tina asked. "I found out last night that Martin has not only bought a new Ducati but he's racing in Daytona next week. Next week! That means he has been practicing somewhere without my knowledge. This has got to have gone on for a while, you know what I mean?"

"He's an adult," Byron said.

"I feel bad. Mad. Sad."

"But not glad."

"No," Tina said curtly. "Sorry. None of this is your business. I'd better get back to class, and you to your work. How is it coming as interim headmaster?"

"Ah...fine. Lots of work, more than I had expected."

"But it's what you wanted, right? I remember two years ago you had been eyeing the assistant headmaster position. You got it. And now you're moving to the next level. God has really blessed you."

Byron smiled. "You know, Tina. You switch

gears a kilometer a minute, and I'm having a hard time keeping up with you."

"Meaning what?"

"I know your heart is heavy that your brother hid his new project from you, and I will pray with you about that, but suddenly you're talking about my career." Byron sat back in his chair. "Is this your coping mechanism? Jump from one topic to another?"

"Why are you asking me all that?"

"I'm trying to understand what makes you tick. How you are as a person—"

"I'm not a science project for your new science wing."

"I didn't say you are," Byron said. "You tried to tell me what's heavy on your heart, and I was listening. Suddenly we're talking about my career. Those two things aren't even connected."

"Do they have to connect?" Tina asked.

"Well, we could wrap up one topic before we go to another."

"Life isn't always like that, Byron. Sometimes life comes in pieces, not in neat little boxes tied with precisely cut ribbons." Tina kept her voice down, but she was getting more irritated by the minute. "Sometimes life is awfully messy. You have no idea how many bikes my brother has wrecked, how many bones he has broken in the last how many years. You have no idea how many times I've wept over his safety and how I've pleaded with God to give him a safer hobby than bike racing."

"I'm sorry."

"You have a wonderful family. Everyone is doing what they should. Like clockwork. Like one of your many checklists. My family is different. I don't know where my dad is. My mom died alone. I have a couple of sisters out there somewhere who never call us. My brother loves to live dangerously. That sort of *messy*, you know."

"I'm truly sorry." Byron stretched an arm across the table and pressed a finger on the back of Tina's hand.

"What are you doing?" Tina asked.

"Giving you a mini hug."

It was the same gesture she had given him on the first day of day camp, when Byron looked rather stressed and tired.

Tina burst out laughing. "You remember."

"I told you, Tina. I remember everything about you."

# CHAPTER FORTY

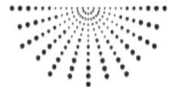

**B**yron lifted his head when he heard his office door slam shut. Veronique strutted toward him, waving her arms and fingers like tentacles.

"Three words," she huffed. "Po-li-cy!"

"That's not three words." Byron said quietly.

Veronique had ranted before, and he had been able to handle her outbursts by remaining calm.

"Syllables. Whatever!" Veronique made waves with her arms. The butterfly fascinator on top of her head bobbed along with her coiffured hair. "Point is, Mr. Interim Headmaster, you're going to lose your job. If you know what's good for your career, I would politely and respectfully ask you to stop it. I'm saying that as your avid supporter and sister in Christ."

Byron stopped signing the forms on his desk and put down his pen. "Stop what?"

"A rumor is starting in the staff break room about you and Tina."

"Tina?"

"Tina MacFarland, the volunteer from Savannah."

"I know who Tina is." Byron sat back. "What are you hearing?"

"Something's brewing between you two."

"Like what?"

"You touched her hand in the cafeteria." Veronique exhaled loudly. "E-ve-ry-bo-dy saw it!"

Byron didn't reply.

"One finger on her hand," Veronique continued. "Fraternizing, Byron!"

Byron cringed. "Would you please calm down? Your voice is echoing in this very small office."

Veronique plopped into the chair in front of the desk.

"Look, I also carried her—and her sprained ankle—to the sick bay yesterday afternoon. What about that?"

"Everyone's talking." Veronique pulled her skirt down to cover her knees.

"Everybody?"

"It's starting to be."

"Starting?"

"They want to know why you took a long time to return from the sick bay to drive the bus to the garage. It was parked outside the school, as you recall, and right in the middle of the narrow road."

"Ah yes. My mistake. I should have parked the bus away from the front entrance."

"What other mistakes have you made, Byron?"

Byron wasn't about to tell her that he had gotten himself involved in Tina's life. His email to his friend Diego Flores had not only reached him, but the pastor of Riverside Chapel had replied. Yes, he knew a couple of private investigators. Why did Byron need private investigators?

"Are you questioning my judgement?" Byron tried to control himself. "Gossip is a sin, Veronique. You know that."

"Our school policy is not gossip."

*She wants a fight.*

Byron wasn't sure how to rebut that.

"I'm speaking now as someone who has worked with you for a very long time, Byron. We go to the same church. You know my family, and you know I speak my mind."

"I appreciate it. Out with it, then."

"You want me to tell you what I think?"

"Yes."

"And you won't fire me?"

"For telling me your perspective?"

"It's the truth as I see it, sir."

"And if I disagree with you?"

"Then correct me, Byron. We both know that you have worked very hard and very long to get Clarke's position. It's now within your reach. Tina is a very attractive girl, but she is an obstacle to your promotion."

"Is there envy?"

"Moi? No." Veronique laughed. "You might not know this, but Tina and I have struck up a friendship since I'm hosting her. She cleans my house very well."

Byron was alarmed. "She what?"

"We made a deal. She cleans my house, and I teach her to sew skirts."

"You're kidding me." *Tina, oh Tina. Surprises at every corner.*

"Now, if she were carrying on with Donovan or Gus—heaven forbid!—that would be different," Veronique said. "But she's attracted to you. You, of all people."

"Is she?"

"It's obvious." Veronique stood up. "If word reaches Clarke or the school board, your career is in jeopardy."

"Nothing's going on between Tina and me." *Except that accidental kiss.*

Then again, it wasn't an accident. He had meant it.

"Good. Of course, if this position is vacated, I'm going to apply for it. I do have a master's in education, you know."

"And I will write you a good recommendation."

Veronique's eyes widened. "After all that I just said to you? You could cite me for insubordination and get me demoted."

"You spoke your mind, and you have no ulterior motives against me. I appreciate your honesty. It's hard to find people who are honest these days."

"Yeah. Like, we still don't know who paid for the new Jesus Loves Me Kindergarten Building."

Byron nodded. "Why would it be a mystery, you might ask?"

"I will find out for you," Veronique whispered.

"No need. If the school board wants us to know, they'll tell us."

"Aren't you a bit curious?"

"Nosy, Veronique. The word is not curious, but nosy."

# CHAPTER FORTY-ONE

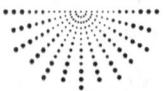

*A*fter Veronique left his office, Byron mulled over what she had said. Surreal as it was, Veronique had overstepped her day camp director position to scold him for something that, ironically, could be a problem for him.

If it wasn't already a problem.

Headmaster Clarke had indicated as much last Friday when he told him to exercise patience.

*Patience to wait on God, wait for Him to carry out His will, wait for the day camp to finish.*

*Patience to focus on the task at hand, to complete the work of the Lord.*

*Patience to know that God works out all things for our good.*

Yes, it was clear there was something happening between him and Tina.

Yet, it could not happen at this time.

The timing was all wrong.

*Veronique is right.*

It was either Tina or the headmaster position.

Byron stood at the window. Outside his office, the wind shook the royal poinciana trees. Petals of red and orange fell and blew about in the wind.

No one walked the grounds at this hot hour of the afternoon. In fact, day camp would be over for the day any minute now.

Day camp.

Tina had only signed up for the Art I session that lasted for three weeks, to end on the tenth of July. A new lead teacher would take over the second art camp, which would end the first week of August.

Byron dared not ask Tina to stay on for any reason.

The longer she worked in the day camp, the longer he had to stay away from her.

However, it only mattered if they had something going on.

A kiss did not a relationship make.

He wondered how Tina felt about him. There was no way of knowing, really. He could ask her, of course, but Tina, being Tina, might not know herself.

He had enjoyed their impromptu kiss in the sick bay—what a place to kiss!—but did Tina too? She had seemed more amused than surprised, as if it was a genuine mistake.

It hadn't been a mistake.

Byron had planned it, albeit at the last second.

Therein was his problem.

"What do I want, Lord?" he whispered into the warm Bahamian afternoon.

*I want to teach.*

Ever since secondary school, he had wanted to be a teacher. It was a noble profession, sure, but more than that, he loved studying the curriculum, preparing his teaching notes, standing in front of his students, and simply teaching.

His assistant headmaster position had robbed some of that. He had been doing more administrative work. Clarke had agreed to let him keep a class. He had taught the secondary school Bible class for seven years, and that continuation had met some of his personal desire to teach.

Now this interim headmaster role had taken that from him.

*All I want to do is teach.*

*And specifically, the Bible.*

That could change once the school board confirmed him as the new headmaster of Chapel by the Sea Christian School. The interim position was only a name; he knew Clarke wanted him to take over as the headmaster. And if that happened,

Byron would be too busy running around dealing with everything but teaching.

"What is my calling, Lord?" Byron had always known that his calling was to point people to Jesus.

He had assumed that when he became a teacher and then assistant headmaster that his degrees in education would lead to opportunities to share the Gospel of Christ with the next generation, from preschoolers all the way to secondary school students. Every grade was here at the Chapel by the Sea Christian School.

But now...

Now he wasn't sure.

As a single man, free of obligations, he could serve God here.

Yet he would serve alone.

In his own mind, the married teachers at the school seemed to be more fulfilled than he was. They had someone to go home to. They had someone to talk to.

He had been living alone so long he probably had no idea what he was missing.

Along came Tina.

A breath of fresh air, a splash of color, a spark of brilliance.

She had touched his heart, like it or not. There was no other way to describe it, Byron thought.

Of all the women in the world, those he had

dated and come in contact with in his life, Tina was the only one who had somehow managed to touch his heart.

But what about the school? And its archaic policy on staff romance. Should he follow it still?

*Or break protocols to make a statement?*

He wondered when that had started such a notion. Probably decades ago when the Chapel by the Sea charter members wanted to segregate the men and women. As honorable and ethical as their reasons might have been, Byron could no longer agree with it.

It seemed to him now that, of all the places in the world, God-fearing Christian schools and churches and establishments were the best places to find like-minded partners in life.

*Partners in life?*

Like Tina and him, maybe?

*Whoa, not so fast. It was just one kiss.*

His desk phone rang, jarring him out of his muse, calling him back to work. It was only almost two o'clock in the afternoon, but Byron felt like it had been a long day.

The caller ID said it was Headmaster Clarke, the person who would remind Byron that he had broken a school rule.

Byron was sure that such an outdated rule

would be changed soon, but not in the next two weeks.

Not soon enough for Tina and him.

He punched the button to let the phone call jump to voicemail.

*God, forgive me. I want this job, but I can't have it and Tina too. What to do?*

A beep on his iPad told him that the voicemail had been transcribed into email. He did not want to read it either.

*Later.*

Byron had always kept a short account of his own sins—

*Sin?*

*Was it a sin to kiss Tina?*

They were both single Christians. Unattached. Never been married. They had known each other from a distance for two years. There was a connection between them this summer. What sort of connection, Byron couldn't define, but a connection nonetheless.

He wanted to explore this potential relationship, to find out if Tina was the...the what?

*The love of his life.*

# CHAPTER FORTY-TWO

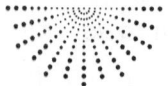

ina hadn't seen Byron since Wednesday's lunch. Even at choir practice at Chapel by the Sea, she didn't see him come and go. It had been his habit to cross the hallway in front of the sanctuary, for whatever reason, but not this past Wednesday.

Back at the school on Thursday, someone had let it slip that Byron had been eating lunches at his desk. How could any teacher or administrator work this hard through the summertime when he was supposed to be slowing down?

She prayed that it wasn't her doing that had caused Byron to change his behavior.

"Ouch!" Tina gasped and dropped the cut fabric from her hands onto the table in Veronique's sewing room.

A small balloon of blood on the tip of her left finger made her stare.

Suddenly she saw Martin on the street outside her pottery studio in Savannah. He was on the sidewalk, his mangled motorcycle nearby, wrapped around a pole. Pedestrians and motorists stopped.

That afternoon, she had been spinning a pottery washbowl on the wheel by the window facing the street when she heard the crash and saw a commotion. In her haste to get outside, she knocked the washbowl off the wheel head. The clay was still wet and squishy and fell apart on the floor like a blob.

She remembered running out the door of Tina's Turn and crossing the busy street to find her brother unconscious and covered with blood.

*Blood.*

*Everywhere.*

She swooned.

"What? What?" Veronique came around the table. "Those pins are sharp."

Tina leaned back against the chair, her shaking finger outstretched.

Veronique grabbed a tissue paper and dabbed it on Tina's finger. "There. All gone."

Tina's face paled. She recalled how they couldn't wake Martin when they had reached the hospital. In a coma for almost two or three weeks,

Martin finally awoke to announce that he had to replace his Ducati.

Tina closed her eyes.

"Let's get you a plaster," Veronique said.

"A what?"

Veronique found it in her first-aid kit, and applied it to Tina's finger.

"A Band-Aid. Thank you." Tina had often forgotten than most Bahamians spoke British English. Even Byron.

*Byron.*

Byron, who had caused her mind to wander while she was trying to pin the hems of her skirt together so she could sew it.

Byron, who had caused her to wonder whether he thought her presence at the school was bad for him.

Bad for his career.

Bad for his life.

"I want to go home," Tina whispered.

"No need to be so dramatic, sister." Veronique picked up the fabric from Tina's lap. "It's just a pinprick. I get it all the time. Do you see me cry?"

"I'm not crying."

"Not yet. I'm trying to preempt any whining behavior there." Veronique laughed. "You don't do blood very well, do you?"

Tina composed herself. "God is sovereign over

all, whether or not a pinprick had triggered a memory I'd rather forget."

"Wow. You recover quickly." Veronique pointed to her. "And that's a good Bible truth. God is always sovereign."

"He is."

"Amen." Veronique put down the fabric on the table. "At this rate, we'll never finish sewing this one skirt. We've been doing this for two weeks now. You can't possibly keep cleaning my bathrooms the entire time you're in town."

Tina had to agree that progress had been slow. "That's because we've been too busy with the day camp. This is only the third or fourth evening we've managed to get back to sewing."

"Yeah, and even on a Friday evening when both of us have no night out. I wonder why Donovan hasn't invited us back to his dinner parties."

Tina shrugged. "I don't care."

"You don't, but I do."

"Well, there's tomorrow's day trip to make up for the missed dinners, right? He invited us to sail with him," Tina reminded her. "You're going."

"And you're not. Why won't you go? Exuma will be fun. Swimming pigs and all."

"Maybe another time."

"Donovan has kindly invited your Savannah team and other volunteers from the other American churches to celebrate your country's Independence Day on his yacht, and you're not going?"

"I guess not. Lucy and Keith will represent our nation." She grinned.

"Byron won't be there." Veronique eyed her. "There won't be a scandal."

Byron was precisely why Tina turned down Donovan's invitation to swim with feral pigs. She had suspected that Byron was jealous of her friendship with his brother. In another week, her art class would end, she would try to have a bit of fun, and then go home. After she was gone, Byron still had to deal with his brother.

It would be best for her not to do anything to cause a sibling rift.

Beneath the table, Tina's left ankle ached a bit. It had been three days since she had fallen into the pothole, and her leg was feeling a bit better, but the ankle sprain was still there.

She got up from the dining chair and hobbled toward a basket where Veronique had placed Tina's tall pile of expensive fabrics she had overbought on a whim.

Byron had paid for them all without a word.

Byron.

Again.

Why must everything remind her of Byron?

Her fingers flew to her lips.

She remembered more than Byron buying her fabric and a dress, fetching all the kids when they had been stranded by the side of the road in the rain, carrying her to the sick bay after she had clumsily sprained her ankle—

And kissing her.

It had been brief, but it was a kiss.

*A stolen kiss.*

Why had he done that?

Tina hadn't had a chance to talk with Byron about it, to find out why he had turned his head ever so slightly to catch her peck on his cheek. He could have left it well alone and there would have been no scandal.

*Scandal? There is no scandal.*

*It was an innocent—no, not innocent at all.*

He had meant to kiss her. He wanted to kiss her. And he had.

# CHAPTER FORTY-THREE

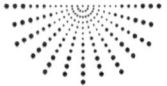

*T*en days.

Surely Byron could avoid Tina for ten more days until she went home to Savannah.

He had avoided her for five days straight, with the exception of church on Sunday, when he had to face the choir with her in it.

Otherwise, at the school, he had worked out a scheme. He had purposed in his heart to steer clear of the art room, the cafeteria, the staff break room, the supply closets, the front entrance, and the car park—or the parking lot, as Tina would say in her American vernacular.

Oh yes, and the quadrangle, fountain courtyard, bougainvillea garden, all of Gus's gardens that Tina might go with her art students, and the great outdoors.

That about covered the entire day camp side of the Chapel by the Sea Christian School campus.

*It has to be done. I have no choice.*

If he stayed away from her until her stint at the day camp was over, then he would quell the rumor that Veronique had said was starting. When Tina left for her home, the speculations would all go home with her.

*Go home?*

*I don't want her to go home.*

*But duty calls.*

All Byron had to do now was to concentrate on his job as the interim headmaster.

As he walked toward the kindergarten playground where workers were dismantling and moving the slides and swings, Byron scrolled through the list of tasks he had given to himself.

On the eleventh page of fine prints, he knew that these were all busywork that he could have delegated to his staffers. He wasn't going to discuss with anyone about them. He was going to simply do the work, check it off, and go to the next one.

If he kept himself busy, he wouldn't think of Tina.

He prayed that everything would go well with her. No accidents. No clumsiness. Nothing that would require Byron to be summoned to solve a problem. He had decided that if that happened, he would send Veronique.

He wasn't looking where he was going and bumped into Gus.

"Keeping busy, eh?" Gus lifted his sunglasses and parked them on the top of his head. His floppy hat hung over a shoulder, its frayed cord—taped over and tied in a knot—wrapped around his neck.

Byron made a mental note to get Gus a new hat for his birthday.

"When's your birthday?" Byron asked.

"Huh?"

"Your birthday."

"Not until the third of September. Why?"

"Just trying to remember family." Byron swiped his calendar, looking for September. He had already written it down. "I have it."

"What's going on, Cousin?"

"Work, of course. What do you mean?"

"So you came all the way here to the kinder-garten area to ask me when my birthday is—when, undoubtedly, you already have it on your calendar."

Byron bristled. "Not really. I came here to see what they're doing with the renovations. What are you doing here?"

"Looks like I need to move some of my bushes. I'm not happy about it." Gus pointed to some plants.

"Whose bright idea is it to go through with the project? I thought the school board nixed it."

"They did. Some anonymous donors made it happen."

"Anonymous?" Gus laughed. "Nothing's going to stay secret for long."

*Secret? What did he mean?*

Byron told himself not to read too much into it. But his guilt was there. He had broken one school policy.

No kissing colleagues.

Technically, Tina wasn't a colleague. She wasn't on staff. She was an unpaid volunteer who had given three weeks of her summer to teaching kids art and pottery.

Such generosity.

Generosity?

*Could she be the anonymous... Nah!*

"Aren't you a bit curious as to who singlehand-edly paid for the new two-floor kindergarten build-ing?" Gus asked.

"I'm told it's not one person. It's probably a group of well-wishers."

"Look at you, cousin. I suspect you know who would donate to such a cause."

"I don't, actually. And I try not to speculate." *Well, he did, but not too much.*

"I say it's Donovan. I bet he had your mother

involved. Maybe your sisters too. Tell me you didn't contribute."

"Not me. I know nothing about it, Gus."

"You went to kindergarten here."

"So did you and all my siblings."

"Right." Gus leaned toward Byron. "But I didn't give a dime. I gave to our church for mission projects instead. It never crossed my mind that the kindergarteners need a new building, and on top of that, I think it's better for kids to be outdoors."

"A mix of both," Byron said.

"Outdoors. I think Tina would agree with me. She spends a lot of time outdoors in the mornings. I think her art class has painted just about every garden I've landscaped."

*Tina. Why did Gus bring up Tina?*

"Speaking of Tina, what's going on with her?" Gus asked.

"What do you mean? Is she ill?" Byron tried not to be alarmed. But this was Tina they were talking about.

"Nothing of that sort. She seems a bit downcast, that's all."

"Downcast?"

"Miserable. Sad. Even dispirited, maybe."

"You don't need to run through the thesaurus."

Gus guffawed. "You asked me what downcast is."

"I didn't. I know what downcast is!"

"Ooooh. Don't bark at me, cousin." Gus shook his head. "Looks like you're irritable today. Over-worked? Exhausted? Worn out? Burned out?"

*Aarrgh!*

Byron pivoted on his feet and stormed off.

# CHAPTER FORTY-FOUR

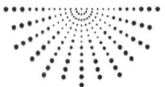

$\mathcal{T}$ina was eating lunch with her art students outdoors under the spreading trees, when she spotted Lucy and Keith crossing the veranda lining the classrooms toward her.

Something was up.

The two of them walked so closely together they were almost holding hands.

Definitely, something was up.

Tina had expected Lucy to warm up to Donovan's advances. Now it seemed that love was closer to home than she had thought.

"Have a minute?" Lucy asked Tina.

"Sure." Tina surveyed her lunch group. Her helpers had spread out over the four picnic blankets, and they all looked fine. She got up from the ground. "We have just a minute before we get back to class."

Tina followed them.

"We've decided to stay and teach at the day camp through August," Lucy said when they reached an empty spot in the courtyard.

*We?* "That's nice."

"Would it be okay if you fly home alone to Savannah next week?" Keith asked.

*Alone.*

"Sure. I'm an adult. Don't worry about me."

Lucy looked relieved.

Tina waited for more. They could have just emailed her, or Lucy could have told her that piece of news when they drove back to Veronique's house.

So why now?

"Is there anything else?" Tina asked.

"Well, yes." Lucy looked at Keith. "We're getting engaged."

Tina whooped and hugged Lucy. "So happy for you!"

She shook Keith's hand. "When did this happen?"

"We're not engaged yet, but you mean, when did we know?" Lucy asked.

"Yeah, everything. Tell me."

"I guess we've known since we both started attending Riverside Chapel back home."

Tina smiled. "Lots of couples there."

"For sure."

*Except me. I'm not a couple with anyone.*

"Would you like to stay too?" Lucy asked.

"Me?" Tina wondered what she was getting at.

"Yeah. Don't they need an art teacher for the second half of the camp?"

"They have teachers lined up, as far as I know. My commitment is only for three weeks. I'm staying in town for a few extra days myself, but not for day camp. I'm scoping out some local potters to display some of their pieces in my gallery."

"Don't work too hard." Lucy laughed.

"Not to worry. I have to get back to my own studio. Have some commissioned works I have to do. I'll be busy as soon as I get home all the way through Christmas. Maybe next year."

But there might not be a next year.

Tina wasn't sure if she could come back to the Bahamas.

*It hurts too much.*

# CHAPTER FORTY-FIVE

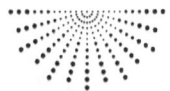

"What do you mean he bailed out?" Byron asked Veronique as they crossed the building to get to the staff room.

Veronique lifted her iPad at him.

As if he could see those little fonts on it.

"He emailed me this morning. He found a job at the university."

"The university is closed for the summer," Byron said. "So why can't he teach Art II for three weeks? It ends on the seventh of August, and he's done."

Veronique stopped at a rotunda, and Byron did too. She paused as if to gather her thoughts. "We'll have to cancel Art II and refund the families."

"Maybe they could sign up for sports or something else. How many kids have signed up?"

"Seventeen."

"Only seventeen? Art I had twenty-seven students before three bailed out."

"Some of the Art II students are continuing from Art I," Veronique said.

"Do you have any suggestions?"

"I'm glad you asked, Byron—sir." Veronique turned toward what Byron had considered a forbidden hallway.

"Where are you going?" Byron tried to remain calm.

"If you talk to her, she might stay for a few more weeks."

"Talk to—No, no." Byron spun around. "She wants to go home next week. Let her go."

"Let her go?" Veronique put her fists on her waist. "But we have no lead art teacher."

"Then we cancel Art II. Nothing we can do about it."

"Lucy and Keith are not only staying for the rest of the summer, but they're engaged to each other."

Byron stopped in his tracks. It wasn't what he wanted to hear.

If Lucy was taken, then Donovan would turn his attention to...

Well, Donovan had tried to propose to Tina and she had told him to get lost.

"Please talk to her," Veronique insisted. "Ask

her to stay through, and we won't have to find another lead teacher for Art II."

"If she says no?"

"Then we tried."

*For the sake of the students. Yep. That's it.*

"All right. Is she even there?"

Veronique nodded. "She's waiting for me to finish work so I could give her a lift to my house. Lucy and Keith are going out tonight, and they're taking a taxi later."

Byron followed Veronique to the art room and took a deep breath before he stepped across the threshold.

Tina looked up from a table. She didn't say a word. Neither did Byron. He let Veronique do the talking.

"I wish I could stay, but I barely have a few extra days after day camp before I need to go home. I have firm commitments for the next four to five months," Tina said. "In fact, I told Lucy and Keith all that when they told me at lunch that they were staying on."

"We could give you some stipends," Byron said. He didn't know why he said it. There was not a lot of money to spare.

Well, if the school didn't have it, he'd pay her out of pocket. He hated to dip into his inheritance, but a large part of him wanted Tina to stay.

Then again, the irony of it all would be that he could not get near Tina until the day camp was over. As it stood, Tina would be done teaching Art I this Friday. If she took over Art II, she wouldn't be finished until the first week of August.

It would be an extra month of woe watching her from a distance and being unable to hold her.

Byron wasn't certain he could handle it.

In fact, he was sure he could not endure another day of avoiding Tina, let alone four more weeks.

Right now, as he looked at her glowing red hair in the afternoon sun streaming into the art room, he felt drawn to her.

Five or six steps, and he would reach her lips.

Byron blinked away the thought.

"Oh, I'm not looking to be paid," Tina explained. "I have work commitments, and I signed contracts to produce pottery for several galleries in Atlanta. Plus, my clients are waiting for their washbowls."

When no one said anything, Tina continued. "I haven't taken a vacation in over a year, and I chose to spend three weeks here with y'all. I'm happy to be here, but I must go home. Besides, I need to go see what my stupid brother is up to."

"He's not stupid," Byron said.

"How would you know that? Wrecking three bikes in two years? Not stupid?"

"Those are angry words."

"And if this were your brother, wouldn't you be angry if he were reckless?" Tina gasped. She stepped toward Byron. "Sorry, sorry. I don't know what overcame me. How did Martin get into the conversation?"

She was close. Close enough for Byron to reach out and pull her toward himself if he wanted to.

But not with Veronique standing here.

Not with the school policy hanging around his neck like an albatross.

Not with God testing his integrity and his patience to live and operate within rules he now disagreed with.

"Don't worry about it," Byron said. "Do you have any suggestions for a solution?"

It didn't take long for Tina to respond. "Raymond Fordham."

"Not a bad idea," Byron told Veronique. She nodded.

"I bet he can easily teach the class," Tina said. "He could teach painting and mixed media in this room. Once a week, you could bus all the students to his studio for clay. Once a week would be enough. That is, if your buses don't lose axles."

Byron laughed.

He couldn't remember the last time he had laughed like this.

He cleared his throat. "The mechanic said it was a rusty bolt. All the buses have been inspected. Cleared for takeoff."

Tina smiled. "Good. Then it's settled? Ask Ray. I hope he says yes."

"I'll call him right now." Veronique whipped out her cell phone and stepped out of the art room onto the veranda and grass, leaving Byron and Tina alone under a slow-spinning fan.

Byron didn't even realize the ceiling fan was on until now.

"I'm sorry about last Tuesday," Byron began. "It wasn't my intention to mislead you."

"Mislead me?" Tina's eyes widened.

"Proverbs 16:9. 'A man's heart plans his way, but the Lord directs his steps.'"

"You're saying?"

"Sometimes what we want is not what we get." Byron frowned. It was painful getting those words out. "I let my emotions get the better of me. Forgive me."

He glanced at the open doors to the veranda. Veronique was pacing the grass. She was still on the phone. She was probably out of earshot.

Byron kept his voice low, regardless. "I have a job to do. I've worked many years for this promotion."

Tina nodded. "Don't let me get in the way."

"You're not—never—in the way, Tina."

"Then what are you saying?"

"I'm sorry about what happened in the sick bay. I'm afraid I've given you the wrong idea."

"What wrong idea might that be?"

"About us."

"I'm leaving next week, Byron. I'm committed to that. You're committed to your job here. That's all there is to it."

The way she put it seemed so final that it tore into Byron's heart five ways to Christmas. He wanted to take back everything he had said about giving her the wrong idea or that his promotion seemed to take precedence over any potential relationship they might have.

But it was all true.

He took his interim headmaster position seriously. He had wanted this job for years.

A stolen kiss had almost ruined it for him.

"We just need to stay out of each other's way until you go home," Byron said.

"Is that your plan or God's plan?" Tina asked.

It was an unexpected question. Yet Byron had an answer for that. "I want God's will for our lives."

"I do too. But what is His will, do you know?"

"It will unfold." It was all he could think of saying.

"Ah, but in the unfolding and unveiling of God's will, how do you know you're not in His way?"

Byron had nothing to say to that.

"I'll pray for you, Byron, for God to reveal His will to you for your life."

"My life?" *What do I want to do in the next sixty years? Or less? Or more?*

"Your entire life," Tina said. "We may never see each other again after this week, but we will always have God."

*Never see each other again?*

*For our entire lives?*

Byron knew he had to let Tina go. While he felt he was losing her, she was not his to lose. She belonged to God.

As for him, he had work to do. No time for—

*No time for Tina.*

Byron frowned.

"Don't frown, Byron. It's going to be okay. Smile for me." Tina stepped back. "Better yet, smile for the Lord."

# CHAPTER FORTY-SIX

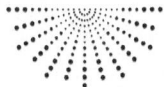

*F*riday had come too quickly for Tina, and the pain in her chest increased. Today would be the day she said goodbye to the kids.

She had asked all the parents and guardians to come an hour early to the art room to view the exhibition of the day campers' artwork, watercolor paintings, mixed-media craft creations, and pottery pieces displayed on several long tables lined up end to end in the art room.

Tina was especially proud of her students' pottery pieces. Since there wasn't a pottery wheel available to them, they did all free-form pieces, but what creativity! There were bowls, plates, mugs, and one ashtray that a student wanted to make for his grandfather.

Oh well. Perhaps they could turn it into a coin dish if the boy's grandfather decided to stop smoking. Until then, an ashtray it was, in glorious colors.

Tina had worn her new skirt that had taken three weeks to make. Veronique had made her resew it a few times because she "just didn't get it," that, in the end, Tina had paid Veronique to sew the rest of the skirts for her.

And that supertalented lady had made her five skirts in five days. Woo-hoo!

Her skirt flowed around her like waves of the ocean as she moved from table to table, from parent to parent, talking with them about their kids' talents and abilities.

She had no idea that Byron was standing behind her until someone started talking to him. His voice was low, but it was unmistakably his.

He had had a haircut. And that iPad was back around his neck the same way it had been the first day she had arrived for day camp.

The last time Tina had seen Byron was on Tuesday when he and Veronique had come to this very spot to ask her if she would stay for the second half of the art camp.

Byron finished talking with one of the parents, and then he returned to the display on the table, either ignoring her or not being aware she was there.

Tina was about to move on, when a warm hand touched her arm.

"Nice job with the art class," Byron said.

There was no emotion in his voice.

Tina knew he was keeping a lid on it. "Thank you for getting the clay shipment in the first week. This exhibition wouldn't be as amazing if not for your effort."

"Don't mention it." Byron shrugged. "We got off to a bad start that first week."

"Did we? I have happier memories than that."

Byron nodded, staring at her skirt.

What could she say? *Thank you for the fabric?*

She couldn't say that in front of everyone. And no, he had not wanted her to reimburse him for the expense.

In essence, he had given her a gift.

The gesture was not lost on her.

According to his brother Donovan in passing, Byron was the tightwad in the family.

But he had done this for her.

"Would you like a guided tour?" Tina asked.

Byron nodded. He followed her as Tina kept her focus on each art piece, the story behind it, including the adventure to Raymond's pottery studio.

"Speaking of whom, did you get an answer from him?" Tina asked.

"Why, yes. He and Veronique worked out a compensation package, and he's going to teach Art II. Good suggestion there."

Tina nodded. "Glad to hear that. Sorry again that I can't stay."

"Nothing to be sorry about."

"Isn't there?" Tina didn't mean to ask that, but at least the words only came out in a whisper.

"If circumstances were different..." Byron's voice trailed off.

But Tina knew what he was going to say. "Don't worry about it."

"When do you leave?"

"Next week. Wednesday."

"Anyone taking you to the airport?"

"Are you volunteering?" Tina smiled.

"I can if you want me to."

"I was going to take a taxi."

"I will be your taxi, Tina."

"Funny man."

"Funny? Am I?"

Tina didn't get to answer the question, because here came Veronique in her spiky stilettos that hit the cement in a sharp rhythm.

"You wouldn't believe the text I just received from Donovan!" Veronique declared. "He's invited all of us to a picnic tomorrow. Staffers, teachers, volunteers—everyone can go."

"Tomorrow?" Byron looked surprised.

"It's a last-minute thing, he said," Veronique replied. She leaned toward Tina. "We're going to *his* private island."

Byron didn't say anything.

"Moss Cay!" Veronique couldn't get any louder.

*Moss Cay? Moss?*

Tina waited for Byron's reaction.

Slowly, he decided to respond. "Donovan thinks he owns everything."

"Doesn't he?" Veronique asked and strutted off.

"Are you going?" Tina asked Byron.

"No."

"All work and no play make Byron a frowner."

Byron stared at her.

"I'll go to the picnic if you go," Tina said.

"You don't need me there. Donovan is entertaining enough."

"But it's more fun with you."

"Fun? No one has ever associated me with fun." Byron chuckled. "Except Mother."

"And me," Tina said softly.

Byron's eyes sparkled.

Tina didn't want to give him any idea, especially since he had apologized about his *misleading* kiss.

"I'd better go mingle. Goodbye, Byron."

She could see the pain in his eyes when she said *goodbye.*

But that wasn't her problem, was it?

Tina continued making her rounds around the art room to meet more parents, and soon lost track of Byron until she saw him exit the art room.

His head was down, possibly because he was staring at the iPad hung on that ridiculous cord around his neck, but possibly for other reasons beyond that.

# CHAPTER FORTY-SEVEN

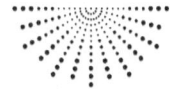

*G*oodbye, Byron.

Not *au revoir*, not *farewell*, not *see you later,* as most of his American friends would say, but *goodbye.*

A finale.

The end.

Byron's legs felt heavy, like they were dragging weights—ball and chain?—as he trekked back to his office to finish up the day.

Tina had said goodbye to him, but tomorrow she was going on a picnic with Donovan to Moss Cay.

Of all the places in the Bahamas, he had to pick the Moss family's private island. That little spot was their retreat, their quiet place, their grandparents' retirement island until they had to move to the nursing home.

Byron speed-dialed Mother as he stared out into the grass, trees, sky.

Before he could say a word, she spoke. "Go to the picnic, Byron."

"How did you know I was calling about that?"

"I know you hold Moss Cay dear, but you gave it up, remember? You wanted to share what your grandparents gave you with your siblings and cousins, and your brother being Donovan, you're getting the whole package of who he is. He likes to party, and Moss Cay will become a party place if you don't reclaim it."

"He's going to ruin our family retreat."

"Yes, and you have no one to blame but yourself."

Byron pressed his forehead against the glass pane on the window. He had the air conditioner on and the window closed, but now he felt hemmed in.

"What do you recommend, Mother?"

"You're thirty-four. Figure out something."

"Make a deal with Donovan? Oh, I hate deals."

"You should have thought of this a long time ago, Byron, being the meticulous planner that you are."

"Thought of what?"

"Thought of the fact that you'd want to leave that island pristine for future generations. If you want to save that island for your wife and kids, you'd better do something now."

*Wife and kids?*

"You thought you'd be single for a long time. That's why you bought that tiny two-bedroom town house. You can't raise a family in that house." Mother minced no words. "I have four kids, and I couldn't fit you all into a ten-room house on a one-hectare plot."

Byron didn't want to say that most other families could raise kids on smaller acreage than that.

"Some of us were demanding of you." Byron didn't name names. "Not me, of course."

"Spoken like my firstborn." Mother laughed. "Truly, you can't always have low-maintenance kids. God gives whom He gives, and we thank God for each person He brings into our lives."

*Thank God for each person.*

*Including Tina.*

# CHAPTER FORTY-EIGHT

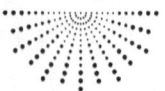

*N*o, Byron did not want to go to the picnic. However, he had to keep an eye on the island retreat that had been in his family for a few generations. His generosity on his thirtieth birthday had backfired, and there was nothing he could do to remedy it.

So here he was on the chartered boat, working on his iPad. Saturday or not, he had a lot of paperwork to read through, administrative issues to resolve, and the new school year to reorganize.

Around him on the chugging boat, people were chatting, taking photos of one another, and generally enjoying themselves.

Well, good. He had been there, done that.

Above the boat, sea birds soared across a turquoise ocean so calm and clear he could see through to the bottom where the sand and corals were.

*Yep, seen that too.*

Byron was sure that some of these people had been out to the ocean before, and seen the clear waters of the Caribbean. Perhaps some of the day camp volunteers had seen them too.

No big deal.

Peals of laughter jarred Byron from his iPad.

*Tina.*

*Of course.*

She and other volunteers, together with several teachers and staffers from the school, were taking turns snapping group photos in which they were all laughing.

"Byron!" Tina called out to him. "Come get in the picture!"

He shook his head and waved her off.

"Come on." Her voice drew alarmingly near, as did the shuffles of flip-flops.

"We'll just come to you." Tina was standing in front of him now, her entourage in tow.

She waved for everyone to stand on either side of Byron, who was still sitting down holding his iPad, and they all smiled at the camera that Lucy was holding.

Byron didn't smile.

In fact, he couldn't believe what she was doing.

"Could you take another one?" Tina held out her iPhone.

Byron saw how happy she was smiling at the camera. No flash went off, because they were under the morning sun, so Byron had no idea if the photograph had been taken with his face turned toward Tina.

*Uh-oh.*

Tina went forward. "I'll take another. You get in the photo, Lucy."

She somehow managed to juggle several cell phones and two or three cameras, rotating them around her neck or in and out of her pockets.

Byron was getting more impatient by the minute.

He had to rework a schedule for the winter break, and that had been what he was doing on his iPad. He had lost his collection of thoughts with this interruption.

"Smile for me, Byron!" Tina shouted.

"He never smiles!" a couple of staffers shouted back to her.

*I do too smile.*

Byron put down his iPad.

That was when he realized how silly, how beautiful, how annoying, how delightful Tina was. The sun and wind in her hair, the beautiful dress he had bought her flowing all around her...

*Exasperating.*

He stood up, and waved to Tina. "I'll take a photo of you all."

"Did you say *you all* or *y'all?*" Tina tipped her head as she handed him her collection of phones and cameras.

"You. All." *Who interrupted my work.*

He wasn't sure if he could hold all those devices in two hands. He placed some on the floor, rotating through them that way.

Through the lenses of the cameras, Byron found Tina stunning while fragile and vulnerable at the same time, as though someone should protect her.

*Let it not be Donovan.*

The glow on her face wasn't because she was pretty, though she was. In fact, her face was covered with more freckles than ever now that she had exposed it to the sun in the thirty-minute boating trip to Moss Cay.

Byron knew that Tina's glow was because she had the joy of the Lord. It was the only way anyone could have such a blissful glow.

When he had returned all the cameras and phones to their rightful owners, he could see the Moss Cay dock in the distance.

No time to get back to work.

He'd do them later.

"Oh look! A tall ship!" someone exclaimed, and

the entire group migrated to the other side of the boat to take photos of the sailing ship coming up on the horizon.

Everyone except Tina.

"You're mad at me," she said.

"No," Byron said carefully.

Why had she said that? Had she read his mind? Heard his griping about lost time?

"Sorry to interrupt your working day off, but our photos of day camp teachers wouldn't be complete without you."

"That so? I didn't teach anything."

"You led us."

"For five days."

"We remember you."

"Long after you've gone home?" Byron didn't know why he had asked that.

"How can anyone forget you, Byron?" Tina motioned for him to stand up against the railing of the boat. "Let me get a photo of you against the blue ocean and sky. They match your shirt color."

With his blue shirt snapping in the wind, Byron dutifully stood where he was told.

Suddenly Tina pointed beyond him. "Look out there!"

She rushed to the steel and wood railing. Byron was glad that her sprained ankle seemed to be healed and she was walking normally now.

"Something on the water—in the water." She lifted her iPhone over the railing to—

And the phone slipped from her hand and disappeared.

There was nary a sound, except a possible faint *plop* that was masked by the boat's motor.

"Oops." Tina's palms went to her freckled cheeks beneath the horror in her eyes.

Byron leaned over to take a look. He couldn't see the phone anymore due to the ripples around the boat. He was sure it now rested on the sand of the deceivingly shallow-looking saltwater.

*Just like Tina to lose things.*

*What am I going to do with her?*

"I wanted to get a picture of that—that..." She pointed.

"The shadow of the clouds on the surface of the ocean?" Byron asked.

Her cheeks reddened. "You must think I'm stupid."

"No, Tina. Clumsy, maybe."

"I lost my iPhone. Cost me a pretty penny."

Byron brushed spirals of ginger hair from her face. "Buy a new one."

"My contacts are on there. So are my deadlines."

"You have deadlines?"

Byron's remark was met with a quick jab of Tina's elbow to his ribs. It didn't hurt.

He held her arm. "Your calendar should still be on the Apple cloud. Sync everything."

"It did *sink*, for sure."

Byron tried not to grin or give away his amusement. "You'll be fine. At least you didn't fall overboard."

"You won't let me."

Byron studied her. "How would you know that?"

"You'll come to my rescue."

"I would?"

"Won't you?"

"Actually, yes, I would."

# CHAPTER FORTY-NINE

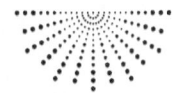

*B*yron's eyes followed Tina everywhere on Moss Cay all morning, as if by his not paying attention to her, she'd get into another accident, like maybe tripping into the ocean, drifting out to the great beyond, and being lost forever.

That thought, cross-checked with what she had said to him on Friday at the end of Art I camp, affected him.

*Goodbye, Byron.*

No, no, no.

It could not end this way.

They could not end this way.

No goodbyes.

Tina was reading a book on a hammock strung between two coconut trees by Moss Cay Bay. She would be safe there as she busied herself trying to keep her skirt from fluttering up and revealing her legs.

Byron appreciated her modesty, but she could have worn shorts and saved herself all that possible trouble, if she had been concerned with unnecessary exposure. The wind on Moss Cay could be calm one moment and then breezy or gusty the next.

Still, he liked the fact that Tina had worn the dress he had bought her, albeit on the wrong day. He chuckled as he watched Tina plop her big tote bag onto her lap to keep the skirt down.

The wind was doing a number on her frizzy hair now. It looked like a giant red candy floss. It would be pointless for her to wear a hat. She'd just as soon lose that too.

Tina's bright-colored hair and multicolored floating dress contrasted sharply against a backdrop of light blue ocean on white sandy beaches, where footprints tracked now.

"What are you looking at?"

Byron didn't think anyone had seen him watching Tina's every move, but apparently Gus had.

His cousin sat down with a bowl of plantain chips. "Want some?"

"Did you have to ask?" Byron reached for a handful.

"I heard that you've successfully avoided Tina for two weeks."

"For the most part." Byron was telling the truth.

There had been only two encounters in the remaining part of the first half of day camp: when Veronique suggested inviting Tina to stay for the rest of day camp and during the student art exhibition on Friday.

The rest of it was not something he could tell Gus.

"Now that her stint here is over, are you going to ask her out?" Gus munched on plantain.

"You remember the last time you talked while eating plantains? You choked."

Gus stopped chewing. "Are you avoiding the issue?"

"There's no issue."

When Byron glanced back at the hammock by the ocean, Tina wasn't in it. Her tote was on the sand to one side of the jute hammock.

Byron scanned the shoreline to see if she might be there. The beach chairs were occupied but not by any redheads. Among the coconut groves, some people were playing beach volleyball.

No Tina there.

His eyes followed the path that led from the volleyball court to the picnic area where Donovan's chefs were grilling their lunch. Leave it to his brother to bring his restaurant chefs to handle a simple picnic.

Near the outdoor kitchen, the path turned into stone and meandered through clusters of flowers that Gus had planted with Grandfather shortly before cancer had taken the latter.

The steps to the cottage were weathered wood, but the beach house was painted bright yellow and green and white to commemorate the past and childhood memories.

Around the cottage, Byron had played hide-and-seek with his brother, sisters, and cousins.

Someday his children would play there too...

Byron's gaze swiveled back to the hammock by the ocean.

It was still empty.

She was nowhere to be seen.

Alarmed, Byron sprung up from the picnic bench and left Gus sitting there texting on his phone.

*Maybe she's inside the house.*

Well, he could wait for her to return to her hammock. After all, she had left her tote bag there.

It would be less conspicuous.

And less unnerving for himself.

Byron kept walking toward the house as those thoughts ricocheted through his mind.

As he stepped up the cottage porch, a sway in

the breeze made him look toward the clump of bougainvillea bushes that Gus had planted a while back. They were growing, not quite replacing the old ones that had been taken down by a hurricane, but they were flowering now with pretty flowers.

*Flowers.*

Byron stepped down the porch and went around the bougainvilleas. The garden path curved around the house into a side garden.

And there she was.

Surrounded by hibiscus of many colors, a barefoot Tina was talking to the flowers.

*Talking, I say, to the flowers.*

Byron stopped for a minute to catch his breath. Tina was oblivious to his presence. She kept talking.

*Oh, I was wrong.*

She wasn't talking to the flowers. She was thanking God for the flowers.

Byron felt ashamed. Such a beautiful paradise here, and how often had he thanked God for this island?

He wasn't sure what to do next.

His head said to let Tina be.

His heart said—

Byron reached her soon enough. In a smooth move, he slid an arm around her waist.

She turned to face him, the surprise on her face

mixed with a happy smile, taking Byron's breath away.

Gently, he lowered his lips toward hers.

Tina didn't pull away. Instead, she wrapped her arms around him, her hands stroking his back through his cotton shirt.

Her lips tasted like a mix of mint with coconut and rose hips. It was a potent elixir. When he surfaced for air, his eyelids were heavy.

"You've been waiting." Tina's voice was as gentle as their kiss.

"Yes. This is the rest of the kiss I started that day in the sick bay."

"The *misleading* kiss?"

Byron sighed. "I was misleading myself. Truly, I had meant it. I meant it with all my heart."

"But you didn't want me to get the wrong idea."

Ah, she remembered things too. Like words. "Two weeks ago, I wanted to keep my job."

"Now we're okay because I'm leaving?"

"Now, I don't care about my job."

"You'd better care, Byron. How are you going to pay your bills if you're unemployed?"

Byron laughed. *I love this woman. So practical.*

And he wrapped his arms around Tina, never wanting to let her go.

# CHAPTER FIFTY

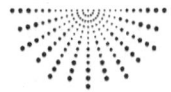

"**Y**ou left it at the hammock," Byron said.

Tina found it interesting that Byron knew where her tote bag was. She had misplaced it again, but Byron had come to her rescue. "Do you ever miss anything?"

"When I was in Boy Scouts, we played Kim's Game. Ever heard of it?"

"No." Tina walked out of garden, and headed for the hammock.

"We'd put little things in a tray, and each of us only had maybe thirty to sixty seconds to memorize everything on the tray. After that we had to write down the items we remembered seeing on the tray."

"Let me guess. You had a perfect score."

"Not at first. But as time went on, I learned to be more observant." Byron sighed. "It's a trivial skill."

"Not entirely useless." Tina picked up her tote that had gathered sand on the ground.

Byron reached for the book on the hammock. "I didn't know Diego writes books."

"It's from his sermon series on how to study the Bible more," Tina said. "There's so much in God's Word. I want to know God's will for my life."

"I thought you already knew His purpose for you." Byron flipped to the copyright page, then the epigraph, and on to the first chapter.

"I know what He wants me to do for my career, but what about the rest of my life?"

"I think your life affects your career and your career affects your life." Byron returned the small book to Tina.

She tossed the book into her tote bag. "So if I know what God's will is for my life, it will inform my career better, you know."

"He has gifted you in such creative ways."

"I could make pottery the rest of my life and be happy, yes."

"But?" Byron raised his signature eyebrows again.

His eyebrows. Sigh.

They weren't bushy or anything, but Tina still thought he wiggled them entirely too much.

"But someday I want to get ma—uh, nothing."

Byron stepped closer to her. "Tina, God will show you His will for your life."

Tina slung her tote bag over her shoulder. Sand shook off the bottom of the bag. "I've had a wonderful time here. The art class went well. We spent a lot of time outdoors. I miss the kids."

"I will miss you when you go home." Byron threaded his fingers through hers.

"I'm still here for several more days."

"When do you leave?"

"Thursday, I think. I forget. I need to check it. I think I have an evening flight or something."

"You forgot?" Byron's voice seemed to be calm, but Tina knew better.

Somewhere at the back of that mind of his, he was probably thinking there was no way Tina would survive this thing called life.

"You must think I'm disorganized," Tina said.

"But your faith is strong and sure."

"But? You said *but*. So you do think I'm disorganized."

"Better that than for a person to be super organized and yet not know the Lord."

"Everything is better with Jesus."

Byron nodded.

"I don't overanalyze things like you do," Tina said.

"That's one of my weaknesses, yes. Sometimes it's better to just trust God and let things be."

"Let God work it out for us." Tina wasn't sure how to say it, but she needed time to sort things out.

It was best that she was going home soon. Best for her to go home and get back to her routine.

Summer had been great while it had lasted, but she could not see a future with Byron.

How could it work out? He was nitpicky. She was carefree.

He planned too far ahead—months in advance. She didn't know what she was going to do that night.

"Maybe we could have lunch a couple of times before you fly home," Byron said.

Tina was glad he couldn't read her mind. "Sounds good. Maybe you can take me to restaurants I've never been to."

"My mother has a terrific cook. She could make us some authentic Bahamian lunches. We'll eat outside on the lanai. That's where Mother likes to eat since Father passed away."

Tina didn't ask why his mother had a cook. She also hadn't asked why the island was called Moss Cay. It was obvious from the way Byron's brother had paraded his yacht and hotel chains and now cruise ships that the Moss family was not poor by any stretch of the imagination.

So why was Byron a school teacher struggling to become a headmaster?

Was this God's will for his life?

Tina didn't want to pry. The more she asked, the more she wanted to know. Curiosity didn't help when she was going home in five days, with no intention to return to Nassau in the foreseeable future.

She would have to let what happened in the Bahamas stay in the Bahamas.

"You've already met my mother at church, so it's not like a first meeting." Byron frowned. "And it's not like I'm taking you to see her."

So Byron had been thinking of the two of them. Why else would it matter whether his mother was in the picture or not?

*How long has he been thinking about us?*

"What's on your mind?" Byron ran a thumb on Tina's jawline.

Before Tina could answer, someone called—no, screamed!—her name.

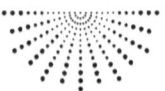

"ononono...no!" Tina hung on to Byron's arm for support as Lucy played the message from her church on her phone speaker.

Pastor Flores's wife, Heidi, was calm, but the voicemail was grave. "We're heading to the hospital now to see what's going on. They said they tried to call Tina but there was no answer."

"Yeah, my phone is at the bottom of the ocean." Tina groaned.

The message ended too quickly.

"Play that again, Lucy."

The words strobed through Tina's ears a second time.

*Martin... Wreck... ER...*

"I knew that was going to happen," Tina finally said. "Lord Jesus, why? Why?"

Even as she asked, she knew why. Cause and effect. Sowing and reaping.

*Play with fire, get burned.*

*Ride your motorcycle at a hundred miles an hour, kill yourself.*

*Martin, I told you!*

Suddenly, Tina felt she was sounding—or had been sounding—like Mom when she had been alive and going after Martin all the time.

Martin could do nothing right in Mom's eyes. When Tina and Martin both left for college, they hadn't gone back to see her the entire time.

Mom had been a difficult woman to live with, and even Dad had run off.

But now, her words came back to Tina, and in spite of the sharpness that had come with it, Mom's favorite phrase was what had popped into Tina's mind this minute.

*Martin, I told you a million times!*

"Could I borrow your phone?" Tina asked Lucy.

"Sure."

Tina returned Heidi's call. "Is he all right?"

"Lots of broken bones, and he's unconscious," Heidi said on the speakerphone.

Tina gasped. She was unable to breathe. "Lord, help us."

"The whole church is praying, Tina. God is always good. Trust Him."

Tina nodded even though Heidi couldn't see her. She listened to the list of things that Riverside Chapel members had been doing since they found out that Martin had collided with another biker while practicing for an upcoming bike race.

"Thank you, Heidi. Please thank Pastor Flores for me. I'll find a way to get home today."

"I'll get someone to pick you up at the airport," the pastor's wife said. "Just call me."

"Will do. Thanks again. See you soon." Tina gave the phone back to Lucy. She turned to Byron. "I need to go home. Now."

Byron nodded. He made a couple of phone calls as Lucy went to tell Veronique what had happened.

Tina felt calmed by Byron's steady voice as he spoke with Donovan, who had arrived in time for lunch and was now giving some ladies a tour of the other side of the cay, wherever that was.

Byron's coolness and the incessant crashing of the crystal-clear waves against the shoreline behind them reminded Tina that not everything was chaotic.

*Martin is!*

Look who was talking, she reminded herself. To some people, she was chaotic.

She wrung her hands until her fingers were red.

Still on the phone, Byron grabbed her hand with his free hand. "Tell him to turn around right now. No, no. No need for a seaplane if Ted's on the next cay."

Byron speed-dialed another number with one hand since the other hand still held Tina's. "The boat will be here in fifteen minutes. Pack up your stuff."

"All I have is this tote bag," Tina said.

Byron nodded as the phone line connected. "Hey, Harold, I need a plane ticket to Savannah this afternoon, as soon as possible. Family emergency."

Tina waited.

Byron handed Tina his phone. "Harold wants your passport number, name, and such."

Tina fumbled through her tote bag for her passport. For some reason, Byron held her hand the entire time she talked with Harold. In fact, he started walking her toward the dock.

He leaned toward her ear when Harold put her on hold. "Tell him we don't care how much it costs. I'll pay for it."

"You don't have to pay for it," Tina said. "I can handle whatever."

"Don't worry about it. The main thing is to get you to your brother, right?"

Tina nodded. They stood at the dock as she waited for Harold to finish the call.

All around them the sea was calm. In the distance, a boat came toward them.

Harold came back on the phone and told her he needed a bit more time to get her connecting flights because there was no direct flight to Savannah today.

Tina hung up and returned the phone to Byron. "Don't drop it into the ocean."

Lucy, Keith, and Veronique came running toward them.

"Is there room for three more on the boat?" Veronique asked, out of breath.

"Sure. It's just going to be us," Byron said.

Lucy put her arm over Tina's shoulder. "I think we should go home with you."

"I appreciate that. Not necessary. Day camp resumes on Monday. You're needed here. Besides, the entire Riverside Chapel is mobilized, and we have God, most of all."

Even as she said that, Tina felt like a hypocrite. She had honored God by remembering Him and yet dishonored her own brother by getting mad at him.

*Well, it's a stupid thing he did, playing with death. Life and death are not games!*

Yet even as she harbored those angry thoughts in her heart, she knew it was wrong of her to focus on those things. What good was it? Martin was in the emergency room. She'd find out how serious it was tonight.

And then what?

## CHAPTER FIFTY-TWO

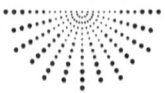

ina had not felt more loved than to have Lucy and Veronique sit on both sides of her in the backseat, their hands holding hers, like they were sisters she never had.

Sisters in Christ.

In the driver's seat, Byron drove and made small talk with Keith on the passenger side. They were becoming fast friends.

"We'll see you in four weeks or so." Lucy began to cry.

Tina handed her a tissue paper from her tote bag. There was a reason she carried a big bag. She could put a lot of stuff in there, including a whole box of tissue paper, which she now passed to Veronique, who also had tears in her eyes.

"Whenever you come to Savannah, you're

welcome to stay with me," Tina said to her. "I have two guest rooms. Oceanfront."

"A five-star hotel." Veronique chuckled amid the tears.

"I'm so glad we met," Tina said.

"Me too. Now that you're going home, I have to put up with those two lovebirds. We're going to have to set some rules before they give my aunt a heart attack with all that courtship dance."

That made Tina laugh, even though she wasn't quite sure what Veronique had meant.

Lucy looked embarrassed.

Keith was totally oblivious to their conversation.

Byron's phone rang, and everyone shut up.

"Okay. Good. Thanks." Byron glanced at his rearview mirror. "Your flight is at 3:30 p.m. That's the earliest he can get you a ticket."

"Thank you."

"That means we need to be at the airport now for the security checks."

"Now?"

"For this flight you can't check in online." Byron paused. "Okay. If you can pack in fifteen minutes, we could make it to the airport by 2:15 p.m. or so, and you should make it."

"Let's pray," Veronique announced.

And they did.

Byron floored the pedal, and they arrived to see

Veronique's aunt waiting at the front door, a concerned look in her eyes. Tina suspected that Veronique had texted her.

With her two friends helping Tina pack her suitcases, they were done in no time, especially since Tina didn't care how they stuffed everything in, as long as they did.

And two pieces of luggage were all she needed. She gave her other two suitcases to Veronique's aunt, invited her to Savannah, and then she and Byron were off.

There wasn't enough room in Byron's small car for everybody, so Veronique drove Lucy and Keith in another car.

Tina appreciated that they had given Byron and her some alone time.

But there was nothing she wanted to say.

# CHAPTER FIFTY-THREE

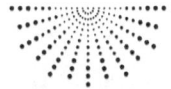

"*D*on't be too hard on your brother." Byron broke the silence in the car.

They were behind a tourist bus, near downtown Nassau, but Tina hadn't complained.

More and more, Byron realized how strong this woman was.

When Father was in the hospital dying, Mother had fallen apart, and it had taken five months for her to get out of the puddle she had been in.

"I warned him," Tina finally said.

"God kept him alive. He's not dead."

"Yet. One of these days he'll kill himself."

"We'll pray for God's continued protection." Byron turned into the airport. "Shall I drop you off and you check in? I'll go park the car."

"Okay."

They were stuck behind a caravan of rental cars and taxis.

"Sometimes people have to realize for themselves the truth of God," Byron said. "You can't do it for them."

"Why didn't he just learn it?"

"We all take time. You know that each of us has different learning styles, and some have to learn things the hard way."

"Martin is pretty uncoordinated on two wheels," Tina explained. "He knew that."

"Yet he's racing bikes."

"Go figure."

"You know, people have been riding bikes a long time, and many have stayed safe." Byron found a spot, but it wasn't near the door.

"Just drop me off here," Tina said. "I'll check in, and see you inside?"

"I'll be there as soon as I park."

It couldn't come soon enough. He didn't want Tina to go. Not this soon. But family emergencies could not be planned.

When he practically ran into the airport departure hall, Tina was standing there with her tote bag, her printed ticket in hand.

"No eticket?"

"My iPhone is at the bottom of the Caribbean Sea, remember?"

"Oh, yeah. So you did leave something behind in the Bahamas." Byron stopped himself. "Sorry. Didn't mean to crack a joke at a time like this."

He didn't see Veronique and her send-off team.

"So soon." Byron planted a quick kiss on Tina's lips. He ran his fingers through her hair and settled his hand on the base of her neck. "I should go with you."

"No, Byron. Your work—your life—is here. You have a school to run."

"I want to be with you through this."

"God is with me. I'll be okay."

"The joy of the Lord is your strength."

"I might seem joyful, but underneath this smile, I have a lot of baggage to deal with."

"Skeletons?" Byron's eyebrows rose again.

*Please don't tell me!*

"Maybe. More like emotional baggage. My family is a mess, Byron. I can't impose that on you."

"What are you saying?" Byron didn't let go of her. He could not.

"We part now. I go home to my mess. You stay on your paradise island."

"I'm going to miss you."

"Me too. Miss you, I mean."

Byron rubbed her arms gently. "We're finally getting along."

"We are, aren't we?" Tina said. "In more ways than one."

"I want to see you again, Tina."

"Maybe someday we will. Maybe not. I need to go home and deal with my brother, and that's all I can think about right now."

Byron nodded. "I understand that. But afterwards?"

"After what?" Tina smiled, but it was a sad smile to Byron.

A very sad smile.

Then she tugged at his blue shirt, and Byron leaned toward her without any hesitation. She pressed a gentle kiss to his cheek.

"We both have work to do, lives to live." Tina's voice began to crack. "This is our summer—"

Shrieks interrupted their moment of solitude.

Veronique and Lucy rumbled through the crowd toward them. Tall Keith was behind them, walking with Veronique's aunt.

When the two women finally caught their breath, Veronique spoke first. "We went to the wrong terminal!"

"Glad you're all here," Tina said.

Byron glanced at his watch. "You have to go. It's past 2:30."

"I'll call when I get home."

Byron thought she said it more to Veronique and

Lucy than to him.

Even as they waved to Tina as she entered the security zone, Byron wanted to run after her to declare that he didn't agree with what she had said to him.

*This is not a short-term summer romance!*

Byron decided he could email, text, or call her to tell her that. But first he had to prepare a rebuttal. In essence, Tina had just said goodbye to him.

He did not like that. Not one bit. Not at all.

But there he stood, waving goodbye to the woman he had fallen in love with, with all her eccentricities of thanking God for the flowers, walking through the school gardens barefoot, being excited about such things as plain and as dull as clay. Messy clay.

And then there were things he had to rescue her from, such as her forgetfulness and clumsiness.

Ironic as it sounded, it had been through those times—abnormal to Byron's organized life—that he had found love in unexpected places.

A kiss in the sick bay.

A kiss in the garden.

And now a premature goodbye at the airport.

*Too soon!*

Was it really as fleeting as it had seemed?

He had met his dream girl.

Or had he been only dreaming?

# CHAPTER FIFTY-FOUR

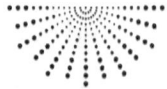

*T*ina paced the waiting room on the intensive care unit floor of the Savannah Memorial Hospital. By the time she had arrived in Savannah, the ER doctors had saved her brother's life, but he had gone into a coma. The damage in Martin's body was extensive, covering all the way from his head to his toe.

The other motorcyclist he had collided with at the racetrack had died on the spot.

At least Martin was still alive, but barely.

The other ladies from church had gone home to get some sleep since it was Saturday night and the morning church service was in less than twelve hours away, but the pastor's wife, Heidi Wei-Flores, had stayed with Tina.

Toggling between being angry and sad at

Martin was probably not the best way to handle the situation.

Still...

"He did it to himself," Tina said.

"Yes, but we've all been there," Heidi replied. "We have all received forgiveness from God for things we shouldn't have done. Shall we now not forgive others?"

Tina stopped pacing. "So you agree with me that it's a stupid thing to race motorcycles?"

"Not everybody who rides motorcycles gets into wrecks."

When Heidi said that, Tina remembered what Byron had said on their drive to the airport in Nassau.

Had it only been that afternoon? This had been a long day indeed.

*People have been riding bikes a long time, and many have stayed safe.*

"But Martin—"

"But Tina," Heidi cut her off.

There was an edge to Heidi's voice that caught Tina by surprise. She had hit a nerve. "I'm sorry."

"No need to apologize," Heidi said. "It's me. I dislike hospitals."

"You and me both, but I dislike the funeral home even more." Tina recalled that awful, rainy day when she and Martin had to view their mother in a casket. Ten or eleven years now, and she still hadn't forgotten it. "And the cemetery too."

"If you have someone to bury," Heidi said. "They never found my parents' bodies. Lost at sea in the South Pacific."

"Oh, I'm sorry. I didn't know that."

Tina had been so busy with her pottery studio and expanding her gallery in a couple of new cities that she hadn't always been around to socialize with Heidi. They knew each other, yes, but Tina was more familiar with the singles than the married adults at Riverside Chapel.

Tina sat down. "I'm so selfish."

She felt ashamed that she had been full of herself, especially today. When the going had gotten rough, she had withdrawn into her shell and turned self-focused.

Back at the airport in Nassau, she had pretty much told Byron to back off. Wasn't he trying to reach out to her to offer his support? She had turned him away.

Now Heidi had been trying to encourage her, and she had not responded graciously.

Heidi sat down next to Tina. "I must apologize."

"No, you don't."

"Yes. A while back, I was here in this hospital, waiting for my own brother to come out of surgery.

"Ming? He was injured?"

"Some years ago now." Heidi sniffled. "But Ming recovered, went on to lead a productive life, and is now a father of two kids. But I still remember that morning..."

"Yet here you are with me." Tina hugged Heidi. "Thank you."

"I'm here because of you, but more so because of Christ, Tina. In the garden of Gethsemane, Jesus asked God if He could let the cup pass from Him, but no."

"There was no other way."

"Right. And when Jesus died on the cross, He died for all of us, including your brother."

"I'm so glad Martin is saved," Tina said. "At least if anything happens to him..."

Heidi hesitated.

*Oh dear.* Tina waited.

"Diego had lunch with Martin a few days ago. They were chatting about church life, when Martin said that although he knew that Christ had died for everybody in the world, he doesn't know whether he had ever truly accepted Jesus personally into his heart. He felt that Jesus was far off from him, like he didn't know Him as his Lord and Savior."

"Oh no." Tina sat up. "Did he mean that he didn't feel saved or that he really isn't saved?"

"That's what I thought at first too. Salvation is by faith, not by feelings."

"Exactly. So?"

"So Diego asked him if he wanted to be sure that he believed in Jesus. Martin didn't think it wasn't necessary, but he agreed to meet with Diego again for another free lunch."

"Free lunch." Tina grinned. "Magic words to my brother."

"They were going to meet this coming Monday to talk some more about what Christ did at the cross. And now this."

"Our church interviewed him and thought he was saved," Tina said. "I thought he was saved. He joined Riverside before I did."

"Diego spoke with the lay counselor who had interviewed Martin at his membership meeting, and the counselor thought Martin was saved."

"So we don't know?" Tina felt exasperated.

"Has anything happened to Martin the last few years that may have caused him to question his salvation?"

Tina couldn't recall anything unusual. "We live a pretty dull life, Heidi. Work, eat, sleep, work, eat, sleep."

"Sometimes when our faith is weak, we could get shaken up a bit by something or other."

"I don't know. I do know that he has wrecked three—now four—bikes in five years. Was that an expression or reaction to something? He hasn't told me anything. Even though I'm his sister, it's not like he talks to me all the time, you know."

"Best thing we can do right now is pray for him. We don't have all the details, so let's leave it in God's hands. If he ever accepted Christ as his savior, he's saved. Once saved, you're always saved."

Tina agreed. "If he's not sure of his salvation, he just needs to be sure. That's all."

"It's sad how there's a lot of confusion these days. If Christ died for everyone, then why isn't everyone saved already?"

"I know. Like, if someone gives you an engagement ring, but you never accepted it, are you engaged?"

"Of course, you can be engaged without a ring," Heidi replied. "Although yes, if someone proposes to you, and you say no, there's no engagement. Now why would you bring up engagements, Tina?"

*Uh...* "Lucy and Keith are engaged."

"Ah, yes. They told us." Heidi seemed to move on. "Along the same line, if you're offered a birthday present, but you never take it, you don't own the present. It's still in a box somewhere."

"The offer is there," Tina said. "The price has been paid."

"Right. Each of us has to accept the gift of salvation from Christ personally. That's why He's a personal Savior and a personal Lord. Someone else cannot accept salvation on your behalf, not your friend or pastor, not your parents or grandparents, not your sister."

They sat in silence for a while.

Tina tried to take it all in.

"Here I am griping about Martin's bike racing when his entire eternity is at stake." She felt a trickle down her cheek. She wiped it off quickly.

"Our God is able," Heidi said. "Who knows? Maybe after that convo with Diego, Martin might have renewed his faith in Christ or accepted Christ once and for all. All it takes is a second of time. And time is in God's hands. He owns it."

*Time. How much time is given to us?*

Tina turned in the direction of the ICU doors. "Wake up, Martin."

# CHAPTER FIFTY-FIVE

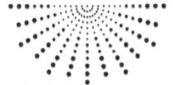

*T*wo days, then three, then whatever.

Byron had been so swamped with planning meetings to reshape and restructure the Chapel by the Sea Christian School in an effort to increase enrollment and funding that he had mixed up Tuesdays and Thursdays in his reports, attended a Friday meeting on a Wednesday, and missed his midweek evening Bible study as a result.

Obviously no one showed up at the Friday meeting on a Wednesday.

To add sparkles to his cone of shame, Byron had shot an email to the science teachers asking them where they were and why they hadn't taken the future of the school seriously.

The physics teacher, in a moment of unprecedented boldness, had replied to his email this way: *Where am I? I'm on a Wednesday in the known space-time continuum.*

Byron could see the invisible ink with the rest of the reply: *What planet are you on?*

Since he was an honest Christian—was there any other kind?—Byron sent a profuse apology to everyone and offered them free dinner after church on Sunday.

The upside of his week was that the science wing—he had nearly called it the space wing after that repartee with Professor Physics—was nearing completion.

Byron prayed that it would be ready for students to tour it on orientation day. It would be a fitting farewell to Headmaster Clarke, whose chemotherapy had taken a toll on him and his entire family.

On Friday morning, after another bout of rain, the groundbreaking ceremony went without a hitch, and the construction of the Jesus Loves Me Kindergarten Building began.

By the time Byron trekked back to his office, he was worn out. He managed to get a few things done. Five messages with photos of the event to Clarke, several texts, and a whole slew of emails he didn't want to read, but one.

One single email from Tina MacFarland.

She had been sending him updates—on her new pink iPhone—but her emails had been dwindling down as the week carried on. Her brother was still in a coma. She said she was still winging and juggling her many pottery orders and going back and forth to the hospital to check on her brother.

Fortunately, the whole church was taking turns. Something like thirty or more people had signed up to spend time at the hospital to pray and wait for Martin to wake up from his coma.

And to pray for his salvation.

Byron thought Martin could accept Christ in his heart. He didn't have to verbally tell anyone about his decision. It was between him and God.

If Tina had assurance that her brother was saved, that would make her feel better. But she was a nonparticipant in his personal decision to believe in Jesus as his personal Lord and Savior.

Or not.

Could one unconsciously accept Christ while in a coma? Byron didn't know.

All he knew was that, even consciously as a believer, he himself had a long way to go in living a life that was pleasing to the Lord. He had made decisions that might or might not be in line with God's perfect will for his life.

Or perhaps he had been in God's will at one

point, and had now deviated from that path he was supposed to be on: teaching.

*Does my job as the interim headmaster please You, Lord?*

Byron scanned his office before he turned off the lights.

# CHAPTER FIFTY-SIX

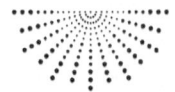

other and Donovan were chatting by the infinity pool when Byron opened the glass doors to the terrace. The fountain at the edge of the pool gurgled. Byron wished it would stop.

"Look what the cat dragged in." Donovan spread his arms across the back of the outdoor settee he was on.

Mother was on an adjacent chaise lounge, drinking a milkshake.

Byron headed for her and planted a kiss on her cheek. He sat down on an armchair across from Donovan.

"Women problems?" Donovan asked.

"Why do you say that?" Byron shot back.

"There. That's proof."

Byron shook his head. "I don't know if I'm cut out to be a headmaster."

"All admin and no teaching makes you a dull boy." Donovan laughed. "A dull boy with no time for love."

"Not helping."

"Trying!"

"Boys." Mother put down her tall glass. She turned to Byron. "How did the groundbreaking ceremony go?"

"Clarke wasn't there."

"Sorry to hear that. What is the school calling the new wing again?"

"Jesus Loves Me Kindergarten Building."

"Well done." Mother seemed pleased. "Give glory to God always."

Donovan shook his head. "I'm shocked, actually. I didn't think that name would fly. I told her—oops."

"Told who?" Byron perked up.

"Nobody."

"Out with it, Donovan," Byron pressed.

"I want to know too," Mother chimed in.

"Well, I told her the school board would never go with the name," Donovan said. "I think they wanted to name it after Clarke."

"Told who?" Byron tried again.

"She said the only way she'd match funds is if the building was dedicated to the Lord."

"She who?" Byron was at the edge of his seat. "Mrs. Michaels? Maybe Jocelyn Peterson?"

Those faithful Christians had been big donors to the Christian school in the past.

"None of the above," Donovan said. "Don't ask me anymore. She doesn't want anyone to know, especially you—oops."

*Tina.*

*Only Tina.*

"You can't keep a secret to save your life," Byron said, to which Mother simply chuckled. "Where did she get the money to match your funds?"

"You know, she's actually an astute business-woman. You and I inherited our estates, but Tina, she worked her way up from ground zero." Donovan pointed at Byron. "You think she doesn't have it together, but it's only when she's around you."

"Me?" Byron looked around.

"All your fault when she looked like an airhead."

"No."

"I'm still commissioning her to make those plat-ters for my new hotel, restaurant, and casino on Lucaya." Donovan leaned forward. "You know what she did?"

Byron didn't know. He really didn't.

"Well, brother, she hired Raymond Fordham to make them for me—to her specs. And she's giving him fifty percent of the profits."

"Seriously?"

"That way the poor man—in more ways than one—won't have to close his studio."

"Close? Why?"

"He's going out of business, didn't you know? Too much debt."

Byron saw it now. "That's why Tina had recommended Ray as the Art II teacher. He could use the work."

"But he's too proud to say he needs the money."

Mother stood up with her empty glass. "Boys, be careful you don't admire a person because of what she has done. Her relationship with God through Christ should hold more weight."

"Hear ye! Hear ye!" Donovan clapped. "Words of wisdom from our supersmart, ultratalented, greatest mother who ever lived."

Mother stopped in front of Donovan. "All right. What do you want?"

"May I have my plane back?" Donovan asked.

"No," Mother said as she waltzed away.

"Figured." Donovan sighed. "Thought I'd ask anyway."

Byron laughed until tears came out his eyes. He hadn't laughed all week. Funny how he felt his stress released. God made laughter, didn't He?

"So what did you do to lose your main mode of transportation?" Byron asked.

"Funny, Brother. Very funny. But here's the deal. God is always full of surprises for those who trust in His Name. If He takes away my jet, He's going to give me something better."

"Whoa. Did you just say that?" Byron's eyebrows shot up. He then remembered how Tina had remarked about his eyebrows.

*I miss her.*

"I did just say that. Mother told me I have to take stock of my life. Can't frolic away my retirement income."

"Good for you."

"I will keep my yacht and my cruise line investment, but no more weekly parties. They cost too much and impressed no one."

"Sure impressed all those gold diggers who hang around your table."

"The people I tried to impress—Lucy, Tina, even Veronique—didn't care."

Byron was glad to hear that Tina didn't care about Donovan's fortune.

"I'm going to do what Gus is doing," Donovan said.

"Landscaping?"

"Ha-ha, Brother. You only think you're funny. Nope. Gus gives to charity work. I'm going to start doing that."

"Good for you," Byron said. "Just be sure you're

not doing charity work to make up for your hard-partying days. You can't earn God's approval that way, you know. If you could earn it, then Christ died for nothing."

"I know. I just wanted to do good things henceforth."

"Great. I'm proud of you, Donovan."

"That means a lot to me." Donovan smiled. "I know what I want. Do you know what you want, Byron Etienne Moss?"

*Who I want? I know who I want.*

*But not what I want.*

"I have this job to do."

"Life is not all about jobs. Someday you'll wake up in your empty little town house all alone. Do you want that?" Donovan asked. "I may be four years younger than you are and seven or eight years younger than Gus, but look at him. He's all alone. And Uncle Richard. Totally alone at seventy-nine years old."

"Uncle Richard wants to be alone."

"Gus couldn't make headwinds with Veronique. Maybe I can help him."

Byron lifted a hand. "Let God deal with them. No need to interfere."

"The point is, if you have someone God has put in your life, better get to her, Brother, before you lose her like I lost Lucy."

"Lucy?"

Donovan waved him off. "And you can take my jet—oh sorry. Lost my jet."

"Don't worry. I'll fly commercial. Trying to collect some frequent flyer miles."

"You'll be flying frequently, if I read you right, Byron." Donovan tented his fingers together. "The question is when. When will you stop listening to your head and start listening to your heart?"

# CHAPTER FIFTY-SEVEN

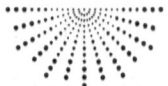

When Tina arrived at Savannah Memorial at eight in the morning with a flower arrangement in a new ceramic vase she had made, and her tote bag and a laptop messenger bag over one shoulder, she ran into her office manager leaving the hospital.

Corinne had signed up to babysit Martin, as had all their friends at Riverside Chapel.

"Hey, I'm on my way up." Tina wanted to be annoyed that Corinne had left Martin so soon, but a second look at the bags under her employee's eyes told her to be quiet about it.

"Someone's up there to fill in for me."

"Oh good. I'm not late, am I?" Tina searched the walls for a clock.

"No, no. You're early, in fact. I'll see you later. I'm going home to get some sleep."

The same routine.

It meant Martin was still in a coma.

"Bye, and thank you, Corinne." Tina headed for the elevator.

Corinne doubled back. "Tina?"

"Yes?"

"Thought you might want to know that Martin and I... Well, we're an item."

*Surprise. Surprise.*

Tina had been home for two weeks and no one had said a word until now. "Please tell me you're not pregnant."

"Oh no. Nothing like that. We're courting."

"What does that mean?" Tina asked. "No kissing?"

"We just hold hands."

"Okay."

"I'm just saying that when Martin wakes up, I don't want you to be surprised."

Tina nodded.

She reached the elevator doors before they closed again. She had forgotten to ask Corinne who was upstairs with Martin, but she'd find out soon enough.

She tiptoed past the glass windows of the ICU.

Martin was still unconscious. All bandaged up and nowhere to go.

*Poor baby brother.*

"Please, Lord, wake him up. Give him another chance at life."

When she reached the ICU waiting room, she saw two people sitting there, one reading the newspaper, the other reading a book. The man reading the book had salt-and-pepper hair and looked haggard and worn out.

Yet, he was unmistakable.

Tina stood unmoving at the door.

The woman put down her newspaper and nudged the older man.

When he looked up, his eyes were red. "You have your mother's hair."

Tina teared up. "Dad."

He breathed a sigh of relief and lumbered toward her. "I thought you'd never call me Dad again."

"How did you know Martin's here? Who called you?"

"Some PI named Helen the Pit Bull."

"Helen Hu?"

"Yes, she's the one. She yaps like a pit bull."

The way Dad talked, he sounded like Martin, and it broke Tina's heart.

"Don't cry." Dad wrapped her in his arms. They were gangly, boney, like Martin's.

The vase nearly slipped out of her hands and onto the floor. Dad rescued it with one hand.

"I'd better put it on the table." Tina took the vase back. She also dropped off her tote and messenger bag, and then said hello to the demure lady still sitting down.

"Ah yes." Dad waved for the lady to come over. "This is my wife, Damaris."

*Wife.*

"Hello." Tina shook her hands. Her palms were rough.

Tina didn't know what else to say to her or to Dad. She was curious, however, about how Helen Hu came into the picture.

"I wasn't hiding or anything, if you must know," Dad explained. "I retired from a job last year, and we got married in Chattanooga. Our wedding announcement was in the papers. But this year, we decided to do some traveling, so we've been in South America for months."

"How did Helen find you there?" Tina asked.

"I don't know. Somehow, she did. Sent someone to track us down in Ecuador."

Damaris held Tina's hand. "I'm sorry about your brother. We've been praying since we heard."

Tina nodded. "Thank you."

More silence.

Then Dad spoke. "How's your mother?"

"I guess you didn't know. She passed away when Martin and I were in college."

Dad's face looked visibly moved. "That long ago?"

"We're not that old. I'm turning thirty this fall." *Only thirty.*

"That makes me sixty-five." Dad's voice was sad. "Are you married?"

"No." Tina wiggled her left hand. *Not yet.*

"If you find the right person, it works out best," Dad said.

Was that the closest he would come to an apology?

"How are you two doing?" Dad asked.

"Martin spends his free time racing bikes when he's not working for me or as a VA."

"VA?"

"Virtual assistant."

Dad nodded. "You?"

"I'm an artist and potter."

Dad chuckled. "Not starving, I hope."

"I manage," Tina said.

"Your mother was a potter."

"Yes. She left me her pottery wheel."

Dad tried to reach for her, but his arm dropped

to his side. He pocketed his hands in his jean pockets. "Again, I'm sorry."

"I forgive you, Dad."

Dad stepped over, wrapped Tina in his arms again, and sobbed. "Thank you. You have no idea how long I've waited for you to forgive me."

There were no dry eyes in the waiting room.

Finally, Tina peeled away, wiping her cheeks with the back of her palms. "When did you get here?"

"A couple of hours ago," Damaris said. "Chatted with that sweet gal, Corinne."

Tina was conflicted about her next question, but she decided to ask anyway. "Do you have a place to stay?"

"Yes. We booked a couple of nights at the hotel one block away."

Tina decided that was enough for her. She could invite them to stay with her later, if things normalized between her and Dad.

Right now all this was happening too quickly.

And Martin was still in a coma.

"We have to pray that Martin wakes up." Tina choked on the words. She turned to Dad. "Maybe you can talk some sense into him when he's recovered."

"About what?"

"Bike racing. It's dangerous."

"For some people, yes, but yeah, I'll talk to him. After all, motorcycles are overrated. What he needs are muscle cars."

Muscle cars?

"Okay, I'll take muscle cars. They have four wheels." Tina hid a laugh. "Martin is uncoordinated on two wheels."

"When he was a kid, he kept falling off his skateboard, remember? Skinned everything."

"I remember, Dad. You suggested putting training wheels on his skateboard."

"I sure did. He never went on them again."

Tina glanced at the clock. "It's almost time for the doctor to make his rounds. Shall we go talk to him to see what's going on?"

"Martin is in God's hands now," Dad said.

To Tina it sounded as though Dad thought Martin was dying. She didn't want to believe that. She wanted God to heal Martin, wake him up, and let her take him home to start over.

*I'll take care of him the rest of my life if I must. This is my baby brother.*

*Please, Lord. Please?*

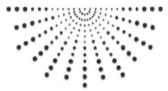

"y dad is alive!" Tina exclaimed on the phone. She sounded terribly excited.

Byron was happy for her. That one email to Pastor Diego Flores had yielded much fruit.

*Thank You, God, for Your perfect timing.*

Byron walked around his condo, listening to her chatter about meeting her new stepmother and how she had prayed with them for Martin to wake up from his coma. It had been two weeks now, and no sign of anything yet.

His whole body was still broken, she explained. The doctors were running tests. "He looks pretty bad. My church has been so supportive. I haven't had to cook in two weeks."

Byron let her drone on until she stopped to catch her breath.

"Chapel by the Sea is also praying for Martin and your family," he said.

"Thank you."

"Glad you sound upbeat, Tina. I was concerned about you."

"I'll feel way better when Martin wakes up."

"I bet. We'll keep praying." Byron felt that as a Bible teacher, he had more to say about matters of life and death. Still, he wasn't sure how to put it without hurting her feelings or scaring her.

"You want to tell me something," Tina said.

"Uh, yes. Remember that regardless of the outcome, God is still good. God is still sovereign. God is still trustworthy. No matter what."

"Yes."

"Even if the path He allows is not what you want."

"Are you talking to me about Martin, or are you speaking about yourself, Byron?"

"Both, perhaps."

"I guess you and I are learning about God more and more," Tina said.

"And seeking God's will for our careers and lives."

"My career is taken care of. I am where I need to be. I'm a happy potter, and I love my job."

*Do I love my job?* Byron wasn't sure anymore.

He sat down on his favorite recliner. It faced the windows and the great night sky. All was dark out there tonight in the cloudy night. He wished Tina were with him, but she was close enough on the phone.

"Uh-oh," Tina said. "Is everything all right?"

"I don't know yet, seriously. The first day of school is the seventeenth of August. Meanwhile, we're still doing the summer day camp. I'll find out when school begins whether everything is all right."

"Are you taking any time off?"

"From what?"

"From school, silly. You can't work year round without a break."

"It has been my job to run the Summer by the Sea Day Camp. This is the first year Veronique has taken over, but she only had to do that because Headmaster Clarke is leaving us permanently, and I have to fill in for him."

"And?"

"I have to redo the schedule I made last year for myself as assistant headmaster this year because I'm no longer the assistant. I have to chuck my own plans."

"Better that than to discard God's plans."

"Indeed." Byron glared at the clock on his iPhone. He could not remember where he had put his iPad. Slowly, he was becoming as forgetful as Tina.

He sighed. "It's almost eleven o'clock, and I need to get some sleep."

"I'm sorry I kept you past your bedtime."

"No, Tina. I like to hear your voice. A soothing elixir to my long week." Byron closed his eyes. "I don't know if I'm cut out to be a headmaster. Too much admin, not enough classroom time."

"If God calls you to be a teacher, you have to teach."

"Right. Pray for me, Tina."

"I have and I will."

"Keep me posted about Martin," Byron said.

"He'd better wake up. Somehow I know that God has a job for him to do."

"He's in his twenties, correct? He can fight this."

"Yeah. This could change his life. There's going to be rehab. Lots of it. Plus, who knows if he'll ever walk again."

Byron sat up. "Trust God. Don't plan too far ahead."

There was silence on the phone. Then Tina spoke again. "Did I hear you advise me not to plan ahead?"

"I said *too far* ahead."

"Like how far is too far?"

"One year turned out to be too far for me this

time around. My life lesson." The verse Mother had invited him to study. "Proverbs 16:9 says that I can plan, but ultimately God directs my steps."

"We like that verse."

Byron wondered how to broach the subject, but headlong seemed prudent. "Have you ever changed a course in life?"

"Like how?"

"Like you're in the middle of a career and you feel a pull to go into another line of work?"

"You mean not be a teacher anymore?"

"I'll still be a teacher, but not where I had thought God had placed me."

"Where you work now?" Tina seemed to want to understand.

Byron found it hard to explain. "I want to teach the Bible."

"And they won't let you at the school?"

"Maybe later, but not this new school year."

"Do what God tells you to do, nothing more, nothing less."

"Would it matter to you if I went back to school —to get another degree, say?"

"Why do you ask me? If God calls you, His plan is the best."

"I like your answer, Tina. Will you support me, then?" Byron asked.

"You mean financially?"

"No. I mean emotionally and spiritually."

"If that is what God wants you to do, I'll cheer you on," Tina said. "However, I would stay put until you are sure you've heard from God. He'll make it so clear to you that you'll have no doubt."

When Byron said nothing, Tina continued. "School hasn't even started, and you're sounding like someone who is burning out. Maybe you're exhausted from all the pressure. Is there any way you can take time off?"

"Well, I can't."

"You don't want to."

"After day camp, our faculty comes back. After that, school starts."

"You're not running the day camp anymore."

"I oversee the building projects on campus. The school enrollment is down, and the board says we're short of funds—oh, internal info. Please don't tell anyone."

Byron didn't know why he had told her those things. Perhaps to justify how busy he'd been running around in circles chasing after his own tail?

"Say no more." Tina said. "Why don't we pray for each other?"

"Now?"

"Yes. This can be our thing. We pray for each other before we say good night."

"We can do that. Maybe we should Skype or FaceTime so we can see each other."

Tina laughed on the phone. "You don't want to see me right now. My nose has sunburn from eating lunch outside today. My freckles are angry."

"I've never seen angry freckles."

"I'm still not sending you any photos."

"Let's pray before I fall asleep," Byron said.

And they did.

And he fell asleep on his recliner.

# CHAPTER FIFTY-NINE

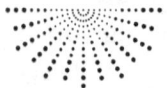

*T*here had been no change in Martin's condition since Dad arrived in town on Saturday. For the next couple of days, friends and family continued to take turns to keep a vigil at the hospital.

After a hearty lunch on Tuesday, Tina had driven Dad, Damaris, and Corinne back to Savannah Memorial to relieve Mrs. Untermeyer, who had the morning shift keeping an eye on Martin, still in ICU, still in a coma.

Quietly they tiptoed into the room. Dad had said he wanted them to pray by Martin's bedside, and Tina thought that was a great idea. They had to wait a bit until the nurses let them in.

Before she could reach the hospital bed, Martin's eyes popped open.

Next to Tina, Corinne shrieked and collapsed into a heap.

"Martin!" Tina rushed to her brother's side, leaving Corinne passed out on the floor just inside the door.

What to do, really? Martin had woken up after something like eighteen days!

Tina pressed the nurse call button several times, a few for Martin and one for Corinne.

Slowly, Martin blinked.

He tried to speak. No words came out.

"Thank You, Lord Jesus!" Tina reached for Martin's hand at the same time as Dad.

Martin seemed to be trying to move his arms and legs, but they were too weak.

"Take it easy," Dad said softly.

Martin's eyes went wide. "Dad?"

Tina began to cry. When she reached for her box of tissue paper in her tote bag, she spotted Corinne on the floor. Damaris had knelt beside her.

Corinne had revived, and she was staring at her phone now, punching furiously with her thumbs, all the while still lying down facing the ceiling.

Behind her, nurses and the attending physician swarmed into the room.

Tina and Dad stepped back to let them work on Martin.

She prayed to God for a quick recovery, but the

doctors had repeated to the family that Martin was going to require extensive surgeries on his spine and bones. He was probably going to have some headaches in the weeks to come from that concussion.

Suddenly, Tina's legs felt weak.

Dad's arm was right there, giving her support.

There was no place to sit in that crowded space.

But it didn't matter.

The most important thing that happened today had happened.

God had woken Martin up.

# CHAPTER SIXTY

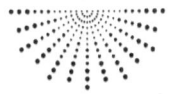

*B*yron was so busy the next two weeks that he was bouncing from one task to another nonstop. The science wing was almost completed, and the Jesus Loves Me Kindergarten Building was well underway.

Health inspectors said that the kindergarteners had to be moved elsewhere for the duration of the construction because of the dust and noise. Byron had to find temporary spaces. Fortunately, the Chapel by the Sea had Sunday School classes that were unused during the week. Byron checked it off his list.

By the time lunchtime came that Thursday, Byron felt he was coming down with a cold or flu or something. His body was worn out to the point of exhaustion, but he had to keep going.

He ate at his office because going into the school cafeteria reminded him too much of where Tina had sat when she had been here.

Sure, he still prayed with her every night over the phone, but he really would prefer to see her in person.

*Yes, in person.*

*Right here, right now.*

In fact, he wanted to wake up beside her the rest of his life...

Paperwork stacked up, Byron turned his attention to a rash of new emails he hadn't expected from the science laboratory suppliers.

"Oh no." The shipment for the laboratory equipment was delayed. It looked like the secondary school students wouldn't be doing any experiments in their new science wing until the end of September.

*The twenty-seventh of September, to be precise.*

Bad news for his teachers.

Byron then spent over fifty minutes composing an email to his science teachers asking for suggestions even as he knew what he would recommend.

There was a private school down the road from here that had secondary school science labs. If Chapel by the Sea Christian School paid the school a fee, could Byron's students use their labs on Saturdays, when school wasn't in session and the labs were not utilized?

Byron knew that the science classes couldn't use any old place—the cafeteria, for example—to dissect rats and cow's eyes.

*More expenses!*

His iPhone rang. He grabbed it before he could see who had called. He wished it were Tina. But it wasn't.

"Mother."

"Would you like to have dinner with me?" she asked.

"Tomorrow night?"

"Tonight. I'm flying out to Ireland tomorrow, remember?"

"Oh yeah. Aunt Eimear's wedding on Saturday." Byron chided himself for becoming more and more absentminded. Perhaps it had been the lack of sleep the last few weeks.

"Getting married at sixty-four. Don't wait that late, Byron."

"Mother, it's not her first marriage."

"Yes, you get to remarry if your husband dropped dead while herding the sheep and rolled down the hill."

"Mother! Have you been drinking?"

"No. Why?"

"Just wondering."

"You sound tired," Mother said. "Take a break and let's do dinner. When do you get off work?"

"I'm working late tonight."

"Then I'll bring dinner to you. Name the place. I'll order and pick up the takeout."

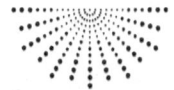

# CHAPTER SIXTY-ONE

"Martin is a mess," Tina said on FaceTime as she proceeded to list her brother's medical issues, some of which would not be covered by her insurance.

Then there were therapies every week, learning to walk and do basic things again, and dealing with their new normal.

Poor Martin.

"How can I help?" Byron asked.

"Other than prayer, there's nothing much you can do."

"I'm glad he woke up and is on the mend."

"A lot to mend."

"Wish I could be there for you," Byron said. "But I'm glad your church is helping out."

"And my dad and stepmom have decided to stay for a few months through Martin's recovery."

"Good."

"They're doing the bulk of the caregiving. I have all these pottery orders I have to fulfill by Christmas." She waved her arms around, pointing at the shelves behind her, but she wasn't sure if Byron could see what she was pointing to.

She was sitting down at a table covered with stray paint and dried acrylic and such. The iPhone was still in front of her, propped up on the table by her hands.

Beyond her iPhone, she spotted an unfinished vase she had been painting glaze on.

It was eleven o'clock at night, and she was still here in her studio.

All by herself.

*So much work to do, so little time.*

"I'm swamped, Byron. Haven't had more than four hours of sleep a night the last week or so."

"Not good, Tina."

"I know, but what can I do?" Tina prayed quickly before she spoke again. "Byron, I need to ask you something."

"Anything."

"Can we take a rain check?"

"A rain check?"

"You're there in Nassau, busy with the new

school year. I'm here in Savannah, dealing with a needy brother and a growing business."

"And?"

"I don't know when I'll go back to Nassau, if ever."

"I can come to see you... Uh, sometime."

"I want more than that, Byron. Virtual hugs are not my style." Tina leaned toward her iPhone camera. "This could never work out."

"We'll pray, Tina, for God to lead us. Maybe we can get together during school breaks."

"If we can match up our schedules." Tina thought Byron wasn't getting it. "I think we're better off with..."

"With other people?" Byron snapped.

Tina didn't remember the last time he had been curt with her. Not this past summer trip to Nassau.

"Like I told you, we had a summer romance," Tina said. "Now it's over."

"No. You have my heart in your hands."

"Do I really? Shouldn't your heart be in God's hands?"

"Ah yes. I suppose so."

"This sort of relationship"—Tina pointed to herself and then to her cell phone—"is not practical."

Byron said nothing.

"You go back to your life. I go back to mine.

What happened to us in the Bahamas stayed in the Bahamas."

"I'm still in the Bahamas, Tina. I have memories of us."

"Memories do not a relationship make."

"That so?"

"We could keep in touch, but it's not going anywhere. We're both too busy for relationships of any kind, let alone across the Caribbean seas."

Byron was visibly shocked.

Tina knew she had to say it. *So here goes.* "Soon, you'll find someone more suitable and available to you."

"Available? I thought you were single."

"I am. I haven't had a boyfriend in who knows how long, but that's because I've been busy with my studio expansions—speaking of which, that's a mess too. Everything's a big old mess, Byron. I can't take on another project."

"I'm not a project."

"A relationship is a project."

"Maybe I can help you sort out your mess. I'm a planner, remember?"

Tina laughed. "I don't want you to plan my life. I want to go where God is leading me."

"Remember that our God is a God of order, not of chaos," Byron said. "Sometimes He sends helpers. Look at how He sent your family and church to help you with Martin. Maybe He's sending me to help you in some way. To be sure, He has sent you to help me look at life from a more well-rounded perspective."

"He did?"

"Yes. Life is not all about checking off goals anymore."

Tina rolled her eyes. "Oh no."

"Oh no what?"

"I'm checking off goals now. Your bad habits have rubbed off on me."

Byron laughed. "And I'm getting forgetful. I misplaced my iPad twice this week."

"I thought it hung around your neck?"

"The cord broke. It was cheap."

"Or overused."

"Maybe both. But the point is that there's more to life than just our careers and obligations."

"My brother needs me, Byron."

"I need you too."

"That's selfish."

"Selfish?" Byron kept his voice low, but Tina could feel his tension. "I know you're overwhelmed, but better not say things you'll regret later."

"You can do everything a person can do, but my brother Martin may never walk again. He has lost bits and pieces of memory and can't retain information. His head hurts all the time. The surgeries are taking a toll on him and us. He has rods everywhere. He will never be the same again. And he's only twenty-seven. Do you understand?"

"Oh, I do understand. Well, Miss MacFarland, I bid you adieu, and don't expect that you will hear from me again. Goodbye."

"Goodbye!" Tina hung up.

*Whoa. Did we just have our first—and last —quarrel?*

# CHAPTER SIXTY-TWO

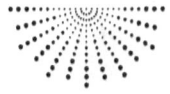

*P*recisely three weeks to the day the new school year had begun at Chapel by the Sea Christian School, Byron lost his verdure for the coveted headmaster position.

Once Headmaster Clarke's throne room, the sparsely furnished office at the corner of pain and suffering that Byron was sitting in now seemed like a prison for his career.

To begin with, he had reluctantly handed over his secondary school Bible class to another teacher who was less qualified than he was to teach the Bible. Perhaps it was presumptuous of Byron to assume that he was a better Bible teacher, though he had been teaching the same class for seven years, with a custom curriculum he had made himself.

Now all that had been pried off his hands.

And the Bible curriculum he had crafted? Well, it belonged to the school. It wasn't his to publish. In fact, the school decided to shelve it perpetually. As far as Byron was concerned, the new off-the-shelf Bible curriculum didn't hold a candle to what he had designed.

*What I have designed?*

*Lord, forgive my pride.*

Yet the Bible class hadn't been all that Byron had to give up. He had to forego teaching Wednesday night Bible studies at church. Often he had to miss Sunday night worship services. All on account of work he had to do in the new school year.

*Administrative work, that is.*

Too much time dealing with school policies, updated Bahamian educational requirements, continued renovations of the science wing, and the construction of the new kindergarten building.

And then there was the money issue. Pressured on all sides to figure out why enrollment was down this fall, it was Byron's job to answer to the school board members and work with them to get more students.

*The islands are small, don't they know?*

*From whence cometh new students?*

As far as Byron was concerned, the school board had itself to blame for voting down more scholarships for students. Fees had gone up substantially in the last few school years. The board's solution to increasing enrollment was to pour money into new science labs. They had expected that with new facilities, parents of secondary school students with an eye on universities would send their kids to the school in droves.

That had not happened, because the plan had backfired. Overruns in costs, unexpected foundation issues in that part of the school yard, and unpredictable summer weather had all delayed the completion of the science wing.

The only thing now that was paid for and on schedule was the Jesus Loves Me Kindergarten Building.

Byron buried his face in his sweaty palms, elbows on the mahogany table that was once Clarke's pride and joy.

Byron had no idea it would be this unsettling to be a headmaster. From afar and from those ideal days of old, it had seemed like the position for him.

Now that he had almost reached it—only one step away to drop the *interim* word—it seems like a bitter pill he could not possibly swallow and live to tell the story to his grandchildren.

*Grandchildren?*

*Are you nuts? You may not even survive this school year, let alone think that far ahead.*

It seemed that Byron had to be more of a businessman and a chief operating officer of the school rather than the academic headmaster he had dreamed of.

The only irony was that his workload at the school had taken his mind off Tina and her last outburst. He couldn't believe she had called him selfish.

He was sure that given time, she would retract her statement. Yeah, it had only been two weeks. She might need more time to think about what she had said.

Then again, they might never meet or communicate again.

Byron winced at the pain in his heart.

The sun began to set above his car—

Car?

Byron didn't know how he had gone from his office to the car park and then on the short drive across the street to his town house.

He unlocked his front door, kicked off his shoes, tossed his laptop briefcase onto his favorite recliner, and threw himself on the Louis Vuitton leather couch that his mother had discarded from her house. The iPad, hanging off his neck, smacked his chest.

He was not looking forward to the next day's battles of increased monetary concerns at the school, curriculum wars, new teachers not adjusting to life on campus, and staffers asking for pay increases for the next school year.

*The next school year!*

This year had barely started.

Byron groaned.

*All I want to do is teach, Lord. I want to teach Your Word. That's all I want to do.*

He could not call Headmaster Clarke to talk about this. His mentor's cancer had spread to his liver, spleen, and stomach.

He could not call Pastor Dixon for counseling. He was the president of the school board. Any rumblings of unrest would cause Dixon to inquire about his inability to handle the workload.

*Go ahead. Find a new headmaster. I'm only temporary.*

Byron had no peace about his own leadership at the school. He had had a lot of help from Veronique since the day camp ended. She was an able assistant and slated to take up his old position of assistant headmaster.

For all practical purposes, Byron himself would nominate Veronique to be the headmaster for the entire school. He would be more than happy to return to his old desk in his old office.

*Lord, I need peace about this. Direct my steps.*

And Byron knew it was a prayer that God

would hear because it had come out of Proverbs 16:9.

Byron had wanted badly to be the headmaster of a Christian school. Now that he almost had it, it tasted bitter.

He just wanted to teach. Really!

He winced. A headache formed at the back of his eyes.

How many Wednesday nights and Sunday evenings at church would he have to miss before his headmaster position settled down to a steady, manageable pace?

Would it ever be manageable? Maybe not anytime soon.

Maybe never.

Would he—could he—make a decent living and support a family if he stepped down from the headmaster position to simply be an assistant headmaster, or even a teacher at the school?

He needed to pray through this. He needed someone to talk to.

But not Tina.

He couldn't call Tina about this. She had dumped him unceremoniously. He had never expected her to be that rude to him.

Thinking of Tina reminded him of his friend at her church. Pastor Diego Flores. Maybe he could advise Byron. Or at the very least, let Byron talk and work through it.

He lifted his iPad from his neck, keyed in his PIN, and emailed Diego a short, unedited email.

Next thing he knew, his iPhone rang.

# CHAPTER SIXTY-THREE

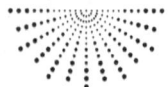

"What's up, old friend?" Diego asked.

"Yep. I feel very old right now, Diego." And Byron unloaded his heart. Uncensored.

When he was done, there was a long pause on the phone.

"Diego?" Byron asked.

"I'm here."

"And?"

"Just making some mental checks," his pastor friend said. "Did you know that you said the words teach, teaching, and teacher something like fourteen or fifteen times?"

"I did?"

"Yeah. And you mentioned Bible and church at least six or seven times."

Byron waited.

"It bothers you that your new headmaster position is taking you away from the things you want to do the most: teaching, going to church, doing Bible studies."

"You make it sound bad."

"It's not *bad* per se, but it seems like there's a lack of order in your life."

"A lack of order?" Byron was stunned. Of all the people in the world, he would never peg himself as being disorganized.

"What is God's purpose and plan for your life?" Diego asked. "Start from there."

"I think He has called me to teach, particularly the Bible. Career-wise, I was happiest in front of the classroom teaching Bible. I'm not doing that now. I'm not teaching anything at all."

"If you don't take this headmaster position, will they still let you teach Bible?"

"They've hired a new Bible teacher. If I quit, I'm out."

"Has God indicated going back to school to get a doctorate or something?" Diego asked. "You know, my wife, Heidi, she has two doctorates in history. She's teaching at the local college here, and she's not only good at it, she's having the time of her life."

"That's what I want to do. I want to teach. I don't care about all these admin and fundraising stuff. Oh, don't get me started on fundraising. It's a nightmare, but if we don't have it, the school won't survive two more years, even with the renovations we're doing."

"That bad, huh?"

"I know I can trust you. Tell me what I need to do."

"I recommend you take a few days of personal retreat and pray to God to show you what you need to do with the rest of your life."

"I don't have any time off." It had been the same thing he had told Tina.

"Then pray every evening after school. And on weekends."

"I'm working almost every weekend."

"Byron."

"Yes?"

"You must get your day of rest or you will burn out."

"I think I'm burned out already."

"You will die a painful, self-inflicted death, old friend, if you don't stop and get this straightened out with God. And you knew that before you called me."

"True." Byron knew what he had to do. "All right. Thanks, friend. Enough about me. What's going on with you these days?"

Byron hoped Diego wouldn't tell him anything

about Tina and her family. That would be too
painful for him to hear.

He had lost Tina.

Then again, she was not his to lose.

She belonged to God.

"Ah, something exciting the Lord is doing,"
Diego said. "Three sister churches—Riverside
Chapel here, Seaside Chapel on St. Simon's Island,
and Midtown Chapel in metro Atlanta—are coming
together to start a brand-new Bible college on the
Midtown Chapel campus."

Byron sat up. "A Bible college?"

"University."

"I know what a college is in your lingo," Byron
said. He leaned back on the couch, which was
highly comfortable, considering the price tag.

"We want to raise up a new generation of
pastors and Bible teachers."

*Bible teachers.*

"They will intern at our three churches, rotating
through different ministerial positions and being
understudies to pastors."

*Bible teachers.*

"That's interesting, Diego."

"Yeah. Never limit God."

Byron wondered what God was up to. "Well, I'd
better let you go. You're opening my mind to ways
that God might work in my life. Appreciate that."

"Never limit God."

"He could direct my steps where I would not expect," Byron thought aloud.

"I'll pray for you, man. Listen to God. Don't make sudden moves until you're very sure you've heard from Him."

What Diego said echoed what Tina had told him almost two months ago when she had called to tell him that her dad had resurfaced after all these years. Byron hadn't yet told her how that had come about.

But in that same conversation in July, Tina had said something profound to him.

*I would stay put until you are sure you've heard from God. He'll make it so clear to you that you'll have no doubt.*

"Call. Email. Text. Anytime," Diego said. "I'm here for you, friend."

"I appreciate it."

"Next time you come out here to Savannah, we'll do lunch."

"You're on." And Byron hoped that would be very soon.

# CHAPTER SIXTY-FOUR

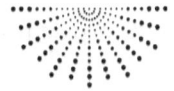

*M*artin had been home for something like five or six weeks—Tina had lost count—and they had settled into a somewhat new normal routine.

Dad and Damaris became his primary caregivers. Living on their social security checks was unacceptable to Tina, so she decided to pay Damaris what she would have paid a full-time caregiver.

Dad, ever proud, didn't want to be paid for anything. He wanted somewhere to park his restored Plymouth Road Runner Hemi and his souped-up Pontiac GTO, and he said that if Tina could swing that, he'd be a happy camper and would do all the driving back and forth to take Martin to therapy.

"Just a garage?" Tina had asked him.

"I can sleep in my cars under the starlight."

Dad must not have realized that his son would have said something like that off the top of his head.

In any case, the deal was struck. It meant that Tina would park her SUV outside on the driveway, but it was a small price to pay for Martin to have his dad back.

Father and son were outside the house now, washing and polishing those two old cars.

Damaris was upstairs taking a nap after having cooked them a hearty lunch. Tina had told her to leave the dishes alone, insisting on doing them as soon as she finished her coffee. It wasn't how Tina wanted to spend her Saturday, but someone had to do the dishes.

Tina had given Dad and Damaris the bigger guest room overlooking the ocean, while she took the smaller one facing the front driveway.

Her master bedroom suite that took up a third of the main floor now belonged to Martin because he couldn't climb any stairs for a while.

Thank God that he could walk some, but he had a long way to go. Most days he was so winded from all that effort he would rather sit in a wheelchair.

But for now, all was calm in the MacFarland household, reconstructed as it were from the ashes of the past and the grime of dysfunctional memories.

Sipping hot coffee in her sunroom with the windows facing the sands of Tybee Island and the Atlantic Ocean, Tina wished that her original family had been one of peace and quiet. It hadn't been so with the constant squabbling between Mom and Dad over money and mortgages. They had been like two big kids with adult problems around them and no solution.

Dad had always tolerated Mom's drinking, but looking back now, Tina knew he had only enabled her. He should have sought help for her closet alcoholism. Instead, he hadn't wanted to deal with it until their marriage collapsed under bottles of vodka. He simply walked away, as if washing his hands off the matter meant he didn't have to deal with it.

And he had been right.

He didn't have to deal with it.

Mom had passed away from acute alcohol poisoning three years after Dad had walked out on her. When Martin and Tina had come home from college to bury her, they were shocked to find that the entire basement of her home was overrun with boxes of empty liquor bottles. The recycling center had a boon that week.

Tina closed her eyes and let the September sun touch her eyelids.

*The past is over.*

Mom had been gone a long time. Dad had a new wife now.

Someday, when it was Tina's turn to be married...

*Lord, I pray You will let me marry the right man.*

Coffee cup empty, Tina left the sunroom to see how the guys were doing. Outside the sunroom, a stone path wound among a small garden that was nothing like Gus's landscaping at the Chapel by the Sea church and school in the Bahamas.

Still, it was Tina's own garden that her landscaper had planted and maintained for her.

The air was still as she made her way to the guffaws and loud male voices coming from the double driveway of the Cape Cod–style home.

In his wheelchair, Martin was hosing the red Road Runner as Dad washed the hood with a soapy rag. Father and son were wet.

And so were Martin's stitches on his arms and legs.

Tina frowned.

"Hey, sis!" Martin smiled. "You looked as freaked out as ever."

And he hosed her.

Tina screamed and jumped back, but Martin wouldn't let up. "Dad! Make him stop!"

Dad simply laughed all the louder. "You missed a spot, Martin!"

"Aarrgghh!" Tina ran.

# CHAPTER SIXTY-FIVE

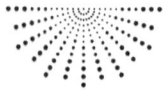

*S*howered and dried, Tina threw on an old tee shirt and a pair of shorts and went downstairs to the kitchen to do the dishes, all the while thinking of how she and Martin had relieved their childhood days, way back when her parents had been together and Mom had been visibly sober.

Family.

Precious.

Yet moments would pass into time and fade like old daguerreotypes if not captured in the recesses of the minds of the next generation.

*I miss you, Mom.*

In spite of who she had been, Mom had tried her best to keep the family together regardless of her own demons.

Perhaps if she had received biblical counseling

or had a Jesus moment, their entire family life would've taken a different turn.

*Still, I will always love you, Mom.*

Tina wiped a stray tear. *Ah, it's that time of month again.*

If she could roll back time and do something different—

No. There was nothing she could have done. What could a teenager do about an adult's deep depression?

Sometimes Tina wished that Dad hadn't given up on Mom. He could have stayed in the family and led them all to higher ground...

It wasn't meant to be.

But now...

Now God was putting some of the broken pieces back together right before Tina's eyes. He had prompted someone to find Dad at such a time as this, to return him to them.

It had been the only reason Tina had returned to Savannah after college. If she didn't leave the town she had been born in, Dad could always find her and Martin.

If Dad had wanted to.

It had taken a near-death experience to bring him home.

*But he is here nonetheless.*

Only God could orchestrate a perfect timing,

and heal Martin so he could spend time with Dad.

Who did God call to make this happen?

Curious, Tina wondered if she would ever find out. She had tried, but neither Helen Hu nor her private investigative firm had returned her emails.

Now why would that particular someone not have called Ming Wei? He also owned a PI business. Perhaps he—or she—didn't know Ming.

*Ah, Ming.*

For a moment, Tina had forgotten that Ming was Helen Hu's brother-in-law.

It was time to call Ming's wife, Sabine. Perhaps she could pry some information out of Helen's sister.

# CHAPTER SIXTY-SIX

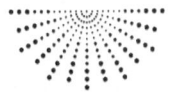

O
n Sunday evening, Tina went alone to the Riverside Chapel service because Martin had a migraine and Dad decided to stay with him. At first Damaris was going to go with Tina. She changed her mind when she didn't trust that Dad would feed Martin a proper dinner. Apparently, since his early retirement from the car parts company, Dad's favorite dinner was a bag of potato chips.

Tina found it interesting that Damaris had pretty much adopted Martin and doted on him. Martin didn't seem to mind all that attention, though Tina was concerned he would be more spoiled than he had already been.

She hoped he would be strong enough to return to work. As it was, Corinne had been covering for

Martin while doing her own job. Martin had also taken time off from working at Saylor Virtual Services.

And Tina had footed every dime of every bill.

*Funny thing, when you love someone, you don't mind.*

So. Who had loved Tina's family so much that they had paid Helen Hu whatever the cost to find Dad in Ecuador and bring him home to Savannah to be with his son?

After church, she hoped to find out.

As she waited in the choir loft for the evening service to begin, she scanned the riverboat dining room for Sabine Wei. She was nowhere to be found. Perhaps she was working in the nursery tonight. Women at the church took turns, though Tina didn't have to because she was in the choir.

She loved singing in the choir.

This choir at her home church.

And also that choir at Chapel by the Sea in Nassau.

She missed the island breeze sweeping through the sanctuary, the way the fan whirred above the congregation, the old pews where everybody sat shoulder to shoulder, and the Caribbean sunlight shining through the open French doors with their stained-glass transom windows.

She missed the people at the school, the excited

day camp kids in her art class, her helpers and assistants, the Chapel by the Sea Christian School staffers she had befriended, even Veronique—who turned out to have a heart of gold—and Gus, who should marry Veronique. And even Donovan, the flashy, splashy trust-fund baby...

And his older brother.

Staid, stoic, solemn Byron Moss.

# CHAPTER SIXTY-SEVEN

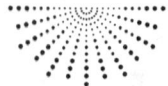

Sabine Wei waved to Tina as she came across the wooden deck on the second floor of the riverboat. Her baby looked cute but sleepy.

In the distance, Tina saw Sabine's husband, Ming, and his firstborn daughter walking toward them, and she knew they didn't have much time to talk. It was time for the babies to go home and go to bed. Tina didn't have any kids, yet that much she knew.

"How's Martin doing?" Sabine asked, popping a pacifier into her baby's mouth. The boy looked like his father.

"I think he's almost back to his normal self."

"Doing cartwheels in his wheelchair yet?"

Tina sighed. "I wouldn't put it past him."

"He's still young, and he should recover. We're all praying for him."

"Thank you, Sabine. We appreciate every prayer."

Sabine nodded. "About your question... Helen won't say much, because her client made her promise not to say a word."

Tina's shoulders dropped.

"But I asked her to nod or shake her head to a series of questions."

"You didn't."

Sabine smiled. "I told her it's a matter of love and death."

"Love and death?"

"Yeah. Only someone who loves you—or your family—would do this," Sabine explained. "Helen looks for missing things—like artwork, musical instruments, relics—and people of all ages all the time. She's very good at it, and she works fast, but she's very expensive. Even I can't afford her."

"Seriously?"

"Yes. That tells me whoever asked her to do this for you—or for your family—has a serious overflow of cash." Sabine rocked her sleeping baby. "That's all I have for you."

"All right. Thank you."

As Sabine started to leave with her family, she stopped. "Oh yes. The call to Helen came from overseas."

*Overseas—*

Tina gasped.

For the entire drive home, the word remained in Tina's mind. Who could it be? She knew no one who cared for the MacFarlands outside the United States.

Dad's grandparents had come from Scotland some hundred or so years ago, but Tina had not been in contact with any of their Scottish relatives ever.

Mom's family... Well, she had grown up in the foster care system and had many families, but no one had kept in touch and no one had attended her funeral.

That left her church family.

Riverside Chapel had been wonderful to her and Martin. But they were in her hometown of Savannah, not overseas.

Who could have called Helen Hu from overseas?

The only people outside the country she could think of who might even care were people she had come in contact with on mission trips. However, she had not developed any long-term friendships with any of the local churches she had ministered in the last several years.

Except Chapel by the Sea in the Bahamas.

She wondered if it was Gus. Gus had been a wonderful friend to her the first time she landed in Nassau two years ago as part of a team of twelve overenthusiastic Vacation Bible School organizers. It had been Tina's first mission trip outside the United States, a steep learning experience for her.

That had been the first time she had met Byron, and it was nothing but static between them. He had wanted the Vacation Bible School run the same way he ran the Summer by the Sea Day Camp, and it was befuddling to Tina to read his ten-page memo and detailed schedule that she couldn't possibly follow.

She had been late to everything, messed up everything, and was on Byron's do-not-call-again list, his permanent blacklist, and whatever other watch lists he had.

Still, this time around, this summer of all summers, Byron had been a good friend.

More than a good friend.

He was a true friend with a kind heart. His words might hurt, his patience short, but Byron always meant well and looked out for her best interest. He would come to her rescue, take care of her, do anything for her.

Of all the people in the world whom Tina knew in her entire life, Byron Moss would be the least—
Selfish.
*Oh no.*

# CHAPTER SIXTY-EIGHT

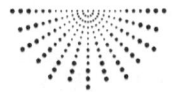

*B*y the time his iPhone and iPad had recharged, Byron had attended two meetings with a spiral-bound notepad in tow, relying solely on whatever he could remember in his stressed-out mind and depending on Veronique to fill in the blanks when details were required.

If there were a competition for the position of headmaster, Veronique would give Byron a run for his money.

And she would win.

In his condition—sapped, spent, and heart-broken—Byron couldn't even will himself to shave this morning.

The last time he had shaved, he nicked his chin.

Today his scraggly beard cast a dark pall over the weekly staff meeting.

Mondays had used to be his favorite day of the week.

Not anymore.

In fact, truth be told, he hated every day of the week now except Sunday.

*Sunday is over.*

*Again.*

As he crawled out of the conference room, the wall clock registered 10:45 am.

*What? Not even noon?*

He knew it was going to be a long day packed with issues and strife he didn't care about anymore.

Byron heard the click-click of Veronique's heels, but he kept walking. Whatever it was, he didn't want to hear it.

"Byron!" she screamed into his ear. "Are. You. Sick?"

"No. Please. Go. Away."

Veronique tapped her iPad hanging off her neck. "Yep. You're sick. Lovesick."

*Lovesick?*

Was there such a thing? Byron ignored her and continued his death march to his tomb—er, office.

"Let me suggest, sir, that you take a sick day and go home." Veronique was right beside him. "Gus can give you a lift."

"I live across the street."

"Yes, but no need to get run over by a lorry when you cross the street."

Byron stopped. "Look, Veronique. I'm feeling unwell, not suicidal."

"Just want to be sure. This school doesn't need a tragedy." Veronique didn't leave. "You haven't had any holiday for the last two school years plus summers. One day isn't going to kill us. We probably won't even know you're not in the office. I can cover for you."

Byron grunted. "Is there anything else?"

Veronique nodded, that plastic butterfly fascinator she still wore fluttered in her hair. "Yes. I went down to the science lab supplier office, and I talked to several people, and I have good news. They're delivering the equipment this Friday."

"This Friday?" Byron perked up. "That's very good news. Good job."

He reached his desk and plopped down on the chair of nails. His iPad and iPhone were pinging endlessly. He should have plugged them into the charger at home last night. He had gone home after the evening church service feeling as tired as a dog and had fallen asleep on his recliner again.

He had barely made it to the eight o'clock meeting this morning.

Again, Veronique covered for him.

In fact, she had been covering for him the last

two or three weeks.

*I have failed.*

*I am not finishing well.*

He realized that Veronique was still standing there on the other side of the desk.

She opened her mouth to say something. But all he heard was, "Never mind. Have a good morning, sir. See you at the next meeting. Two o'clock. Don't be late."

*Don't be late?*

What was Byron turning into? Whatever happened to his old self, always on time, on top of things, on top of the world?

He knew it! It was Tina's fault.

He remembered what he had told himself when Tina first arrived in Nassau back in June.

*That woman is going to be the end of me.*

It had all come true.

Everything he had worked for—to be the best organizer, the best planner, the best scheduler ever —had all come to naught.

*My plans are all up in smoke.*

He caught himself.

*My plans.*

He closed his eyes as an old hymn ran through his mind, the hymn that the choir had led the congregation to sing only the day before in the Sunday morning service.

*All to Jesus, I surrender,*
*All to Him, I freely give...*
*I will ever love and*
    *trust Him,*
*In His presence daily live.*

Byron finished ruminating through the words of the old nineteenth-century Judson Van DeVenter hymn, with a prayer for forgiveness and a renewed commitment to God.

*I surrender all...*
*I surrender all...*
*All to Thee, my blessed*
    *Savior,*
*I surrender all.*

All?

Yes, even Tina.

By the time Byron finished praying, he felt a huge burden lift from his heart. A peace overcame him the same way he had felt the day of his salvation in Christ way back in secondary school.

He knew he was now on the right path with God.

*Ping-ping-ping!*

And then there was work.

*Sigh.*

# CHAPTER SIXTY-NINE

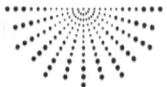

"*T*wo things." Tina had kept her voice as soft and as quiet as she could, but her words still startled him.

Byron rolled off the trim around the fountain and dropped like a sack of rice onto the green, green grass of the lovely Bahamas.

He used a hand to shield the morning sun from his eyes as he squinted up. His jaw dropped.

"Clumsy," Tina announced.

Byron scrambled to his feet, freshly cut grass stuck to his hair and all over his blue polo shirt, the very same one he had worn to Moss Cay back in July.

As Tina stared at the blue fabric the color of the entire Caribbean ocean, a stroboscope of snapshots of that Saturday a while back—and yet so recent, it seemed—flooded into her mind.

She remembered the photographs they had taken on the boat to Moss Cay, their kisses in the hibiscus garden beside the Moss Cottage, their walks on the white sandy beach by the crystal-clear water of Moss Bay.

Tina could still feel her panic when the news of Martin's wreck had come, and the relief in her heart when Byron had taken charge and helped her get back to Savannah without a hitch.

Then there was the possibility of his behind-the-scene costly undertaking of tracking Dad's whereabouts and bringing him to her brother's bedside as he was in a coma in the ICU...

And Tina's poor response to such generosity.

She had called him selfish over the phone and had hung up on him.

Tina sniffled. "I didn't know."

"Didn't know what?" Byron brushed off grass, pollen, and dry bits of stuff from his hair and shirt and navy pants.

"The other night, on the phone, I called you selfish. Please forgive me?"

"Of course." Byron closed the space between them. "I always forgive you. There's nothing you can do—well, except dump me—that we can't reconcile on."

"I felt bad for days after I found out what you had done."

"What have I done? Oh yes, I ticked you off."

"Not that." Tina sighed. "I had no idea it was you who hired Helen Hu to find my Dad."

"Who told you?"

Tina grinned. "So it was you."

Byron cringed.

"I only guessed. Why, Byron?"

"Ah..."

"It's not a secret anymore, so tell me."

Byron reached for Tina's hands. "All right. I lost my father suddenly. I don't wish that upon anyone else, especially you."

"See, you're not selfish. I accused you falsely."

"Don't mention it. Sometimes we say things we don't mean."

"I meant it that evening. Every word."

"You did?"

Tina nodded as she tried to reel back tears. "I called you selfish for not thinking of my brother's condition, when it was I who was selfish for not considering your well-being."

"Let's forgive and move on."

"I was unkind."

Byron held her hands. "Looks like you need to forgive yourself."

"Huh?"

"'If we confess our sins, He is faithful and just to forgive us our sins and to cleanse us from all unrighteousness,'" Byron recited.

"I know that one. It's 1 John 1:9."

"Yep. We have all sinned and fallen short of the glory of God, Tina. You, me, everyone. If we have asked God to forgive us, and He does, then don't relive the guilt of it."

Tina nodded.

"Pray with me?" Byron asked.

Tina closed her eyes and waited.

"Father God, we come before You now to ask for Your forgiveness for our tongues. With them we praise You, and with them we cut down other people," Byron almost whispered. "Forgive us, Lord, and cleanse us from all unrighteousness."

"In Jesus' Name we pray. Amen," Tina added.

When she opened her eyes, she tilted her head toward Byron, who was still holding her hands. "You should teach Bible classes."

Byron didn't say anything.

"What's the matter?" Tina felt Byron's palms sweat.

"I'm not teaching anymore."

The sharpness in his words grazed Tina's heart. "I thought you taught high school Bible."

"Someone else is. I'm too busy with admin work as the *interim* headmaster."

The way he had emphasized *interim* was telling. Tina wondered what was going on in this man's life right now.

"What about your Wednesday night Bible study at the church?"

"Ah, I had to give that up too."

"Why?"

"No time."

"No time for God's work?"

Byron bristled. "Something like that."

Tina could tell she had hit a nerve.

She could also tell that Byron was going through something painful.

He rested his head on hers and groaned.

The agony in that groan was not lost on Tina. She let him hug her as long as he wanted. His shirt smelled like dryer sheets and warm sunshine. She snaked her fingers through his waist and held him close.

Her cheek touched his rough chin.

"What's with the scruffy beard?" It was obvious to her that not everyone could keep a proper beard. Byron's was messy and poorly trimmed. "No time to shave either?"

Byron managed a smile. "You don't like it?"

"It might get in the way," Tina said.

"In the way of what?"

"Of this." Tina ran her fingers up Byron's

jawline toward his ear, and wrapped her hand around the base of his hairline as her lips met his.

Byron's response was immediate. He held Tina tightly, as if letting go would be the death of everything they ever had.

# CHAPTER SEVENTY

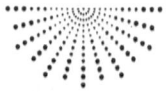

"What's the second thing?" Byron asked when they came up for air, the Bahamian sun rising and beating down on them, though the fountain provided moisture in the courtyard to balance out the year-round heat.

"What?" Tina rubbed her hands on Byron's back.

Byron felt his back muscles relax. It had been a difficult month—or two months.

"You said two things. What was the second thing you wanted to tell me?"

"I forget."

*Just like Tina.*

"It wasn't just a summer romance." Byron offered. "I never forgot you."

"Nor I you."

"I want to know how you feel about me."

"I have no idea how this is going to work." Tina's voice cracked. "We live in different countries. We have careers in different cities. Our schedules don't match up."

"Just tell me how you feel about me," Byron repeated. "We'll sort out the rest. If God wants us to be together, He will work out the details, will He not?"

Tina nodded. "I feel pain when I'm not with you, like something is not right."

"Me too. I don't want you to leave me again, but you will. When do you go home?"

Tina breathed in the sunshine around them. "Thursday. I'm meeting Raymond to go over our plans for the two hundred platters and serving bowls your brother wants us to make for his restaurant in Lucaya."

"Oh, so this is a business trip." Byron tried not to show his disappointment. "Where are you meeting Ray?"

"He's picking me up as soon as I call him so we can go to his studio. We might make our first platters this afternoon." Tina stepped away. "Speaking of business... Uh-oh."

"What?"

"School hours. Shouldn't you be in your office right now?"

"It's my day off. Veronique's sitting at my desk right now."

"But you're here. Ah, no wonder you're not wearing a dress shirt. I wondered why you're in that polo shirt."

"Because it reminds me of our trip to Moss Cay."

"Funny. Same thoughts. Back to work. You could have taken a real day off so you're not thinking school all the time."

"Can't get away." Byron shrugged.

"Are you addicted to work, you workaholic you?"

Byron laughed. "I've worked so many extra hours the last two months I could take weeks of holidays. I also haven't taken a sick day in years. Besides, we don't have any meetings today, and everything is in place. The school is good to go, and everything is well."

"Everything may be well, but not everyone is."

Byron averted Tina's eyes on his. "Ah, but the school must go on. We've got a system in place, and I'm happy about the way things are shaping up for the school. Veronique knows what to do... In fact, she'd make a better headmaster than I would."

"Let me understand this. You don't have to work today, but you came in anyway, just to nap by the fountain in the courtyard." Tina waved her arms. "Is this your happy place?"

*Busted.*

"Well..." Byron wondered how much to tell her. "When I'm at home, I have nothing to do. Since I live across the street, I could just come here. I figured that if Veronique needs my input, she could text me."

"She could text you across the street."

"Well, yeah. Anyway, keeping busy is good for me. I don't miss you too much, think of you too much."

He knew now that he had started to love Tina the first time she had left Nassau two years ago. It had been a slow process, but Tina's second summer trip to the Chapel by the Sea Christian School had solidified his feelings for her.

"I missed you so much, Tina."

"I feel the same way." Tina looped her arm around his. "Now let's walk back to your office before someone sees the headmaster goofing off. You might get reported, fired, quartered, and thrown into the ocean."

"Now that you've come to see me, I don't care about anything else."

Tina pulled him along. "You will care, because Dad said I can't date losers."

Byron laughed so hard that birds in nearby trees flapped their wings and flew away.

When Byron looked at Tina again, she was tugging his face toward hers, and it was the longest kiss she had ever given him. So far.

If not for his time to spare, it would be all wrong for him to stand in this courtyard that his cousin Gus had made for the school. He should be in his office right now, mired in the grime of stress in a job he was never cut out for. He knew that now.

Yet his conscience didn't feel the guilt of being out of his office while school was in session this morning. In fact, he hadn't planned on showing up at the school today, having considered Veronique's suggestion that he take the day off.

His mental health break.

But the school had pulled him when he got up this morning, as if something was there waiting for him.

Now he knew. It wasn't something waiting for him. It was someone.

*Tina.*

And here was his therapy, his anodyne, his panacea...

Could Tina be the partner in life that God was

providing for him to navigate those weary, unknown paths on earth?

Could she be the love of his life, his helpmate, his buddy, his best friend, his—

*Wife?*

# CHAPTER SEVENTY-ONE

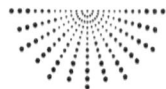

*T*ina kept her foot on the pedal, spinning the wheel head at a steady pace as the big serving bowl rose over six inches high from the potter's wheel. Using her open palms, she shaped the lip of the bowl as her foot pedal slowed down the wheel motor. She kept at it until the bowl was perfectly circular.

She sensed someone at the door that led to the painting tables and easels in the outer area of Raymond's pottery studio, but she kept working on her new creation.

The figure at the door was still there. She looked up. "Byron. Oh."

"Oh what?"

"You shaved."

"Yeah." Byron ran his fingers over his smooth chin. "I can't keep a beard."

"You tried."

"And failed."

Tina brushed it off. "You're early. We don't have to leave until five o'clock, right?"

Byron nodded. "The weather is going to be lovely tonight, and I hope we'll have a nice sunset at or after dinner."

"It's only a little after four o'clock now. Long way until sunset."

"I wanted to see what you do at the potter's wheel." He walked toward her.

"You might not want to get any closer. It's very messy. You'll get clay on that nice shirt." She pointed to his striped shirt.

His dress pants and dress shoes made him look spiffy.

He looked like his old self again—that clean-cut, meticulous, orderly, everything-in-place Byron Moss.

Suddenly she remembered something. "Oh dear. It's not a formal dinner, is it? All I have for a change of clothes are a tee shirt and the crumpled skirt I wore this morning."

"Doesn't matter what you wear as long as you show up," Byron said. "It's a private beach, and we'll be alone at dinner. Well, the chef and servers will be nearby, but you're the only one I invited to dinner."

*A private beach?*

Tina ran a wire across the base of the bowl and removed it from the wheel. She picked up the bowl and took it to a countertop. If Raymond could fire it in the kiln tonight, she could glaze it before she flew home on Thursday.

Now she wished she didn't have to go home.

At a large, rectangular sink, she washed her hands and arms. Water splashed over her apron and her shirt. She turned off the faucet.

A hand towel appeared in front of her eyes.

"Thank you." Tina dried her hands and arms.

Byron pointed to her forehead, then to his own.

"What?"

"You have streaks of clay on your forehead and on the top of your hair."

Tina reached for her forehead. Yep. Something hardening was stuck to it. There were clumps in her hair. And she was going to dinner tonight?

"I was trying to get hair off my eyes earlier while I was throwing the clay."

"I love your eyes, Tina." Byron held her hands. "You have such pretty eyes the color of the deep-green sea around Moss Cay. Do you remember the island?"

"Before or after the news of my brother's wreck?"

"Everything." Byron lifted a curl of hair away from Tina's cheek. "God wants us to be thankful always, whether times are good or bad."

Tina nodded. "Because He is with us."

"Always."

# CHAPTER SEVENTY-TWO

$S$unset swept across Paradise Island in such a way that the entire sky was bathed in purple and pink and marigold and burning red, God's brushes painting swaths of intense colors across the private beach like a canopy over Byron and Tina.

Byron thanked God repeatedly in his heart for this moment. The rain didn't come, but the sunset did around 7:15 p.m. He wasn't sure how it would have worked out had it been a cloudy night.

Chef Giuseppe had outdone himself again with the five-course meal that included lobsters, lamb shanks, and a three-layer pineapple upside-down cake. How the chef had married the seemingly disparate dishes and dessert, Byron couldn't begin to guess, but he reminded himself to send Donovan a thank-you note for letting him borrow his restaurant chef at such short notice.

Across the folding table covered with white linen, Tina ate quietly in her covered chair. She was obviously enjoying herself, but seemed a little nervous.

He had told her over and over that it didn't matter that she was wearing a rumpled tee shirt over an even more rumpled skirt, but he didn't know how else to make her more at ease.

"I'm stuffed," Tina finally said. "Felt like I was on a cruise."

"A cruise?" Byron's eyebrows rose.

He was fully aware that if he had to make his move, it had to be soon. The paper lanterns were shining brighter now that the sun was setting, and soon it would be too dark for him to see her reaction to what he had rehearsed all afternoon.

Tina nodded. "The last time I had lobster tail that good was on a cruise."

"Where did you go?"

"Cozumel."

"Did you enjoy it?"

"Yes, but I spent most of the time alone because Martin disappeared to who knew where."

"Next time you go on a cruise you won't be alone." He picked up a small gift bag, from under the table, that Mother's maid had hidden for him.

He placed it on Tina's side of the table. "Something for you."

"What is it?" Tina looked excited. She pulled out the silk scarf so bright that it was still colorful in the sunset and under the lanterns. "Oooh. Love the colors!"

"I bought it from the same shop you got your fabric. Remember that?"

Tina scrunched up her nose. "I remember losing my debit card."

"We found it. Let's not recall that. But this scarf goes with that dress you bought."

"You mean the one you paid for," Tina corrected him.

Byron said nothing as he watched Tina drink up her favorite soda.

A flutter of wind caressed through their outdoor dining table.

Tina got up and floated the scarf in the gentle wind. It sailed in the air. Byron caught one end of the scarf, and he left his chair.

Tina wrapped the scarf around Byron's neck and pulled him toward her. Slowly, she kissed his chin and cheek.

He said nothing.

She stopped at his lips.

Byron didn't wait for her to decide against kissing him. He didn't know how long they stood there, the colorful scarf around their necks, binding them as they kissed. She tasted like Fanta Grape.

"This is a pretty scarf," Tina said. "Thank you."

"Will you wear it?" Byron sensed something that Tina wasn't saying.

"I'll keep it. I will."

"But?"

"I don't wear scarves."

"Oh. I'm sorry."

"Don't be. It's just me," Tina explained. "I have this fear of things tied around my neck, like I can't breathe or something."

"It is around your neck now," Byron pointed out.

"But you're with me."

"If I'm with you, then you're okay wearing it?"

"Yes, because if anything happens, you'll rescue me."

Byron kissed her again. "You know I will."

"Like, if the ends of this scarf get caught in a door—you know, an elevator door, bus door, suchlike —I could get strangled."

Byron laughed. "You crack me up. I keep forgetting you're... Uh..."

"Clumsy?" Tina asked.

"Uh...that's not the word I was looking for." Byron cleared his throat. "Let's go stroll off some of that pineapple upside-down cake, shall we?"

# CHAPTER SEVENTY-THREE

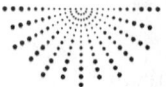

"It's so beautiful out here. Only God can make such a lovely ocean and sky." Tina locked her arms in Byron's as they walked barefoot along the shoreline.

The September evening air was cooling around them, and the tide was coming in.

Byron had rolled up the hem of his dress pants. Even as he listened to Tina, he was rehearsing in his mind how he could broach the subject.

He went for it. "Do you remember what you said to me the night we talked about your dad?"

"The night I broke up with you?"

"I guess it was in the same conversation. You said, 'If God calls you to be a teacher, you have to teach.' Or something like that."

Tina nodded.

"As the interim headmaster—and word is they could confirm me before the end of this school year—I'm not teaching at all, and I don't foresee myself ever teaching again in this capacity. There's just too much work to do. The school is not doing well financially—oh, I guess I should stop right there."

"I hear you. Financial troubles can cause problems for the school board and leadership."

"This is confidential."

"I can keep a secret." Tina's hand rubbed Byron's arm.

"If you must know, the only new project paid off in full is the Jesus Loves Me Kindergarten Building."

"Good to know."

"The science wing is a money pit, and the other unpaid debts in the other parts of the campus..." Byron winced. Maybe he shouldn't tell her all these things.

Then again, he knew he could trust her. "If I had known all that, I would never have agreed to step in for Clarke."

"So as the assistant headmaster, you didn't know?"

"My job was to deal with the day-to-day stuff in the school. I didn't have to report to the school board or take orders from them. Whatever I needed to do,

Clarke told me the filtered, practical, doable editions."

"Now you see what's behind the curtains."

"I don't think this job is for me. I think my work at the school is done." Byron felt a little sad—but not too sad—that the chapter had closed. "I want to teach."

"If God calls you to teach, you have to teach."

Byron cleared his throat. "If I go to seminary, would you still marry me?"

Tina didn't say a word.

"Tina?"

"Hmm?"

"Would you still marry me if I go to seminary?"

"Did you just switch that question around? It's the same question."

Byron stopped at the edge of the ocean. The darkening sky was foreboding, portending a rejection. He wished he had—

Well, he wasn't sure what else he could have done. If he didn't pop the question now, Tina could be too busy on Wednesday to meet with him, and she would be going home on Thursday.

Byron knelt on one knee. Waited.

Tina leaned down and kissed him on the forehead. "My love for you is not predicated on whether you go to seminary. If God calls you to go to seminary, why would you not go?"

"You do love me."

Tina nodded, smiled, and sat on his bended knee.

"Tina Gracielle MacFarland, I love you. Will you marry me?" Byron didn't know how the engagement ring he had bought this afternoon at Tiffany's in downtown Nassau—without looking at the price tag—suddenly appeared in his grip.

"Forever, yes."

"Well, technically, according to the Bible, marriage ends at death. There's no marriage in heaven. So... Till death do us part—"

"Byron."

"Yes, ma'am?"

"This is not a graded assignment." She wiggled her left ring finger at him.

He placed the marquise-cut diamond ring there. He could barely see it with the sun setting all around them. "Please don't lose the ring."

"I knew you'd say that." Tina chuckled. "It's a bit tight, so I don't think it's going to come off. I bet you insured it."

"Ah yes. They gave me a great deal on the insurance. I had to take it."

"Figured."

"I'm sorry. I do irritate you, don't I?" Byron tried to hide the hurt in him.

Tina pulled him to his feet. She wrapped her

arms around his waist and rested her head on his shoulder.

Then she smiled at him in the dusk. "I love you, Byron. I told you that."

Byron nodded, relieved.

"Including your pedantic moments, your prickly attitude, and your sometimes peculiar idiosyncrasies. All of you, Byron."

*Yikes. A laundry list.*

"However..." The word trailed into a mischievous grin on Tina's face.

"Uh-oh."

"I expect you to do what's right in the eyes of God."

Byron wasn't sure what Tina was going for. "Yes, ma'am."

"I'll be looking to you as the leader of our family, the head of our household, and the resident pastor for our future children. Can you handle that?"

Byron straightened up. What happened to the previously befuddled, scatterbrained Tina? This one seemed self-assured. Perhaps she had lost her nervousness around him.

*This is good, right?*

"Sure. Trusting God, we can do anything," Byron said over the waves swishing and swashing back and forth on the soft sand around their feet. The tide was coming in.

"I'm glad we agree," Tina said. "We'll worry about the other details later."

*Details?*

"What details?" Byron's eyebrows shot up.

"You know, like where are we going to live after we marry? Are we going to reside in two countries separately and only see each other on weekends or school holidays? If so, how are we going to be man and wife and parents to our children? How many children do you want to have? What are we going to name them? Details like that."

*Details like that?*

Byron knew he wasn't going to be able to sleep well for nights until he had prayed through and analyzed and planned and—

*God will direct our steps.*

"The future is in God's hands," he finally said. "Let's pray for direction and then follow God, step by step."

"Good answer, Byron."

Byron picked her up and swung her around in the ocean breeze. "Was that a pop quiz?"

"And you passed with flying colors," Tina said as her new scarf unfurled from her neckline and flapped away into the wind.

# CHAPTER SEVENTY-FOUR

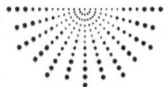

O n this fresh June morning, the rain had come and gone on Moss Cay, leaving behind clear blue skies and calm aquamarine seas all around the private island where wedding guests had arrived in boats from Nassau, where they had all stayed the night before at one of the Moss resorts. The wedding party from Savannah had been there most of the week, preparing for the wedding.

Byron hadn't been antsy since the rehearsal the evening before. He had prayed for patience, and God had given it to him. Standing on the pristine beach and breathing in the fresh morning air, he smiled and lifted his eyes to the heavens and praised the Lord in his heart.

*Today is the day!*

Byron had waited for nine months for this day

because he and Tina had prayed and sought the Lord for wisdom. They had felt His leading for Byron to finish the school year as the interim headmaster of Chapel by the Sea Christian School. That way, he would not leave the students and staff in a lurch by quitting during the Christmas holidays and moving to the United States.

Everyone at the school had been happy with his sacrifice, from the school board to the staff and students—except for Veronique, who had coveted his headmaster office from day one. Still, she had accepted all of it as from the Lord and had exercised patience as well.

*Patience.*

Between September and June, Byron had seen to the completion of the new science wing and had presided over the opening ceremony of the new Jesus Loves Me Kindergarten Building at the school. Sadly, his predecessor's health had dwindled to such a degree that he could not attend any of the ceremonies.

Byron had brought video recordings to Gowan Clarke's bedside and explained to him in person that he would not be accepting the position of headmaster.

Clarke had been sad at the new development in Byron's career and life, but he understood that the ways of the Lord trumped man's ways. They had prayed that day.

It had been the last time Byron saw Clarke alive, as the cancer-ravaged headmaster passed into glory shortly after Christmas and was now safe and sound in the arms of God in heaven.

*Glory, glory hallelujah!*

*No more tears, Headmaster Clarke.*

Byron wiped his eyes quickly before anyone could see him at the edge of the beach, in front of the array of swaying coconut trees.

With the passing of his mentor, Byron's time at the school had come to a closure that was easier for him to bear. Before his last goodbyes there, Byron had done everything he could to help the fledgling Christian school, cutting expenses by freezing any new expansions, focusing on hiring superb teachers who loved the Lord and loved teaching—in that order—and raising the quality of core academic classes.

He also strengthened the morale of the staff after the death of their beloved headmaster by encouraging more staff Bible studies and prayer hours at the school, reminding them that the Lord was their comfort and the joy of the Lord was their strength.

Keeping busy had been his thing. However, throughout the busy school year, Byron had managed to spend Christmas in Savannah with Tina's family and had developed a friendship with her brother Martin, who had now traded his motorcycles for muscle cars.

On her part, Tina had flown to Nassau once a month or whenever Byron could not make it to the United States. Tina's hours were more flexible, and she had saved her pottery studio expansion to Atlanta for after the wedding. She had also scaled back the rest of her business, and had sold her third studio in Charleston to a potter friend.

And now, all that flying around would come to an end once the wedding was over and they hopped on the Moss Gulfstream back to the United States. All their luggage had been packed on board, as were the wedding gifts from friends and family. The jet had been fueled, and the pilot was waiting at the hangar in Nassau.

All that was left was to attend the biggest event of Byron's life, next to the day he had accepted Jesus Christ as Lord and Savior.

Standing there, breathing in the morning that the Lord had made, Byron heard someone call his name.

# CHAPTER SEVENTY-FIVE

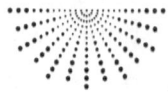

"What in the world is a staycation honeymoon?" Donovan spread his arms wide as he traipsed across the sand toward his older brother.

"Atlanta is a new place to both Tina and me." Byron smiled, knowing that he didn't have to explain to Donovan a third—or fourth—time that this was how it was going to be. When Donovan got married, he could do whatever he wanted with his own honeymoon.

Byron made his way toward the arch covered with flowing sheer fabrics fluttering in the morning breeze. Between the arch and the Moss Cottage, rows and rows of benches had been arranged in the widest area among the coconut trees and hammocks. Benches instead of folding chairs—whose feet would sink into the shifting sand—had been the wedding planners' idea, and the team had gotten up super early this morning to do this after a bout of rain the night before had threatened to postpone the wedding.

Well, if it had rained, they would have held the wedding inside Moss Cottage, where the back covered porch that Grandfather had built could seat over two hundred people. Plus, they could always add tents to make more room.

However, God had parted the skies.

And here they were.

The benches would have been lined up on the beach itself if the destination wedding planners had had their way, but Tina had insisted they leave the beaches alone.

"What in the world are we doing setting up the wedding under the coconut trees?" Donovan pointed up and out. "What if the coconuts fall on your wedding guests? Did it ever occur to you the liability it would cost the Moss family?"

Donovan's fists were on his waist, his white linen shirt halfway unbuttoned, showing off a physique that had been in the family for a few generations, the genetics of which had somehow skipped Byron.

Tina hadn't minded that Byron was not as tall and hunky as Donovan. She loved him anyway.

And Byron got the girl.

*Yes, only by the grace and mercy of God.*

Quietly, he thanked the Lord for Tina MacFarland, soon to be Tina Moss in two hours and—he glanced at his watch—fifty-nine minutes.

Reluctantly, he had packed away his iPad in his carry-on that was already on board the plane. He could check his email later on the flight out of Nassau. There shouldn't be anything important since he was no longer working at the Chapel by the Sea Christian School.

His student visa to the United States had been approved a while back when the seminary had accepted him, and they'd sort out his new immigration status as the spouse of an American citizen later. Everything was fine.

So. No emails to worry about.

Funny. He didn't miss his iPad at all. His iPhone was in his pocket, shut off, but there in case of an emergency. One never knew with Tina, and Byron wanted to be prepared.

Still, Tina's entire known family was here somewhere—her brother, Martin, and her father and his wife. Tina herself was inside the Moss Cottage doing whatever a bride and her matron of honor did.

Byron had wished for Tina that her own mother could be here to watch her daughter get married, but some things were not meant to be. For that, he had to trust a sovereign God.

Family and friends and people aside, today was a big day between Tina and him and between the wedding couple and God Almighty who had created and ordained holy matrimonies.

It was God who had brought them together. Yes, indeed.

"My offer still stands. Five nights at Moss Lucaya—with its brand-new honeymoon suites—and all excursions included." Donovan lowered his voice as guests milled about the sandy beaches in their flip-flops and sandals, saving seats for their preferred views of the marriage ceremony.

"May we take a rain check?" Byron asked.

"A rain check? Who takes a rain check on honeymoons?"

*We do.*

Byron smiled again. In fact, he hadn't stopped smiling all morning. "I told you last night at the rehearsal dinner, remember?"

"Uh, what again?"

"No time, Donovan. Tina's new studio in Atlanta opens in a month. My Greek and Hebrew classes start next week. I need them so I can hit the ground running this August."

"I still can't wrap my mind around the fact that you're going to seminary. Of all places, in Atlanta.

Isn't it landlocked? Don't they have seminaries in the Bahamas or maybe even south Florida on the beach somewhere?"

"I'll miss you too. We'll have a guest room just for you whenever you come to town."

"You'd better, Brother. Can't believe you're leaving town." Donovan placed both hands on Byron's shoulders. "Then again, you need the training if you want to teach the Bible."

"What I want to do the rest of my life. My calling."

"Well, my calling is to be the richest hotelier in the world," Donovan declared.

"Your own calling or God's calling for you?"

"Ah, Brother. You love to live the life of poverty." Donovan swung his lanky arms about. "You could buy an island bigger than this with cash, and yet you squirrel away every dime. You give away to charity and do the anonymous Samaritan things way too much!"

Byron didn't feel the need to explain that he and Tina had worked out their joint account and had started new funds for various projects they wanted to do—like scholarships for needy secondary school students to go to the university, support for the new Bible college that those three churches were starting in Atlanta, and of course, education funds for their future children.

Somehow, after all that, they had enough to buy a new house outside metro Atlanta, where they had decided to honeymoon.

Why not? It was on fifty acres of land filled with green grass, old oak trees, and the sky.

They would be landlocked, yes.

But oh so in love.

# CHAPTER SEVENTY-SIX

*A*s the live musicians played a Caribbean variation of *Pachelbel's Canon in D*, Tina prayed that she would not trip on the sand on her way to the arch where Byron, his best man, Donovan, and her matron of honor, Lucy, stood on both sides of Pastor Flores.

She could see through the veil, but her nervousness had returned. Yes, she had slept well in the very comfortable Moss Cottage back there, but she could hardly eat even a light breakfast this morning.

*I'm marrying Byron.*

*Today!*

*Right now!*

*Aarrgh...*

The sand beneath her bare feet was smooth and lukewarm. Now she wished she had worn her flip-flops, just in case there was a nail or something in the sand. Too late for such thoughts.

Besides, if she tripped, she was holding onto her beaming Dad who strutted beside her like he were a hundred feet tall, his chest puffed out and chin held high, his haircut a tad too short, making him look more like a biker dad than a muscle-car dad.

But Tina was thankful to God, nonetheless, for bringing Dad home to her and Martin.

Martin.

There he was, sitting beside Corinne in the front, near Damaris. Martin was staring straight at her, and Tina could see that his eyes were red.

She winked at him. He nodded.

She thanked God for keeping Martin alive and restoring him to a new life.

And best of all, Martin had accepted Christ at her wedding rehearsal the night before.

*Woo-hoo!*

Byron had talked to Martin about life and death, and explained to him as simply and as clearly as possible the step of faith needed to receive God's gift of salvation through Jesus Christ.

And Martin had finally believed that Jesus had indeed died for his sins—all of them—on that cross so long ago. Walking with Byron on Moss Cay, he had asked Jesus into his heart once and for all.

*Finally!*

So many good things had happened in such a short period of time that Tina's heart was overwhelmed with joy.

When Tina reached the arch, she thought she would pass out. This was too much, too good to be true, and yet it wasn't, was it?

A good God provided for His children blessings upon blessings, grace upon grace. Sure, life had its ups and downs, good and bad days, but here they were, safe in the providential hand of God.

Still, the rest of the wedding was one big blur to Tina.

She decided she'd watch the video later. Someone was recording all this, right?

All of a sudden she heard Pastor Flores pronounce them man and wife.

Tina gazed at her new husband, Byron, and then at the gold wedding band on his ring finger.

She glanced at her own left hand. Her wedding ring shone in the morning sun, right next to the sparkly diamond engagement ring—that she hadn't lost, by the way.

Byron lifted her veil.

*Oh, his kiss is coming!*

On top of her head, Tina's natural red curls sprung up to life—freedom!

The veil rose from her hair, and a gust of wind blew it right off Tina's head. No doubt it had to be the same Caribbean wind that had taken her scarf the night of Byron's proposal on Paradise Island back in September.

Tina's right hand, still holding her bouquet of hibiscus, instinctively reached for her hair, but there were only pins left, a few of which embedded themselves into her bouquet. When Tina lowered her hand, two hibiscus and half a leaf from her bouquet remained attached to the pins in her hair.

The crowd laughed heartily as Lucy, her matron of honor and two months pregnant, chased after the veil, now floating in the air down the beach.

Tina grinned at Byron, who seemed to be pretending not to notice anything the matter. She knew he was aware that she had been leaving pieces of things in the Bahamas—an iPhone in the ocean, a scarf washed out to sea, and now a veil that might not be recovered.

She hoped she wouldn't get fined for littering all over the Caribbean.

"We'll get another veil," Byron whispered in her ear.

"No need," Tina replied. "We're only getting married once."

"Yes." Byron's eyebrows lifted. "Once and for all."

Tina eyed his lips.

Her husband seemed to know what she wanted.

And he gave it to her, the wedding kiss she had been waiting for, and with it, the promise that he would kiss her like this for as long as they both lived.

DEAR READER:

Thank you for reading *Smile for Me*, book 1 in my Vacation Sweethearts series. While *Smile for Me* is a coastal beach romance, the next novel in the series is set in a mountain hideaway. In *Reach for Me*, we travel to a remote retreat in the Great Smoky Mountains, where an optimistic disabled veteran from Britain and a pessimistic prodigal daughter from America meet in the valleys of their lives. There is love on vacation in those misty mountains, and there is danger in the shadows. Find out what our British veteran hero is doing in the mountains of Tennessee in this small-town contemporary Christian romance novel with a side of international suspense.

Reach for Me (Vacation Sweethearts Book 2)
JanThompson.com/reach

Before we take a sneak peek at *Reach for Me*, book 2 in the Vacation Sweethearts series, I'd like to mention two friends from my Savannah Sweet-

hearts series who made special appearances in this Vacation Sweethearts novel. Did you know that Diego Flores (Byron's pastor friend) and Heidi Wei (Tina's friend from church) have their own story to tell in *Know You More* (Savannah Sweethearts Book 1)?

Know You More (Savannah Sweethearts Book 1)
JanThompson.com/know

Tina MacFarland's home church in the USA, Riverside Chapel, is also the hosting church for my Savannah Sweethearts series featuring Christians looking for God's will in their lives.

Savannah Sweethearts
JanThompson.com/savannah

Are you on my book news mailing list? Get book release news, sales and special deals, promotional notifications, and behind-the-scene-information about my books. Keep up with my publication news as I write more novels for you to enjoy.

Subscribe to Jan's Mailing List
JanThompson.com/newsletter

Back to this novel you just finished reading. If

you enjoyed *Smile for Me*, would you please write a review of the novel? Reviews are very helpful to other readers, especially those who might be new to my books. Follow the link below to post your review on a retailer site.

Smile for Me (Vacation Sweethearts Book 1)
JanThompson.com/smile

Continue reading for a preview of *Reach for Me*.

# THE NEXT NOVEL IS REACH FOR ME

## VACATION SWEETHEARTS BOOK 2

*He leaves his homeland to protect his family.*
*She flees her hometown to abandon hers.*

At a remote mountaintop retreat, an optimistic triple amputee veteran meets a pessimistic beauty in the valleys of their lives.

A Christian romance with suspense, *Reach for Me* is book 2 in *USA Today* bestselling author Jan Thompson's **Vacation Sweethearts** collection of clean and wholesome, sweet and inspirational Christian vacation romance novels set in some of her favorite vacation places. Travel with our friends to the coast and to the mountains, and cheer them on as they celebrate the immeasurable grace and undeserved mercy of God through Jesus Christ. These **Vacation Sweethearts** novels are a spin-off of Jan's **Savannah Sweethearts** series.

In *Reach for Me*, we visit the Great Smoky Mountains bordering the states of Tennessee and North Carolina in the USA. It's the fall season and the leaves of autumn color the mountaintop retreat where our friends' story begins.

## IN HIS VALLEY OF DETERMINATION...

His friends call him O'Tierney the Optimist. Even after having lost two legs and an arm in a bomb blast and having undergone numerous reconstructive surgeries, disabled United Kingdom Special Forces veteran Keenan O'Tierney is still excited about facing unknown new challenges in life.

Highly decorated for his heroism in fighting terrorism on behalf of his grateful nation, Keenan has given enough to his country. Yet, his enemies are going after him and his former team members as an act of personal vengeance. To protect his family, Keenan leads a trail away from Britain. Off the grid, he is incognito at a remote resort in the mountains of Tennessee.

While waiting for his storm to pass, he meets an American girl who is hiding for a different reason in the same misty mountains...

## IN HER VALLEY OF DISCOURAGEMENT...

Bearing the burden of a mistake-riddled life, prodigal adopted daughter Phoebe Pace has nowhere else to go. She finds solace in the Great Smoky Mountains, living in quiet regret, not forgiving herself, and being unable to ask God to forgive her.

She thinks her days are merely for survival, with her job at the funeral home not improving her grim outlook on life.

Now the most intriguing guy Phoebe has ever met is sharing her swing on her log cabin porch over-looking unparalleled spectacular vistas. She has no intention of seeking any friendship outside her small and safe circle of friends. She would rather be left alone to wallow in her own personal loss and remorse.

What is she going to do with her new neighbor

encroaching in her private personal space? Why is he so friendly toward her? So delightful to be with? So charming? So inquisitive...?

## DANGER FINDS THEM ON THE MOUNTAINTOP...

Visitors come and go at Mendenhall Retreat, but Keenan is different somehow, offering a distraction for Phoebe from her daily routine. However, just when Phoebe begins to think that she might open up her heart to Keenan, the ex-soldier's unfinished business pulls her into a crisis she has never experienced before, and danger comes knocking...on the wrong door.

Continue reading for a sneak peek of *Reach for Me*.

# REACH FOR ME CHAPTER 1
# SNEAK PEEK

## VACATION SWEETHEARTS BOOK 2

Keenan O'Tierney didn't see her until she was standing right in front of him on the rustic porch overlooking a mellow sunset that dimmed the lights across the Great Smoky Mountains.

It didn't help that she was dressed all in black in the dying light.

His eyes had been closed, a failed attempt to stay awake for a few more hours. The jet lag was wearing off as his body clock tuned in to Tennessee time.

It would be midnight in Dublin, Ireland, where he had been staying the last few months—moving from house to house—until he had found his way here, as far away as possible from his family and close friends.

Now she blocked his view of the waning sunset in the western sky that stretched from this part of the mountain range, over Gatlinburg some ten miles away, and beyond.

To the north—his right—he could see a faint hint of Mount Le Conte in the blue-and-purple haze.

He had been told that an eagle's flight away to the south of this cabin in the Mendenhall Retreat was Clingman's Dome.

This little stretch that wrapped around one of the mountain slopes was a prime property that had been in the Mendenhall family for two hundred years.

It was the perfect place for Keenan to retreat and rest.

*Well, save for this interruption.*

"I charge five dollars for that seat." Her voice was neither harsh nor sweet. It was even. She seemed neither annoyed nor amused.

It was a flat statement, given with no air of familiarity, though Keenan was sure she would have remembered that they had nodded to each other at dinner at Mendenhall Lodge on the top of the mountain the night before.

Dinner had been around three long tables, seating about twelve people each, with guests eating in shifts. Somehow they had both ended up at the same table at the same shift.

And it had been Keenan's business to notice people.

*Just in case.*

Keenan couldn't place the accent, but he would hasten to guess it had been cleaned up from a possible southern drawl.

Well, he shouldn't be critical of this woman—this stranger—when he had often portrayed himself as more English than Irish, especially when duty called.

All in the name of protecting his country and, at present, his family and loved ones.

Those death threats—

Ah.

Keenan had lost his pursuers now, having enticed them out of Britain and Europe, having turned them over to his buddies, who had then led those criminals on a wild chase through Australasia.

The trail should be cold by now, some thirteen months after it had flared up.

He smiled a little bit.

His parents, siblings, cousins, grandparents, granduncles, relatives were all safe now.

*I hope and pray.*

"Five dollars, dude," she repeated.

Keenan didn't move. "Considering I'm sitting on only a third of this swing, I say a five-dollar fee is grossly overpriced."

If she wanted to sit down, she was welcome to do so on the other end of the swing.

*What's the fuss?*

"You can't pay me with wit," she said.

She hadn't given him her name.

Back in the days before the ambush, Keenan would've countered that with two words.

*Identify yourself.*

Not today. A continent and several years removed from the battlefront, he had no wish to return to musty, dank, underground interrogation chambers, where the pain his team had inflicted on enemies of the state had then found its way back to his team after his time in Her Majesty's service had ended.

Tit for tat.

He had been fortunate to survive the bomb blast.

Well, parts of him, anyhow.

What had remained...

And now with rusty people skills, he didn't know how to respond to this woman, svelte and tall, her hair pulled back into a ponytail, revealing a soft widow's peak in the waning light.

He couldn't tell the color of her eyes, only that it was turning fiery, a different look than when he had first seen her at dinner nearly twenty-four hours before, eating her turkey meatloaf and side salad silently at the lodge, and not talking to anyone before she left hastily after dinner.

But she had dressed the same as this evening—in black from head to toe. A different fabric—he'd been trained to notice such things—but the same dark color.

*What kind of darkness is she staring at?*

"I'd offer to weed the garden in exchange for half a swing, but I don't feel like it," Keenan said, not trying to defuse the situation.

He had arrived to the swing first, right?

This cabin was a part of Mendenhall Retreat, was it not?

He had paid in full for his two-month stay and felt that he had the right to sit wherever he pleased on the mountaintop property.

He was staying in the main lodge at the moment, but the owner of the retreat had given him a map to the various walking trails in the area. Lamar hadn't said a thing about off-limit cabins.

"You're offering to weed my garden?" Her lips stretched. "Do you see a garden here? It's all stone and dirt and then a whole forest all around us."

"There are a couple of flowerpots out on the front porch."

"So you walked around my cabin? Didn't see any sign?"

"Lamar said I could choose whichever cabin was available." Keenan produced a wrinkled map.

The woman sighed. Pointed a pretty finger at a wooden sign nailed to one of the porch pillars. It was facing out toward the backyard.

Truly, Keenan hadn't paid much attention. He had made a beeline for the swing.

"This is private property," the woman said.

She was beautiful standing there, her hair effusing a muted glow under the porch light—

*Ahem.*

"Exactly. That's why I chose to spend my extended holiday here. It's private, and there won't be busloads of people making all sorts of noise. It's peaceful out here."

For good measure, Keenan waved his paper map again.

The woman breathed deeply, exhaled, and looked like she was losing the battle. "I'd asked

Espy to print a new map. This cabin is not for guests."

"Oh, that sort of *private* property. Silly me. This is your home."

"Yes, sir."

*Sir? She called me sir. I'm not that old.*

"Yes, sir, this is your home, or yes, sir, I'm stupid?"

The woman's face softened.

"Ivy Mendenhall willed this cabin to me after she passed away." Her voice cracked—or so Keenan thought—as if she was still grieving.

Keenan had heard of Ivy Mendenhall, the matriarch of the family. She had passed away a few days shy of her hundredth birthday a couple of years ago. Left the whole mountaintop retreat to her grandnephew, who happened to be an old friend of Keenan's.

Well, it turned out that his welcome at the Mendenhall Retreat didn't extend to this cabin.

"I apologize. I didn't know I shouldn't be here."

Keenan tried to get up from the swing.

His legs locked up, and he couldn't stand up.

He tried again, his good arm reaching for the chains that held up the swing armrest. He hoisted himself upright.

Clumsily.

And for some unfortunate reason, his carbon-fiber legs buckled underneath him, sending him down, his torso and thighs smashing against the wide pine slats of the porch floor as he heard the unmistakable sound of his microprocessor knees rebooting.

Keenan did the best thing he could do, considering the circumstances: he laughed.

And laughed some more.

Reach for Me (Vacation Sweethearts Book 2):
JanThompson.com/reach

Vacation Sweethearts:
JanThompson.com/vacation

Subscribe to Jan's book news mailing list:
JanThompson.com/newsletter

# ACKNOWLEDGMENTS

Many thanks to my Georgia Press publishing team for keeping up with my writing schedule.

For this novel, I thank my outstanding copyeditor, Dori Harrell, my patient proofreader, Lenda Selph, and my beta reader, Debbie Jamieson. Their eyes for details are from the Lord.

I am grateful to God for my husband and son for their support and encouragement.

And I'll always remember my beloved mother and my late father for having instilled in me the love of reading and writing from a very early age. I miss my father here on earth, but I will see him in heaven some bright day.

Most of all, I am eternally thankful to my Lord and Savior, Jesus Christ, who died on the cross to save me from my sins and rose again from the grave to give me eternal life. Without Him, I can write nothing (John 15:5).

Jan Thompson
John 3:16

# BOOKS BY JAN THOMPSON

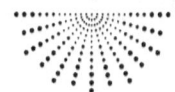

## CHRISTIAN ROMANTIC SUSPENSE & BEACH ROMANCE

### BINARY HACKERS (NEAR-FUTURE INSPIRATIONAL ROMANTIC THRILLERS)

- Book 1: Zero Sum
- Book 2: Zero Day
- Book 3: Zero Base

### PROTECTOR SWEETHEARTS (CHRISTIAN ROMANTIC SUSPENSE)

- Book 1: Once a Thief
- Book 2: Once a Hero
- Book 3: Once a Spy
- Book 4: Twice a Fighter

- Book 5: Twice a Convict
- Book 6: Twice a Soldier

DEFENDER SWEETHEARTS (CHRISTIAN
ROMANTIC SUSPENSE)

- Book 1: Never a Traitor
- Book 2: Never a Hostage
- Book 3: Never a Fugitive
- Book 4: Always a Maverick
- Book 5: Always a Champion
- Book 6: Always a Guardian

SAVANNAH SWEETHEARTS (CHRISTIAN
COASTAL CITY & BEACH TOWN ROMANCE)

- Prequel: Ask You Later
- Book 1: Know You More
- Book 2: Tell You Soon (Romance with
  Suspense)
- Book 3: Draw You Near
- Book 4: Cherish You So
- Book 5: Walk You There
- Book 6: Love You Always (Romance
  with Suspense)
- Book 7: Kiss You Now
- Book 8: Find You Again

- Book 9: Wish You Joy (Christmas Year Round)
- Book 10: Call You Home

## VACATION SWEETHEARTS (CHRISTIAN TRAVEL ROMANCE)

- Book 1: Smile for Me
- Book 2: Reach for Me (Romance with Suspense)
- Book 3: Wait for Me (Romance with Suspense)
- Book 4: Look for Me (Romance with Suspense)
- Book 5: Pray for Me
- Book 6: Care for Me
- Book 7: Cheer for Me

## SEASIDE CHAPEL (CHRISTIAN SMALL TOWN BEACH ROMANCE)

- Book 1: His Longing Heart (second edition of Share with Me)
- Book 2: His Wake-Up Call (second edition of Step with Me)
- Book 3: His Morning Kiss (previously published as Sing with Me)

- Book 4: His Quiet Serenade
- Book 5: His Waiting Love
- Book 6: His Beach Retreat

Subscribe to Jan Thompson's mailing list:
JanThompson.com/newsletter

# SEASIDE CHAPEL

Welcome to *USA Today* bestselling author Jan Thompson's Seaside Chapel Christian beach romance series. These novels are set on real-life St. Simon's Island, Georgia—a beach town where history is all around and the future is a moment away—and the neighboring fictitious Seaside Island, where the rich and famous live.

Savor the small-town atmosphere and the warm southern beaches of St. Simon's Island and the idyllic Golden Isles along the Atlantic Ocean. Enjoy the music of the orchestra and hymns of the church, and hang out with our Christian friends who attend Seaside Chapel, a little church by the sea known for its beach weddings and fair share of love and life.

As these Christians grow in their knowledge and understanding of God, they are tested in their spiritual maturity, their love lives, and their relationships with others. Share their heartaches and healing, and cheer them on as they celebrate faith, family, and friends.

JanThompson.com/seaside

- Book 1: His Longing Heart (second edition of Share with Me)
- Book 2: His Wake-Up Call (second edition of Step with Me)
- Book 3: His Morning Kiss (previously published as Sing with Me)
- Book 4: His Quiet Serenade
- Book 5: His Waiting Love
- Book 6: His Beach Retreat

# SAVANNAH SWEETHEARTS

Welcome to the new south! From *USA Today* bestselling author Jan Thompson come these clean and wholesome, sweet and inspirational Christian romances set on the romantic beaches of Tybee Island and in the coastal town of Savannah, Georgia.

Meet a group of multiracial and multiethnic churchgoing Christians who love the Lord, work hard in their careers, and seek God's will for their love lives. Against a backdrop of ocean, sand, and sun, these inspirational romances showcase aspects of the human need for God and for one another. Have some tea, settle in a comfortable reading chair, and enjoy these sweet celebrations of faith, hope, and love in Jesus Christ.

JanThompson.com/savannah

- Prequel: Ask You Later
- Book 1: Know You More
- Book 2: Tell You Soon (Romance with Suspense)
- Book 3: Draw You Near
- Book 4: Cherish You So
- Book 5: Walk You There
- Book 6: Love You Always (Romance with Suspense)
- Book 7: Kiss You Now
- Book 8: Find You Again
- Book 9: Wish You Joy (Christmas Year Round)
- Book 10: Call You Home

# VACATION SWEETHEARTS

Travel with our friends from Savannah, Georgia, to the coast and to the mountains. Cheer them on as they celebrate the immeasurable grace and undeserved mercy of God through Jesus Christ.

The Vacation Sweethearts novels are a spin-off of Jan's Savannah Sweethearts series, and fans will recognize familiar faces from Riverside Chapel, a church in the coastal city of Savannah, Georgia. In fact, we might even visit the beach town of Tybee Island from time to time to visit old friends and beloved families...

~

JanThompson.com/vacation

- Book 0 (Prequel): Time for Me
- Book 1: Smile for Me (International Romance)
- Book 2: Reach for Me (Romance with Suspense)
- Book 3: Wait for Me (Romance with Suspense)
- Book 4: Look for Me (Romance with Suspense)
- Book 5: Pray for Me (International Romance)
- Book 6: Care for Me
- Book 7: Cheer for Me (International Romance)

# PROTECTOR SWEETHEARTS

Private investigator Helen Hu and her associates specialize in searching for missing persons and hunting for lost treasures. Join them in their adventure suspense around the world in *USA Today* best-selling author Jan Thompson's Protector Sweethearts, a series of Christian Romantic Suspense with a side of mystery. Protector Sweethearts is a spin-off of Savannah Sweethearts and Vacation Sweethearts.

~

JanThompson.com/protector

- Book 1: Once a Thief

- Book 2: Once a Hero
- Book 3: Once a Spy
- Book 4: Twice a Fighter
- Book 5: Twice a Convict
- Book 6: Twice a Soldier

# DEFENDER SWEETHEARTS

Defender Sweethearts is a sister series to the Protector Sweethearts Christian romantic suspense collection. While the heroes in Protector Sweethearts search for lost treasures and lost people, the Defender Sweethearts novels focus on protecting the helpless and hopeless. The main characters in Defender Sweethearts come from the supporting cast in Protector Sweethearts.

JanThompson.com/defender

- Book 1: Never a Traitor
- Book 2: Never a Hostage

- Book 3: Never a Fugitive
- Book 4: Always a Maverick
- Book 5: Always a Champion
- Book 6: Always a Guardian

# BINARY HACKERS

Like more suspense with your Christian romance? Like to read suspense thrillers? If you're looking for clean near-future romantic suspense without compromising the Christian faith, these books are for you.

From *USA Today* bestselling author Jan Thompson come these inspirational near-future cyberthrillers combining technothriller and romance, starting with Binary Hackers that feature computer specialists living at the edge of cyber-space, where they have to juggle being law-abiding truth-telling Christians while carrying out their assignments by any and all means possible.

The Binary Hackers series is set in the same story world as Jan's other books, and characters from the other series may make cameo appearances in this series and vice versa.

JanThompson.com/binary

- Book 1: Zero Sum
- Book 2: Zero Day
- Book 3: Zero Base

# ABOUT JAN THOMPSON

*USA Today* bestselling author Jan Thompson writes clean and wholesome contemporary Christian romance with elements of women's fiction, Christian romantic suspense with an air of mystery, and inspirational international thrillers with threads of sweet Christian romance. Jan's books are for readers who love inspiring stories of faith, hope, and love in Jesus Christ.

Raised on a tropical island in the eastern hemisphere, Jan now lives and writes in the western hemisphere. Her international background gives her a unique multicultural and multiracial perspective to her novels and books. The island has never left her, and she reminisces about beach life in her beach romance novels.

When Jan is not busy writing small-town stories, she writes big-city romantic suspense and international technothrillers, a nod to her previous career in computer science. She weaves technology with human interests, reflecting the current and future digital world. And romance. There's always romance.

Beyond the printed page, Jan is a wife, mother, family scribe, avid reader, occasional artist, erstwhile pianist, and chief of staff to the family cat.

For God so loved the world,
that He gave His only begotten Son,
that whosoever believeth in Him
should not perish,
but have everlasting life.
—John 3:16

www.ingramcontent.com/pod-product-compliance
Lightning Source LLC
Chambersburg PA
CBHW030753260626
47169CB00001B/36